The

Middlemen

Christine Brooke-Rose

VP Festschrift Series:

Volume 1: Christine Brooke-Rose
Volume 2: Gilbert Adair
Volume 3: The Syllabus
(Edited by G.N. Forester and M.J. Nicholls)

Reprint Titles:

The Languages of Love
The Sycamore Tree
The Dear Deceit
The Middlemen
Go When You See the Green Man Walking
Next
Xorandor/Verbivore
by Christine Brooke-Rose

Three Novels — Rosalyn Drexler
Knut — Tom Mallin
Erowina — Tom Mallin

other Verbivoracious titles @

www.verbivoraciouspress.org

The

Middlemen:

A Satire

Christine Brooke-Rose

Verbivoracious Press

Glentrees, 13 Mt Sinai Lane, Singapore

This edition published in Great Britain & Singapore

by Verbivoracious Press

www.verbivoraciouspress.org

Copyright © 2015 Verbivoracious Press

Text Copyright © 2015 The Estate of Christine Brooke-Rose

Cover Art © 2015 Silvia Barlaam

Introduction Copyright © 2015 Francis Booth

All rights reserved. No part of this publication may be re-produced, stored in an electronic or otherwise retrieval system, or transmitted in any form or by any means, electronic, mechanical, digital imaging, re-cording, otherwise, without the prior consent of the publisher.

The Estate has asserted the moral right of Christine Brooke-Rose to be identified as the author of this work.

ISBN: 978-981-07-9387-6

Printed and bound in Great Britain & Singapore

First published in Great Britain by Secker & Warburg 1961.

Introduction
FRANCIS BOOTH

Clearly the silencing of women critics and writers and especially of women experimental writers, is true, is constant, and is done by ignoring them, or, more often than might be supposed, by stealing from them without acknowledgement. I have experienced both myself and simply put up with it.[1]

Christine Brooke-Rose refused to be silenced, though she said it was "not only more difficult for a woman *experimental* writer" to be accepted than for a woman writer in general "but also peculiarly more difficult for a *woman* experimental writer to be accepted than for a male experimental writer." But although she was a great exponent of and apologist for the experimental novel, not all her novels were experimental. They fall into three groups of four—what might be called early, middle and late —plus another four individual novels that might be called very late. The first four are: *The Languages of Love* (1957), *The Sycamore Tree* (1958), *The Dear Deceit* (1960), and *The Middlemen: A Satire* (1961). Although these are all relatively conventional, *The Dear Deceit* has already begun to question the nature of narrative by telling the story in reverse. Then, in 1964, she began a sequence of experimental novels: *Out* (1964), *Such* (1966), *Between*, (1968), and *Thru* (1975), in between which came a book of short stories: *Go When You See the Green Man Walking* (1970). Brooke-Rose called the third series the Intercom Quartet: *Amalgamemnon* (1984), *Xorandor* (1986), *Verbivore* (1990) and *Textermination* (1991). She also published *Next* (1998), a

---

[1] 'Theories of Stories' in *Stories, Theories and Things*. Cambridge University Press, 2009, pp. 225/226

novel with 26 dispossessed narrators (chronologically in the middle of the late novels group but not part of the Quartet), and *Subscript* (1999), a story of evolution told from the viewpoint of a developing cellular organism, as well as two autobiographical novels: *Remake* (1996) and *Life, End of* (2006).

During her career as a lecturer, then professor of European Literature at the University of Paris VIII at Vincennes, from 1969 to 1988, she also published several volumes of lectures and criticism, two books on Ezra Pound and translations of Alain Robbe-Grillet. Even though her experimental phase did not begin until 1964, Brooke-Rose had already shown an historical and stylistic appreciation of the "anti-novel" as early as 1958, three years before the publication of *The Middlemen*. In a review of Beckett she said:

> It seems necessary to the development of the novel or play that every now and then anti-novels or anti-plays should be written, which for various purposes turn the form inside out, hold it up, perhaps, to ridicule, and give it a thorough beating, or at least an airing. These are often considered to lie outside the history of the novel proper, and yet they are indispensable to our knowledge of the form: *Don Quixote*, Furetière's *Le Roman Bourgeois*, *Tristram Shandy*, Hoffmann's *Kater Murr*, *Epitaph of a Small Winner* by Machado de Assis, Gide's *Les Faux Monnayeurs*, Irzykowski's *Paluba*, Thornton Wilder's *The Skin of Our Teeth*. And now we have Beckett. Even if I have missed out some names, the tradition makes a sparse alignment compared with the vast body of 'straight' novelists whose main concern is to tell a story about persons recognizable as human beings in recognizable situations.[2]

The Middlemen, which, in the above definition, is a 'straight' novel, is a good title for a Christine Brooke-Rose novel: being in the middle, being between—socially, linguistically, geographically—is a key theme of her

---

[2] 'Samuel Beckett and the Anti-Novel'. *The London Magazine*, December 1958, volume 5 no. 12, p. 38

life as well as her work. Born in 1923 in Geneva, Switzerland to an English father and a Swiss-American mother, she grew up speaking English, French and German. She went to school in England and during the Second World War she worked in intelligence at Bletchley Park, where all the intercepted German messages were decoded by middlemen and particularly middlewomen—she may have known Alan Turing. Her native Switzerland was in the middle of Europe but not involved in its war. After the war she attended Somerville College, Oxford then University College, London, where she wrote a doctoral thesis on mediaeval French and English philology, completed in 1954, writing about a period of linguistic intersection, when the English language itself was between ancient and modern, between English and French, when educated men and women would move between both as well as between Latin and Greek. And, of course, a professor of literature is a middleperson by definition (as is the writer of an introduction to a novel), standing between text and student; a conduit, an interpreter, looking for meaning and pattern, shaping a story. In the 1968 novel *Between*, the narrator is a also a middleperson: a simultaneous translator, always shifting—between ideas, between conferences, between languages, between genders. S/he translates other people's ideas without trying to interpret or alter them, without adding language or ideas of his/her own; but, Brooke-Rose asks, is this possible?

> The I / central consciousness / non-narrating narrative voice / is a simultaneous interpreter who travels constantly from congress to conference and whose mind is a whirl of topics and jargons and foreign languages / whose mind is a whirl of worldviews, interpretations, stories, models, paradigms, theories, languages. Note that in this metastory the simultaneous interpreter has no sex.[3]

In every identical hotel room s/he reads the labels on the bathroom supplies, their language being the only clue to what country she is in,

---
3   *Stories, Theories and Things.* p. 6

their physicality her only reality. This emphasis on the thingness of things, this *chosisme*, is one of the debts she acknowledges to Robbe-Grillet.

But *The Middlemen* is no *nouveaux roman*. It is important to remember that *The Middlemen*'s subtitle is *A Satire*; it is a comedy of manners, written in a *style indirect libre*—"Serena felt very smart in her new Italian swimsuit" (p.177)—that Flaubert would have been perfectly comfortable with, and Brooke-Rose's views of her characters are as Olympian, certain and as self-justifying as Jane Austen's, an authorial position she reversed in her next novel, *Out*, where the characters have no character at all. Some of her sentences might almost be from Austen herself, or at least Virginia Woolf.

> When women make dramatic gestures and write to say that all communication must cease, they are sometimes a little pained, secretly, after the anger has died down, to have been taken literally. (p.192).

The characters in *The Middlemen* are part of a social critique, something Brooke-Rose never did so directly again, though social criticism is present in more oblique and surreal ways in later novels like *Out*, published only three years later but a generation away in style and intent. Although it was published in 1961, the world *The Middlemen* inhabits seems more '50s than '60s, more post-war Britain than Swinging London. As Larkin pointed out, the '60s didn't really begin until the advent of sexual intercourse in 1963. Precise details like Serena offering £6,000 for a freehold house in Camden Town, which would now be worth millions, anchor it firmly in time and place, something Brooke-Rose would never do again. Another episode also dates the novel as exactly as the mention of floppy disks in her late novels: Dick Barber, a literary agent, is trying to sell a novel about TV advertising called *Mass Medium*[4] to "a newish firm that had done well on beatnik howls of protest, the new school of Nuclear Fiction, and the re-

---
4   Marshall McLuhan did not use the phrase "the medium is the message" until 1964.

action against it, the Antinuclear Novel." (p.98) And, shortly after the *Lady Chatterley* jury were swayed by a barrister asking them whether they would want their servants to read it, she has Stella say: "Rusty, you really must not quarrel with tradesmen and servants". Rusty replies: "My dear Stella, you're living in the past. There are no servants any more, except in underdeveloped countries and the bedraggled remains of the British Empire". (p.168)

Brooke-Rose does not enter into an authorial discussion of middlemen until later in the novel:

> Middlemen have one thing in common with souls in hell, which is that for the most part they do not know that they are middlemen, any more than the souls in hell know that they are in hell, hell being a mere negation of heaven, of which they catch occasional glimpses, too agonising in their positiveness to be borne or remembered for more than a flash of eternity. (p.132)

Like sinners, middlemen can be separated into the self-confessed and the unaware. Some, like lawyers and diplomats, deal in abstracts (as do novelists, though she doesn't mention this); some are "merchants and shopkeepers or their modern extensions, agents and salesmen, who take their percentage on the way, frankly for being there." One of the central characters of *The Middlemen*, Rusty Conway, is a representative of a generation of senior military officers who have moved after the war into corporate life. He has the ultimate middleman job: Chief Public Relations Officer of U.V.I., a company that makes dress fabrics out of sand and saltpetre, contemporary alchemists. Unfortunately, their dresses tend to explode; Rusty's job is to present the public with an image of safety, to shape a story, create a vicarious version of the truth that will calm them, make them feel safe. "It's all a matter of relating... One must, one simply must relate." (p.11)[5] Rusty sees a psychiatrist named Serena, to whom he relates his dreams, so that she can be the middlewoman between him and his imagination, vicariously shaping a story for him, one that will make him feel safe, though "he was hardly the sort of chap to have premonitory dreams. Bluff and easy-going, that was him." (p.9) Serena herself seeks to be totally unlike middlemen such as Rusty.

> But with a name like hers, Serena knew that she had to acquire, earlier than most, that tranquillity of the heart which can be read in the eyes of so few and such scattered people—a small tobacconist in a Paris suburb, a bartender in a Moroccan village or a nun in Notting Hill. (p.26)

Rusty's spiritual godfather, the man usually called the father of Public Relations, Edward Bernays, was a nephew of Sigmund Freud, but before him was Ivy Lee, who published a "Declaration of Principles" in 1906.

> In brief, our plan is frankly, and openly, on behalf of business concerns and public institutions, to supply the press and public of the United States prompt and accurate information concerning subjects which it is of value and interest to the public to know about.

This statement implies a belief in absolute facticity, the possibility of uninterpreted, unstoried facts, independent of viewpoint and context, that the middleman can transmit unaltered, a belief almost all of Brooke-Rose's work seeks to confound. Hughie Hill, a middleman TV producer represents Lee's side; he presents a programme called *Focus on Facts*, "to a gay little tune which turned out to be, if one listened carefully, an exceedingly jingled version of *It's a Sin to Tell a Lie*". (p.39) Hill has "Faith in the

---

5   The Forster quote, from *Howards End*, that Rusty brings to mind goes, in part: "Only connect the prose and the passion, and both will be exalted, and human love will be seen at its height". This is no doubt exactly what Rusty wants to do.

beauty of truth and of course the truth of beauty. For Hughie Hill unquestioningly believed in the objective reality of the Facts on which he Focused." Edward Bernays' view of facts versus truth is less Keatsian, and closer to Rusty's and Brooke-Rose's:

> The conscious and intelligent manipulation of the organized habits and opinions of the masses is an important element in democratic society. Those who manipulate this unseen mechanism of society constitute an invisible government which is the true ruling power of our country... We are governed, our minds are molded, our tastes formed, our ideas suggested, largely by men we have never heard of.[6]

Rusty is one of these men. U.V.I.'s agency is Screen Persuaders Ltd, a *Mad Men* organisation containing "the Philosophic Rulers of our Mental Republic, from which Poets and Artists had, however, been eliminated." (p.19) Their offices have internal walls of pink glass to alter reality, "to give everybody a rosy outlook, and their pink strip-lit world a tropical, sunkissed aspect". (p.12) Their account director, Ted Baker, who alters his own reality by dyeing his hair blonde but pretending it is bleached by the Greek sun, suggests a radical approach:

> "Since we were, before the last campaign, I mean, flogging Process-Confidence, why not go the whole hog? What about a really corny documentary? Telling the truth, I mean?"
> "Good lord," said Rusty, jocularly but seriously shocked as well. (p.15)

The idea of showing the public the truth is of course shocking to Rusty, though in fact the film the agency have prepared is a fake and shows completely different factories.

One of the few people in the novel Brooke-Rose seems fond of is Stella,

---

[6] Edward L. Bernays, *Propaganda*, New York: Horace Liveright, 1928

Serena's non-identical twin, whom Rusty at one time considered marrying. Stella's speech slips in and out of Italian, Spanish and German as she moves

> in the pseudo-cosmopolitan, neo-colonial and sub-diplomatic world of large international good-will organisations, small consulates, and companies trading in tea, cotton, oil, nuts or rum, according to the secretarial job she happened to be in. (p.30)

Secretaries of course are middlewomen too, both connecting and separating their bosses from the outside world; both conduit and shield. G.K. Chesterton said "a million women said we will not be dictated to and promptly became shorthand typists", but Stella will not be dictated to; she is "a real original, those who knew her would say, she's quite extraordinary." (p.8) With Rusty's colleagues, she

> had somehow been made to feel ill at ease by these smart people who had no intrinsic value in each other's eyes except as intermediaries to something else. Their very middlemanship was their identity, they were one-up by their mere existence. No effort was needed and so, like all middlemen, they tended to sell each other gossip when they had finished selling each other their wares. But Stella was in effect her own middleman, alone in the world, selling her personality, and very badly. (p.24)

In all this realist social comedy, a rare hint of what is to come in Brooke-Rose's work comes in a heated conversation between Stella and the journalist Cliff Morrison, a natural middleman, interpreting the work of another journalist.

"Poor man, there's a fundamental dichotomy there. Yes, in-

deed. A fundamental dichotomy. Great turmoils deep down below, dear me."
"Really, Cliff, how on earth can you know?"
"Ah my dear Serena, it's written in his every phrase, his very syntax."
"What is? The deep turmoils?"
"Serena my dear, you're a very clever woman. Very clever. And attractive, if I may say so. Oh, yes. The White Goddess and all that. You understand life and its dark ancient rituals, buried deep down in the collective—"
"For Christ's sake."
"*But*, my dear Serena, *but*: you are not a stylist. Rupert will understand me there. How do young lovers in their first speechless discovery of the flowery paths that wind their scented, colourful, enchanting ways to the deep abyss, try helplessly to cover their inarticulateness, their verbal nakedness, how? By copying out poetry, quoting half-remembered lines they learnt at school perhaps and will doubtless never quote again, using our poets as messengers and heralds, interpreters if you like, translators—I began as a translator, so I understand the problems, no, more, as communicators, in an agreed code, of those ineffable, inexpressible—"
"Turmoils," put in Serena.
"You may laugh. But the English language—"
"Phooey!"
She went out and slammed the door. (p.112)

Brooke-Rose later said "I do not know myself where the novel will go"[7], but, after *The Middlemen* she found the direction her own novels should go, a direction no one had ever taken before, and she went out and slammed the door.

---

7 *A Rhetoric of the Unreal: Studies in narrative and structure, especially of the fantastic*, 1981, Cambridge University Press, p. 338

1

IT is the sixties in the century of middlemen.
Middlemen of course, have always existed, indeed have made themselves very necessary, ever since merchant adventurers began to persuade people into coveting the produce of the men in the next valley, the next island, the next continent, who were paid, more often than not, with useless trinkets they too were persuaded into coveting. In this way gold, tobacco, coffee, even ideas, soon became indispensable. Naturally, the middlemen profited most.

So much so that nowadays everyone waits to be a middleman, which used to be rather disreputable. The class is becoming larger and larger, like the middle class, pushing its own extremities out of existence, and few people are producing more than a small part of something. The age of giants has vanished. For there was presumably a time when giants could talk to pygmies, when, if Mahomet did not come to the mountain the mountain could quite easily come to Mahomet. Now the giants hide themselves in mist and every mountain is covered with pygmies, a sprawling ant-heap of middlemen. We are all middlemen, selling to others something we do not own, something we have not made, something we do not intimately understand, and the profit, though larger of course than that of those who make, is less than it used to be when there were fewer middlemen, except for the bigger middlemen, who then need more middlemen to interpret their middlemanship to other middlemen lower down.

These disloyal thoughts were not precisely verbalised as they turmoiled through the hazily discontented soul of Rusty Conway, Chief Public Relations Officer of U.V.I. They came and went like odours rather than thoughts, leaving no trace whenever a nice fresh puff to his *raison d'être* sprayed into his office, which fortunately happened quite frequently.

For Rusty was not the usual kind of smooth, faceless young man one finds in public relations, though he had several such specimens of humanity under him to do the actual work, the seating arrangements at industrial banquets, the press parties, the image-foisting. Sometimes Rusty wondered whether his job had not perhaps been created specially for him, like a chair for a distinguished but obsolete scholar, as a reward for his existence and survival. He knew the theory of his status well enough, but he was tired of reading about himself as a social engineer or a lubricator of the human machinery for getting things done. In practice that simply meant doing other people's jobs, indeed, his job was forever spilling over those of other people like oil on troubled waters. Business consultants made it all sound so electronic, so military, with Divisional Controllers and Unit Managers and transistorised carrier equipment, as if everyone were playing at war, for practice. But it wasn't like that at all: not in U.V.I., which still had room for old-fashioned individuals like himself and, say, Harry Thorpe; not in England, where the O.K. thing was still to muddle through in a School Club way, the School Club having merely become much larger. But that was precisely what made him uneasy. He would have liked things to be more clearly defined, as they had been during the war for instance. Or did he, on the contrary, feel that they were becoming too clearly defined, with more and more middlemen taking over below him, slowly pushing him to the top, a useless non-executive sort of top? The organisation trend was there. He could sense it, hear it even, like that winged chariot.

He certainly had a very elegant office, airy-modern but comfortable and high up in a curtain-walled skyscraper overlooking the Thames. At fifty-one, Rusty Conway had had quite enough of seeing the world. At first it had been for his country and his service, mostly as a youngish Wing Commander—Rusty Wing, they had called him in Colombo when he got promoted, but in Cairo it was usually Wingcon, in Tunis Winkaway, and by the time he was occupying Germany he had shot through a group-captaincy to air-commodore in the general prestige scramble that marked the difficult relationships between the four victors, not to mention the conquered, at the end of the war. Then, later, the travelling had been for U.V.I., almost every non-productive aspect of which he had represented in almost every one of its numerous and far-flung outposts from Chile to Japan. Ah, yes, those were the days, though he felt more sentimental about his almost young man's war than about his later jobs which, however varied geographically and however generously bestowed with high allowances, never seemed to give him quite the touch of glamour that he had derived from being a Senior Liaison Officer in a blue-grey uniform with three rings round his wrist. Then four. Then a big broad one and scrambled eggs. He had never forgotten the day when he had bumped into Harry Thorpe at the Interservice Club on his last leave, for Harry was still only a Colonel, whereas an Air Commodore, as Rusty couldn't resist translating—unnecessarily, he knew—was equivalent to a Brigadier. Harry had been one of the many Sales Managers at U.V.I. before the war, and as such one financial rank above him, a mere Personnel boy then, but now Harry was head of Sales Promotion, Southern Division, and had his eye sharply focused on "U.K. Sales", as the top Home Consumption job was called. And although Rusty was also head of his department now, there was no doubt at all who had done best, so that Rusty tended to treasure that incident like a tender memory. It soothed his scornful envy of Sales Managers in general, who, as middlemen, were at least theoretically concerned with the goods produced.

Today, however, he felt more important than all the sales departments for every area in the kingdom, because all the sales departments suddenly depended on what safe image of U.V.I. he could persuade the public to accept. There had been an emergency meeting that morning, with three of the directors and everyone from General Manager and "U.K. Sales" down. And although, as usual, this was strictly speaking a job for Publicity, he Rusty, Conway, had been charged with getting out a final statement that the Press would print as news, though of course Statistics and Consumer Research would produce the actual information. And Lab, naturally. So far he had kept the Press at bay with the phrase "our laboratories, are, making exhaustive tests", which the Press was free to interpret as "there's a tremendous flap on" if they wished, since there was.

Then a report would have to go to the Parliamentary Sub-Committee. There had been questions in the House. And no wonder.

"Any statistics you can think up," he said down the telephone, "as long as they're correct. You know the sort of thing, only .000 something of every ten yards sold, has gone up in flames, or only one and a quarter persons per twenty million has been burnt to death. Or try a regional approach. It only happens in old-fashioned houses with draughts and open fires, never where there's central heating. Use your loaf man. And quick."

"Wilco, sir," said Statistics, to appease him.

"Any luck?" she asked down, the same telephone to another extension, and Lab replied, "we're carrying out exhaustive tests."

"I want to speak to someone responsible," Rusty said, optimistically. "Who actually discovered the formula? You know, invented the stuff?"

A pause the size of a proton occurred as Lab registered its shock. Then Lab said,

"The team—"

"I know the team invented it, all in group harmony. But I can't talk to a group harmony. Haven't you a conductor?"

"Yes, well, the team—"

"O.K., you win, three cheers," Rusty interrupted wearily.

"But what can I tell the Press pending?"

"You might remind them that all scientific progress involves some mishaps at first," snapped Lab, queered out of its scientific composure. "When we first put cinderella on the market there was trouble too, and look how we've perfected it today. It'll be the same with nitron."

"Well, well. But the old margin of human error won't wash with either the Press or Parliament, you know, or the public that's led by them. We're not supposed to market a product until—"

"I'll let you know as soon as the team have reached some formula," Lab said curtly and put its receiver down.

So Rusty at once transferred the curtness and the snappiness down the very same telephone to Consumer Research, and, for the rest of the morning, to the other, smaller Public Relations Officers who worked in a consecutive series of less well-furnished boxes on the same floor, at his beck and call.

But he did not, that evening, tell his psychoanalyst about that, only about the harassing time he had had, and how deeply worried he was about it all.

"You see, I feel personally responsible," he wallowed, "although I know with my mind that the scientists are to blame. All those lovely girls blown up in their cinderella frocks. Brrr."

"You mean nitron?" said Serena gently.

"Yes, of course nitron."

The silence barely covered the space of time it takes to say, "an interesting mistake", and Serena went on, with a professional courtesy of enquiry.

"Can you tell me why you think of them as girls?" For she knew they were really seven housewives of thirty-five and upwards. As she expected, Rusty Conway smirked, winked, smirked, again, then erupted into a long and, noisy clearing of the throat.

"Floozies, don't you know!"

Serena waited patiently.

Though the Venetian blinds, the setting sun threw a tiger, tiger burning bright upon the forest of an explosive abstract on the wall of Serena's consulting room. Serena herself glowed pink. Rusty smoothed his greying ginger hair sideways across the top of his head, then stroked his brush moustache with his index finger, rather lovingly.

"The first one was a girl," he said with a slow nod of recognition at his own perceptiveness, "years ago when we marketed cinderella. You remember those ads we had?"

"No. Tell me."

"But you must remember them. A girl standing tiptoe on top of a volcano, with a wand. Later on we had the volcano itself suggesting a wide crinolined ball-dress. Cinderella, you see," he explained laboriously, "is a synthetic fibre we make from fine volcanic sand." He suddenly felt she was rather stupid. Fancy not knowing that after all this time he's been coming to her. Serena looked at him expectantly. "We alone have the formula," he added out of habit.

His lower lip drooped a little and was permanently wet, as if his moustache were dripping onto it, though it wasn't. His eyes were small and piggy, and though astute enough in office hours or at the club, could look as lost as a baby's in the pink flaccidity of his present face.

"Of course, that publicity was unfortunate. When the first girl's dress exploded near the fire, you can imagine what play the Press made with it, though in fact there's no connection, none whatsoever. Volcanic sand is just sand, it's black, that's all. Have you ever seen a black beach? There's one in the Canary Islands, between the blue sea and a yellowy-green lagoon. Looks quite astonishing. Really beautiful in an odd sort of way. Hmm! Well anyway, no amount of heat can turn the processed stuff back into lava or smoke or whatever it was when the bloody thing erupted. Besides, exploded is their word, in most cases it just shrivelled, though of course, so did the flesh. But it could happen to nylon, or anything." He gesticulated to convince himself, but failed. "Anyway, that was all put right, and cinderella was a great success, as you know. Why, I do believe you're wearing it yourself. Isn't that skirt—" he leant forward in his armchair and suddenly broke through their professional relationship—"Why, Serena, you drip-dry, non-iron, crease-resisting, dirt-repelling mother-surrogate, you, why don't you lie down on that couch you never use. I'll lie on you. I'll explode and shrivel you, you bitch, you dot-dot-dot-dotting great . . ." His voice tailed off in sudden loss of interest as he saw Serena watching him with a scientific eye. "No offence, old girl, hmm, I did that to—er—for light relief; you know how it is, the show must go on and all that . . . Well, anyway." He gathered his scattered thoughts. "Yes, cinderella caught on all right. Spread all over the world. Sin-drill-on over the old channel," he punned heavily. "Hmm! But then the stink-boys had to produce nitron, made, if you please, out of saltpetre! Potassium nitrate, you see. And blow me if the publicity crew didn't go and think up a selling line about gunpowder plots and heaven knows what else. Even I know that gunpowder isn't just potassium nitrate. Shot-silk taffeta, they burbled on, and Guy Fawkes never knew what he began. The same mistake showing off the how, not the what. Process-confidence they call it. Well, that was bad enough. But then they suddenly thought they'd have fun with a little understatement: Marketing Meiosis. Oh yes, there's usually some solitary chap airing his education. We don't say it's the Best but it's going with a Bang. And it is, by Jove. But I'm the one who has to face the music."

"Tell me," Serena said in a soft, motherly voice, "how do you visualise those girls blowing up?"

Rusty put his head in both his palms and, concentrated hard under Serena's watchful eye. The silence was almost as tremulous as the dusk pervading the room now that the sun had vanished behind the roofs, and she quietly switched the reading lamp just behind her armchair. He didn't hear it, so that no knowledge of it having been switched on caused any glimmer of light to penetrate beneath his eyelids, tightly screwed shut behind his wrist-bones. But then he moved his hands and opened his eyes a moment, which, having glimpsed the light, now saw fiery visions under the same shut eyelids and the same curved wrist-bones. Explosive visions quite impossible to speak.

"I've just remembered a dream I had when I woke this morning," he said at last. "Do you want to hear it?"

"By all means," Serena said, unruffled by his evasions.

His manner was quite jovial now.

"It was about Stella, you'll be interested to hear. She was sitting under a huge cactus, but huge, you know, frightfully signif, I'm sure. In her W.R.A.F. uniform, and very hot she looked, too, and she wore no hat, though the sun was beating down, and blow me if she wasn't typing. On her knees, a dainty little sky-blue typewriter. And Harry Thorpe was fanning her with a huge palm-leaf. He was wearing a magenta-coloured turban, by jove." Rusty chortled heartily for some time, because the rest of the dream was considerably less symbolic, involving himself and Stella under Harry Thorpe's unexpectedly lecherous eyes and the tickle of that large palm-leaf. Stella, in some curious way, went on typing to Harry's dictation.

The next day, oddly enough, a letter from Stella arrived at the office. She was coming home on leave in July, she wrote, and might give him a tinkle at U.V.I. to see if he was free for a drink. And because of his dream, which had certainly astonished him, he quietly decided not to mention Stella's letter to his wife.

Not that Jean objected to Stella, at least, from afar, and in principle. She knew, as even Stella herself didn't know (for they really were just "good friends") that he had once toyed with the idea of marrying her; and after Stella had stayed with them once or twice she understood why he had funked it, why, in fact, everyone seemed to funk it. But she also understood why he had remained in casually avuncular touch with her, or rather, why he willingly and passively accepted that Stella should remain in touch with him, Stella being the letter-writer, the home-comer, the descender. For there was an element of blackmail in Stella's originality. A real original, those who knew her would say, she's quite extraordinary. So that anyone who didn't appreciate her extraordinariness felt guiltily ordinary. In fact, as Rusty was subtle enough to apprehend, if not in words, certainly in whiffs of uncertainty, Stella appealed mostly to very ordinary people, precisely for that reason. And from the little he had seen of her friends over the years, it seemed that Stella too, preferred to surround herself with the nice but dull, in order to feel more unusual. So that Rusty's admiration for Stella when she arrived like a breath of fresh air also managed to make him feel very ordinary, and by the time he had seen just that amount too much of her that Stella never knew when to suppress, he agreed with Jean and with his finally funking nervous self that she was rude, aggressive, and exhausting, in short, impossible.

Yet never before had he dreamt of her in that way, at least, not since Cairo, when such dreams had been in general somewhat redundant. He really never thought of her, and he was hardly the sort of chap to have premonitary dreams. Bluff and easy-going, that was him. But not today. He kept dropping things, snapping at his secretary, jumping when his telephone buzzed, standing up to examine one of the numerous charts and graphs on the wall behind him, sitting down again and swivelling round to stare morosely at the ugly blocks of flats the L.C.C. were putting up across the mud-grey river in a vain attempt to develop the South Bank. There was no doubt about it, these explosions had upset him more than any office intrigue of ambition and jealousy. Surely he wasn't heading for another breakdown? For that was the name the office had politely given to the devouring, paralysing sense of futility that had led him to Serena Scott-Buttery in the first place.

In his mind, Stella's tinkle occurred at that very moment.

'Is that you, Rusty? Oh, I'm *so* glad you're here, and not in Iceland or Peru. I desperately need your help . . . But how *are* you?'

Stella always spoke, and wrote, in italics, so that even in his imagination he both heard the emphasis in her voice and saw the underlining in her letters. There was always some drama, too. What would it be this time? She had got the sack, she was stone broke, there was a revolution in —where had she written from, now ? Or, more likely, her latest love affair had come to grief and she had broken her contract with whatever firm had sent her wherever she was, so that she had paid her own fare home, was looking for a job, for some digs. . . . He would ask her to call for him at the office, and then, when the reception desk telephoned through, he would have her shown up. Rusty always had people shown up, instead of going down to meet them in the reception hall, even when he was lunching or drinking with them, because he liked them to see him in his fine office with the luxury carpet that came with his seniority. She would blow in, exotically elegant, and be exuberantly impressed. 'But *Rusty*, you must be *madly* V.I.P. these days.'

Actually it was Harry Thorpe who blew in, or stormed, really, for his manner was worse than breezy.

"What the devil d'you think you're doing, staring at the bloody river?"

Harry had worked his promising way up from the Leeds branch of U.V.I. and had never lost his North Midlands accent. Or rather, he had once tried to lose it, in his younger, more resentful days, before the war when accents counted against a man or so, at any rate, those who had them firmly believed; but he had done well during the war, when the backbone of the nation had to be flattered as well as the stiff upper lip, and now, since the democratic revolution, he tended to over-emphasise the strong velar vowels and the rich sing-song, for they gave others, and especially his superiors, confidence in him as a sharp, efficient, reliable no-nonsense man. All of which qualities he certainly possessed, but then so did many others, and he was the one to be noticed. That was the image of himself he issued, like a publicity handout. 'I come from the great working masses of the North,' he seemed to say, 'therefore I'm more real,' as if reality were not a purely individual matter. He was grey and wiry, with a slight twist about the mouth and a calculating expression in the eyes that could denote either irony or suspicion according to how one viewed him. Rusty viewed him as perpetually sarcastic. Also as more "real", but only on account of being Sales Promotion Manager, rather than Public Relations Officer.

"Keep your hair on, old boy. I'm thinking."

"And to what effect, may one ask? Sales have dropped seventy percent in the last week, you know."

"How's cinderella doing, by the way?" Rusty countered, "any effects?"

"Oh, steady enough. The public don't connect, you know. Still, there's no upcurve either. What I want to know—"

"My, dear chap, I've shot down the first wave, but I'm paralysed by Lab and Statistics. Ever since automation you can't get a thing out of Statistics. Or Consumer Research. The machines are overfed, so they say. A spot of indigestion, a little wee ulcer, an executive neurosis, pooh. Anyway, let Publicity think up a few emergency tactics for a change. They're always lost in their long-term projects and strategic campaigns." Rusty sounded rather hurt.

"I know, I know," Harry said, more gently. "I just looked in for a glance at the Press-Book. And to see if you had any of your cocky ideas. Most of Publicity's better notions seem to come from you in the first place," he added kindly as he flicked through the Press Book on the side-table, and Rusty felt both flattered and alarmed. "Young Jim Fawcett's none too bright, let's face it, lad."

Rusty could never quite tell whether Harry Thorpe's sudden lapses into indiscretion were sincere or nothing more than fairly crude attempts to play heads of departments against one another by prodding their ambition. As an efficiency technique it seemed risky enough, since it could just as easily lull them all into a false sense of security; though it was true that Harry sometimes praised the others grudgingly, but sky-high for him, the sky of his opinion of others being rather low. Rusty could imagine the same scornfully "real" vowels to Jim Fawcett. 'Let's face it, lad, our friend Roosty was over with the war.' In spite of all this, he felt ridiculously pleased.

"Some of the gen's coming through, old man, and my boys are working on it. They'll be staying on late, the whole night if need be, they're all keen as mustard. I promise you a new image first thing tomorrow morning. Or several. The next meeting's at ten, isn't it? Meantime I'll have a pow-wow with Jim." Harry nodded slowly as Rusty was reacting the way he wanted. He even allowed him a grand finale of the same salesman's platitudes with which he himself had already soothed "U.K. Sales" and the Managing Director before the meeting the previous day. "After all, look at what happened with cinderella. Public memory's short. At the worst we can lie doggo till it dies down. Turnover can take it. But don't worry, old chap, you'll get your image."

"It's all a matter of relating," Rusty went on, for he was fond of the phrase Serena used so often. "Yes," he muttered at the door Harry Thorpe closed behind him, "one must, one simply must relate."

2

JIM FAWCETT and Rusty Conway walked together in the palace of polaroid glass, their steps dully clocking their progress along the mock-marbled thermoplastic floor. The heating was sub-tropical. On all sides, pale pink glass partitions flanked with wilting vegetation separated them from typing pools, comptometers, secretaries, directors in conference, designers bending over their drawing boards, artists gesticulating, copywriters cogitating, cutters measuring the air with spools of negative, indeed on a dull day the effect was of moving through a silent but three-dimensional colour-film. Only the studios were allowed the privacy of walls, and even the reception hall had been a vast elongated open-plan of fibreglass lounges muralled on one side with pink mirror and on the other with technicolour photographs blown up to inapprehensibility, each lounge separated from the next by bamboo partitions, fountains, palm trees, fish tanks and, last but not least, a fierce and fiery-plumed parrot silver-chained to a perch of pure jade.

The idea of the pale pink glass was to give everybody a rosy outlook, and their pink strip-lit world a tropical, sunkissed aspect; at the same time, no one could slacken without being seen by someone else, even by the offices opposite, for the outer walls were of glass too, and it was difficult not to feel that the entire staff might step out one by one into the void above the street any moment from now. Even the lift-shafts were transparent and so were the lifts. The suggestion had originally come from a time-and-motion expert peculiarly insensitive to the limitations of human charity, not to mention other ailments like agoraphobia, scoptophilia, and vitromania. Or even a simple weariness of window cleaners.

By the time Jim Fawcett and Rusty Conway had reached Ted Baker's office the details of their arrival had been noted and relayed to all the relevant sections of Screen Persuaders Ltd., so that Ted Baker had the U.V.I. file already on his desk, together with charts, designs, film scripts and of course the U.V.I. account book.

Ted Baker rose, it seemed, out of a silvery film-projector, though in fact the projector was built into the pink glass partition behind him, just above his head so that he could switch it on without moving; it was fed from the room next door, at his bidding through the talking-box, by an assistant as rosily ethereal as Homer's dawn herself, who had, however, broken the office rules and arranged the silver filing cabinets in an L-shaped wall that cut her off from other offices, but not from Ted or the sub-tropical light outside.

He came forward with an outstretched hand, like a friendly Swede, all bleach and suntan. "The Greek sun, dear," he would say to admiring women, who usually knew the difference between the sun, Greek or Roman, and a bottle of peroxide, but admired his courage nevertheless, for he was on the weedy side of five foot seven and the blondness gave him height by analogy with Tall Teutons, as opposed to little latins.

"Jim, my dear fellow, how nice to see you. I hope things aren't as bad as they sound?"

"No, everything's fine, fine, all under control. This is Rusty Conway, our P.R.O. Done a splendid job, quite splendid. Wanted to come along and see what you could cook up."

It was impossible not to get on with Jim, Ted would say, he was so affadaptable, and euphoric to the point, sometimes, of imbecility, perhaps as a result of graduating in Business English and Human Relations in a School of Management run on American lines.

"I should think U.V.I's so tipsy with riches they could take three months' No Sale and hardly feel the pinch."

"Steady on," said Rusty.

They sat down to proffered cigarettes and lighters on their respective sides of the curved executive desk. Jim didn't smoke and instead kept smoothing down a Henry the Fifth fringe which robbed his face of what little character it had. Even in his well-cut suit he looked more like the Dauphin in Saint Joan than Harry for Saint George.

"Did you watch the programme last night?" Jim's voice throbbed with enthusiasm, and Rusty blushed because he hadn't wanted to mention it himself.

"No," Ted lied. "What programme was that?"

Rusty was disappointed.

"*Public Inquisitor*," he said, and blushed again. Now he disliked his own tawny hair, which gave him such an unruly complexion, especially in this light, but then they all looked glowing with something.

"Rusty was on it, he's probably practically a star by now."

"Steady on," said Rusty. "They really wanted one of our scientists, you know, but I told them that was impossible. All working late, doing exhaustive tests. So they had to be content with poor old me. Still it was rather fun, you know."

Ted was a Cambridge man who liked to indulge a feeling of immense scorn for the world he publicised, to which in fact he was selling for a high salary, the result of his higher education. In his flat he kept the idiot-box, as he continued to call it, on the floor behind an armchair, but when alone he would often enough turn the armchair round and dutifully watch the advertisements he himself or his firm had created, or programmes relevant to his firm's clients, and sometimes even others. He had seen last night's *Public Inquisitor* and thought it lamentable. There had been a prim and tearful housewife from Dugwharton where two of the accidents had happened, and some alarming female from a magazine—or maybe she was a reporter, anyway he had never heard of her, which showed she couldn't be anybody—and Tom Stevens, M.P. for Dugwharton, and Rusty Conway humming and hawing his statistics, and of course the great Johnny Green himself, chairmanning the whole show for the People, Vox Dei. Tom Stevens had managed to get in a political plug for his party —"of course this would never have happened if we had State Private Enterprise"—which hadn't made Johnny Green turn a shade bluer than he already looked. The result had been, as usual in such discussions, a draw, nil-nil.

"It went down marvellously," Jim was twittering on, "Viewer Research rang Rusty this morning to say they'd had simply hundreds of phone calls and they expect hundreds of letters to follow. Splendid tactics, Rusty, splendid."

Rusty tried to look modest and stroked his moustache sideways. He felt as if he had just received the D.S.O., which was absurd from this mere boy of, what would he be, thirty-four, thirty-five? But then he himself had also been thirty-fours thirty-five, and a Wing-Commander, a Group Captain. An Air Commodore.

"Anyway, I've come on more strategic matters. Our general policy is to let it ride for a bit, isn't it, Rusty? But in the meantime we want to get a commercial out, or even a film, to be ready in about, say, three months' time, or even longer, depending on the approach. We don't want it to look as if we'd rushed to make an apologetic explanation because of all this."

"At the same time," Rusty put in, "it had better be pretty convincing."

"Yes, that's it. Pretty convincing. That's exactly it."

"You know, Jim, I've been exercising the little grey matter on your problem," Ted announced with quite a lot of deep exhaling and waving away of the exhalation as he spoke. "Looking through all this—volcanoes dancing Victor Sylvester style, guns shooting puffs of smoke that descend as parachutes and turn into brides, Guy Fawkes, pictures of the Houses of Parliament, fireworks scintillating into spangled ball-dresses, cannon balls turning into balls of soft wool, and, er, yes, Marketing Meiosis—" He was turning the pages of the file as he enumerated his past bright ideas with a characteristic mixture of pride and mockery. "All this stuff we've sharpened our trim little geniuses on in fact. And I've been wondering ... I think I've had rather a brainwave." There was more exhaling and waving away to create an expectant pause. "Since we were, before the last campaign, I mean, flogging Process-Confidence, why not go the whole hog? What about a really corny documentary ? Telling the truth, I mean?"

"Good lord," said Rusty, jocularly but seriously shocked as well.

"Or . . . can't we?" Ted inquired with mock caution. "But of course we can. I think it's a perfectly splendid idea." Jim's affirmation sprang automatically from both his zeal for U.V.I. and the elementary skill which even the most ordinary middleman possesses by instinct: never tell anyone more than he needs to know, he may turn up in a rival camp. The truth, after all, was only that someone had blundered, and it could be presented with garnishings that made it sound a little less stark, or even different altogether. Jim, who was not only happy in his work but good at it, understood this basic principle very well, indeed, he could be said to live by it, and his life too was fine, perfectly splendid. Rusty was less confident.

"I don't quite visualise—"

"You leave the visualising to me, my dear Conway, that's what I'm paid for. As long as I have Jim's general O.K. to carry on. First samples on approval and all that."

"Yes, but I don't see how," Rusty insisted. "I mean we can't have whole film units in our labs and factories. Apart from the disturbance—"

"Which I imagine you can well take in your stride on the production line at the moment. No, but seriously, that wouldn't be necessary, I feel sure. What I have in mind is a real documentary—we can easily put one together from our library. I've found some shots from a caramel factory which would do very nicely indeed, and of course any old labs will serve. That sort of thing. Though of course we'd come along for location-shots as well. Look, let me show you a few sequences."

He switched on his talking-box and gave a few orders to Rosy-fingered Dawn, who got up and walked towards them. Jim obediently turned his swivel-chair round towards the opposite glass pane and Rusty imitated him. Ted pressed several buttons. There was a whirring sound and several clicks as a white blind unrolled over the glass wall while thick black velvet curtains drew themselves across the window and remaining walls. Then a complex of machine-wheels, cogs, pistons moving up and down and from side to side, moulds, spikes, grids and pouring caramel was flung like moving entrails on the sudden screen. The caramel bubbled in a cauldron as vast as a crater. A white gaseous column shot up like a geyser through the caramel. The caramel flowed like a mighty river down a ravine of steel into a big round lake of milk. A cascade of dark lava poured into the caramel from above. The caramel swirled and glubbed round and round and was gradually sucked down the centre until it vanished altogether. The caramel reappeared wound round a steamroller, or was it a printing press? The caramel was spiked and torn. The caramel was stretched like cat-gut.

Rusty felt suddenly depressed, as if a swarm of locusts had moved in with the buzzing darkness and devoured his jovial enough mood. He kept thinking of Jean and all her miscarriages. Nothing could be done, the doctors said, it was the way her pelvis was built. Every single time in the fifth month. They had stopped trying now. She got pregnant so easily.

Jim sat entranced under the beam of images that radiated in luminous dust above his head. His nose prickled with a longing to be picked, a longing that had to be restrained since Ted was sitting obliquely behind him, watching the silhouette of his reaction.

Which was, in the final black silence:

"Splendid. That's wonderful, Ted. Absolute stroke of genius. Extraordinary thing, it really looks exactly like some parts of our factories. If you hadn't told me I'd never have known. Quite extraordinary."

The velvet curtains slid open again, catching Rusty's forlorn expression just before it changed to one of bemused cynicism.

"I expect the machinemen would know."

"You'd be surprised, Mr. Conway, at these people's lack of visual ability to relate."

"Yes," said Rusty, and was.

The documentary had struck him as quite primitive. The sort of thing he used to see even as a schoolboy.

"Of course," said Ted, "it's a little primitive. This is only the raw material. And only a bit of it. You wait till our experts have had a go at it and set the whole thing to the Modern Jazz Quartet." He added mock pompously: "Surely you know our standards of sophistication by now?"

"The real difficulty's in the selling, not the making," he went on, after a further exchange of smoking civilities. "I doubt whether Isabel will buy an ad masquerading as a documentary. I mean TV's rigidly fact, farce or jingle, isn't it. We might wish it on general release cinemas as a subsid to go with one of those epics, but then it would have to be a full-length shorty. What I have in mind is a five-minute affair—and you'd be surprised how much it takes to fill five minutes of screen-time," he added to Rusty's raised eyebrows, but Rusty nodded sagely, as a now experienced performer. "To go into one of those *Focus on Facts* programmes. I think Hill's our man. But Isabel's worth a try and as a matter of fact I've got her hooked for lunch. Why don't you join us?"

Rusty pleaded a previous engagement with the industrial correspondent of *The Express News*, a fact which was only true in the sense that he had lunched with him the day before. He excused himself with a polite throwing back of pigeons and went off, trying not to show his relief through the walls of the glass palace.

Isabel Gormley had been in radio ever since the 2LO days, and talked as if she had invented it. So pioneering did she like to appear that she often gave the impression she had thought up and organised the whole of the B.B.C. European Broadcasts during the war, had begun B.B.C. Television single-handed (though she consented to an ambiguous and possibly royal we), and then been begged by one of the new independent companies to teach them, image by image and for a very tempting salary, the fruits of her long experience. Having lived on air all her life, she was no doubt entitled to her fantasies. And now as Director of Advertising Time for TV-X, she by no means lacked the mechanically exaggerated charm of social intercourse, on the contrary; but she lived her job in every nerve and inevitably brought her work to every dinner table, course after course until well beyond the brandy. Lunches, however, were paid shop, whosoever's the expense account, depending on who was selling what to whom. In this case, Ted Baker's.

They looked a little like one of those brash triangles, the ageing woman with a fondness for boy-lovers, one of whom was on the way out, having supplied a successor. Both the young men wore suits that seemed to taper off from the shoulders down, with a plainness that allowed no flaps, turn-ups or sleeve-buttons, though the starkness of this latest cut was relieved by Jim's pale mauve tie. Ted's milieu made other demands of differentiation so that he contented himself with a silvery sea-grey shirt and a plain black tie, to mourn perhaps, the passing of his devotion to Truth. Everyone in Screen Persuaders Ltd. wore well-cut lounge-suits, suede shoes and pure silk ties—often with horizontal stripes to suggest some new kind of old school—in an attempt to look both artistic and established at the same time. Establishment no one denied them, indeed, they were the Philosophic Rulers of our Mental Republic, from which Poets and Artists had, however, been eliminated. The great thing, therefore, was to look artistic, or even intellectual, though naturally no one was, or would have dreamt of wearing what intellectuals actually wore, which was thirty years out of date. In view of all this it was important to singularise oneself a little.

"So then this character turned up in my office, large as life, if you please," said Isabel to her glass of wine. "And I can tell you, she was bigger than the three of us put together. Well, as I say, nay secretary had already written that it was no use—we have to be careful, you know, there's the Television Act and all that. No private persons allowed to advertise, we wrote. She wasn't having any. I ignored four more letters, and the next thing, I knew there she was on the other side of my desk. She must have hypnotised my underlings—or isn't that what they do? No, they go into a trance themselves, don't they? Oh, well, whatever she did, there she was. Oh, she could pay all right. That's what was so amazing. A full minute advertising her seances, every night for a week. She must have roped in a packet for years. She'd even had the film made, of herself in a trance. Said she'd got a message from 'Yonder' that this was what she must do. 'I'm a mass medium,' she said."

A bibulous roar of laughter erupted from their table. But when the suitable time came round for Ted to explain the matter of the meeting, it was settled almost as soon as mentioned.

"Darling Ted, clearly as I love you I can't give you time that isn't mine to give. What you need is someone like Hughie Hill. Unless you'd care to let me have another of those pop-adaptations of yours. What was it called? Gunpowder Rock, ah, yes, rolled across by Danny Dago. Danny (Hip) Dago as he's trying to get the fan-mag columnists to call him. Poor boy, he wouldn't need a tag like that if he were really at the top."

"Ah, but if he were really at the top he wouldn't need to appear in your beastly little half-minutes."

"Which you don't find so beastly when I allocate them to you, darling."

Ted never wasted his pressure, and their shop soon became the usual bubbly mud of smart gossip, squelching with loud guffaws. Jim basked in it like a happy rheumatic.

But when he goggled at the door of the restaurant Isabel was annoyed at the loss of attention. She turned round and saw only a middle-aged man with flat ginger hair and a ginger brush moustache, accompanied by a tall striking woman of about forty, who wore bobbed hair and a ravaged look. Isabel was about to go on with another story, but Ted now followed Jim's gaze and laughed. Their table was so near the entrance they couldn't ignore him.

"Why Rusty, you old fraud."

"Steady on, old man. This is a very old friend of mine, from my Cairo days. Friend of my wife's too," he waffled unnecessarily. "Turned up unexpectedly from abroad, you know, so cancelled the other lunch. May I introduce, Miss Stella bruin, Ted Baker, Jim Fawcett, and, er—"

"Miss Isabel Gormsley," Jim said.

"Oh! What gorgeous blond streaks you have in your hair," said Stella to Ted, and stroked it. "Do you use Glo-gold? It's marvellous, though one has to have the highlights put in professionally first."

"Well, no, the Greek sun . . ."

"They're in television, Stella," said Rusty.

"Oh, but how exciting. Are you terribly important producers? Oh, Rusty, do ask your friends if we can join them. I've never met any TV producers before, all my friends in Nairobi will be absolutely green with envy if I can say I actually had lunch with *three* television producers."

"Well," said Rusty.

"But by all means," said the host, delighted at the prospect of a larger bill to claim on expenses. "I invited you in the first place, Conway. Oh, waiter."

"I think I'm going to have sole by itself," said Stella primly as she studied the menu, rather as if it were a question of morals. "*On mange à la français!* Everyone's always *so* amazed in London when I order no vegetables," she went on unaware that no one was, except at her saying so, "'What, *no* potatoes and greens?' they say. They simply can't understand, they're absolutely rooted to the old idea of meat-and-two-veg. *Mais moi, je mange à la français.*" She turned to the patient waiter and said disdainfully, as if he hadn't been standing there all the time. "I'll have sole, by itself, please." Then she seemed to notice Isabel for the first time, and making up for the lapse, granted her a precipitous allocation of personal attention:

"What's that stuff?" She stretched across Rusty to finger the neckline of Isabel's dress. "Oh, pure silk, I'm so glad. I can't stand all these synthetic fibres Rusty's selling. They're useless in the tropics, you, know."

"Are they really?" said Jim brightly. "Oh, dear But I'm the one who has to try and sell them. Rusty just explains when I fail."

Stella looked at him with total lack of interest and said, "Oh!" Then she smiled nervously all round.

"Everyone's always *so* amazed when I order no vegetables," she repeated when her bare sole came, presumably because there had been no particular reaction save a wary exchange of looks she half-apprehended rather than saw. She added mechanically, "*moi, je mange à la française.*"

"So, you're in Nairobi?" Ted flashed his smoothest charm straight at her. "What on earth are you doing in that dump?"

A smile is sometimes said to dimple a face with pleasure but Stella's closed-in expression seemed literally to split open with a smile that was both frank and coy at the same time. The contrast was startling, but usually gone in a flash. The disarming enthusiasm of the introductions had at once been replaced with her prim, discontented look during the shuffling of chairs and places, which in turn had given way to the aggressiveness of her uncertainty. Then the smile returned at Ted's attention.

"Oh, do you know Nairobi? But how marvellous! When were you there?"

"Only briefly. On my way to Zanzibar to make a film, two years ago, I think."

"But how extraordinary I should have missed you! I suppose you went to the *English* Club, everyone does. The English are so absolutely sheeplike abroad they simply rush for the *English* Club like rabbits to a burrow. Don't they, Rusty?" Now everyone else was smiling nervously, because Stella's own smile during this harangue expressed nothing less than pure delight at her own originality. "You can always spot the English abroad at once, they look so absurd in their creased suits. And their wives! With their perms and their shapeless flowery-glazed cottons. Glazed cotton in the heat of Africa. It's just the last thing one should wear. The skin can't breathe. It's the same with this stuff Rusty produces. All the little English typists come out with their hideous nitron dresses and their frilly cinderella slips and nitron nicks and they nearly die. One of them went out in the midday sun and the stuff actually shrivelled up on her, it was terribly funny. But English women haven't a clue," she went on as though she wasn't one. "They *all* dress badly, it really is quite incredible . . . Did you go to the Bangwoko? The Bangwoko's marvellous, *don't* say you missed the Bangwoko!"

"No, no, I went to the Bangwoko," Ted murmured, overwhelmed by the torrent of her insistence.

"But *didn't* you think it was marvellous? Kali, the doorman, is a tremendous admirer of mine, whenever I go there he races down those gorgeous steps and *snatches* whatever I'm carrying and races up again. The first time I thought I was being robbed. I was absolutely terrified."

Isabel was furious. Not only was she being done out of her luncheon ration of shop-talk, but she had hoped to sell Ted Baker an idea of her own, that is to say, her new friend Tamara as a designer for Screen Persuaders Ltd. But it wasn't even possible to talk to Jim or the ginger-haired man, for Stella's voice filled the whole space of the table and more. She was attractive still, Isabel admitted with an expert eye, slim and exquisitely dressed in clothes quite unmistakably made abroad. Too slim, even. Then Isabel's cattiness took over and she noted that Stella's exalted opinion of herself had obviously quite distorted her features, for her eyebrows were permanently up, thoroughly creasing her brow, and the corners of her mouth permanently down, further lengthening her face. But her grey eyes, with the slight droop of the eyelids, were extremely sexy.

However, even Ted was now trying to stop Stella's avalanche of attempted mutuality.

"I thought the place was terrible," he said dryly. "The whites made me sick. There they are in the most beautiful countryside and all they can think of is Clacton-on-Sea. Or rushing to the local cinema to see *Saturday Night and Sunday Morning*."

"Oh, but those are only the officials, the petty clerks, we take no notice of them," Stella exclaimed, without bothering to explain who "we" was. "You're absolutely right, they're perfectly awful people—"

"Did you know Hughie Hill is becoming a Catholic?" Isabel decided to use ruthless measures and Rusty felt more and more miserable. Jim looked like a young priest modestly disclaiming responsibility, a pose which successfully hid his total lack of real interest. But Ted was visibly relieved.

"He can't be!"

"Who's Hughie Hill?"

"A television producer," said Rusty, and sighed.

"Oh! How exciting."

"But Isabel, are you sure? It's impossible."

"He's under instruction." Isabel was triumphant at Ted's reaction.

"But he's only interested in making money!"

"What's that got to do with it?" Stella asked. "In Argentina all the most powerful beef magnates are madly pious."

"That's different," Isabel said impatiently. "It's a Catholic country. Anyway, you don't know Hughie."

"Oh, but you're wrong about Argentina, I assure you. I've lived there for years."

"We're talking about Hughie Hill."

Stella pursed her lips, which Rusty knew was a sign that she was crushed at last. But she came back, with some spirit, he thought.

"Well, I still don't see why your Hill Billy or whatever his name is shouldn't become a Catholic despite his faults, that's rather the whole point, I mean isn't it? I know I'm a Catholic and I let no one except my confessor tell me about my faults, it's *simply none* of their business, and that's the attitude in Latin countries, and they really under*stand* these things. That's why I *simply* can't live in England any more, it's just *so* awful. In Argentina, for instance—"

She was off again. Rusty tried to smile all round, then went on eating miserably. He knew Stella like the back of his hand. He knew she was at her worst, like this, because she had somehow been made to feel ill at ease by these smart people who had no intrinsic value in each other's eyes except as intermediaries to something else. Their very middlemanship was their identity, they were one-up by their mere existence. No effort was needed and so, like all middlemen, they tended to sell each other gossip when they had finished selling each other their wares. But Stella was in effect her own middleman, alone in the world, selling her personality, and very badly.

The waiter brought Ted his bill and he scribbled his signature at the bottom, calculating the tip as Stella talked and sliding the silver on the plate. They had had their coffee and could go at any time but it was difficult to judge whether any of her pauses would be quite long enough to make a pre-leaving remark without appearing to interrupt.

"But perhaps it's different, now, with television," she was saying. "Ted, couldn't one of you possibly get me a job here, because you're quite right, really, Kenya is pretty awful. And in fact I've chucked my job with the coffee company there and I've come home to look around. I speak French,

German and Spanish fluently, my typing speed is 60 and my shorthand too. Though of course I've been dreadfully spoiled and got used to dictaphones now and I far prefer an electric typewriter, they're so marvellous, they just brr along without any effort. I don't know how England can be so old-fashioned, I'm so terribly sorry for the poor secretaries here who are still slogging away with shorthand and hammering at those heavy machines. England always was years behind everyone else. But TV must be marvellous. I'd adore to be in TV. Though I often wonder about pure sound, the poor old B.B.C. just seems to have given up, I mean, they don't even try to compete, even with their own television. And pure sound is after all unique, it provides something *none* of the other mediums can provide, not the theatre, the cinema or television, which are *all* predominantly visual. I mean—"

"How's Cambridge?" Isabel interrupted with absolute determination, turning her face pointedly at Ted, who had been there for the weekend. If there had to be a drift away from shop, she liked to remind people that she had been a Girton girl, however far back in the Testament of Youth days. And at last the battle was won.

The waiter brought back the slip of Ted's bill, or rather, the slip of another, much higher bill left by a naïve customer, and Ted pocketed it, nodding his thanks to the waiter who had been very handsomely tipped.

Apart from that, the lunch was a total failure from everyone's point of view except that of Jim Fawcett, who thought it had been great fun. Splendid, really.

3

SERENA SCOTT-BUTTERY had spent the second twenty years of her life working hard to justify her first name. The previous twenty had been the usual procession of confusions, uncertainties and sudden withdrawals of love that make up childhood and adolescence, indeed, the whole human lot from the first yell of the newborn to the last gasp of the dying. But with a name like hers, Serena knew that she had to acquire, earlier than most, that tranquillity of the heart which can be read in the eyes of so few and such scattered people—a small tobacconist in a Paris suburb, a bartender in a Moroccan village or a nun in Notting Hill.

She had, therefore, pursued serenity with a relentlessness that did not go unrewarded, for by her twenty-seventh year she was a fully-trained psychoanalyst who had herself undergone, as all good soul-healers should, three years of painful self-revelation under the guidance of one of the best psychiatrists in the profession, who still sent her such patients as could not afford his fees. There was no conflict in Serena which had not been resolved, no single word or action whose unconscious motive had not been plumbed, sounded, graphed and interringleted into the recurring patterns of dream-currents and the layered cosmography of oceanic compulsions and desires.

Serenity was her aim, not only in herself, but in others, those poor distraught every one of us who have not had the money, the time, the courage or even the inclination, to do more than play at mercilessly knowing ourselves, and who in our late twenties, or thirties, or forties, suddenly cannot face the next decade and seek humiliating love affairs, run away to China, quietly take to drink, or just develop asthma instead. To those such patients who, somewhere along their downhill track, were directed or otherwise found their hesitant way to her, she sold serenity at the cost of an endurance in scrutiny which only the self-absorption of the average human being made possible, and of fair, but regular cheques. She was, on the whole, successful, a modern middleman between body and soul, a perfect salesman of the unconscious to the conscious. Having herself made a success of her life, her marriage and her career, she managed to inspire enough confidence at the start and to impart enough serenity throughout, for her patients to leave at the finish with fresh personalities, refashioned at least to fit the coming decade, if not perhaps exactly in the style intended by the original designer.

Serena was her name, serenity was her life. To this unruffled composure there was, however, one irritant which went about the world by the name of Stella Druin. And Stella was Serena's twin.

"I am *quite* unable to find a *single* fault in you," Stella had written in one of her numerous wads of airmail paper epistles from, was it La Paz, or Kuala Lumpur, or Hong Kong, "*except* that you allow yourself to be irritated by me *beyond* measure."

They were not identical twins. It might have been easier for them if they had been, for identical twins often love one another with a love more loyal and more mysterious than blood-blackmail can normally account for, a love more devoted and from which no Echo could lure Narcissus. But Stella and Serena were as different as any two sisters, and as alike, twins in a sudden tone of voice, a fleeting expression, a gesture, carried by the brother sperms in one and the same spasm of angry pleasure, expanded and inter-imitated perhaps in that dark soft cradle they had shared for many shaping months.

"Stella's coming," Serena announced once again to her husband on the morning she received the unsurprising news.

"In July, of course."

"Oh, yes?" said Rupert, who was reading *The Times Literary Supplement*.

"I wonder whether she'll ask about the flat." Serena looked down beyond the sentence, 'and now I have some surprising news for you,' which was in fact as far as she had read. "Let me see, 'Nairobi has become sheer hell ... my boss ... and on top of that ... and besides, Omar, my beautiful black horse, died . . . a fearful swindle by a horrible Indian merchant and I was heartbroken . . . great hopes of a job in New York . . .' no, there's nothing yet."

"I suppose she's coming in July?"

"Yup."

"And the small matter of the flat?" For so Stella had referred to it after their first big quarrel about it, and the phrase had stuck.

"Not mentioned yet." And she laughed, partly at Rupert's slowness—he heard, as it were, with the back of his mind, and then brought it forward as his own—but also at her own expectancy over Stella's tactics. One of the faults of the psychiatric milieu was knowingness, to which Serena was by no means immune: she derived a special strength from feeling—and not always rightly—that she could see beyond appearances into motives unknown even to those who put on the appearances.

Stella's descents had not been so bad in their early days, when Serena was still under training and living in a bedsitter. Stella would stay with a friend, or take a room nearby, and if she thought Serena's world, of which Serena was them volubly full, incomprehensible and therefore absurd, she at least could admonish her twin on other matters. For although Serena had left her sickliness and compensating tomboyishness behind in the neurotic bogs of childhood, not even the draining of those bogs could turn the plainness of her face into anything but an unobtrusive restfulness, and she had little time to develop more than a conventional taste in clothes. She was, therefore, grateful for the tips, even when the brand of lipstick or style of shoe she had dutifully adopted was derided in extravagant terms by Stella the following year. But later, when these criticisms spread to her home, her life and her husband, her gratitude slowly changed to what she hoped looked like, but frequently was not, a patient but weary tolerance.

In the early days of her marriage she had actually put Stella up on the drawing room sofa. But gradually her visits were firmly changed to dinners and drinks, for their flat off the Finchley Road was extremely small and geared to their professions. They had a sitting room, made to look smaller than it was by Rupert's piano and where Rupert, who was a freelance critic, did most of his work; and an attractive L-shaped bedroom which Serena used as her consulting room by partitioning off the bed with a smart folding-door. Stella of course never just occupied one room but left traces of her existence all over the flat, in the form of nail varnish bottles, pots of cream, stockings or underwear; during sessions she would play hot jazz on the piano or sing loudly in the bath, and if her presence was by any chance not felt, the silence probably meant that she was preparing *the* most marvellous Abyssinian dish in the kitchen, using up all the eggs intended for supper and leaving the place looking like a dustman's delight.

"Oh, *Reeny*," she had urged at dinner during one of these trials, "why don't you turn your horrible drawing room into a consulting room, it's quite good enough for all your rich nymphos, then we could use your room, which is *so* delightful." Stella's criticisms, Rupert observed safely afterwards, usually came paired with a piece of facile praise, as if to atone for her rudeness as a guest, but the emphasis was nearly always unfortunate.

"I can't, Stella." Serene had said. "It's very important that patients should be in a pleasant room. And anyway the piano wouldn't really fit there, because of the odd angles, you see, that bit of wall that juts out."

But Stella had worn her waiting-for-her-turn face.

"And then the drawing room is a bit *caffone*, you know." She used words like a season's fashions, to death. That year, too, everyone was running up gumtrees, we had simply sold the Arabs down the river, and there seemed to be a great many absolute critters around. "I mean since your social life is *completely* centred on the drawing room and you insist on these ghastly evenings with half-a-dozen dreary people just sitting round the fire and *talking*, well, you might as well do it in the *nicest* room you've got." She had smiled nervously and at once sought anonymous authority for her statement: "They're called *soirées à l'anglaise* by all my Mends in Algiers." Or had it been *tardes ingleses* by all her friends in Argentina? Serena couldn't remember.

"And anyway you could easily keep the piano in here—all the more space in the other room, in case your boring intellectual friends actually went mad and wanted to dance or something. Rupee could play it in the evening, after your patients have gone."

They had got used to the slightly ridiculous, rather than affectionate nickname she gave him. She also called him Butterscotch, though here she was not as original as she thought, for many rival critics did the same. She had caught from the middlemen she worked for the habit of deriding other people's worlds to boost up their own, and most of her names for people and things half-known were derogatory. And half-known Rupert certainly was, for she never showed the slightest interest in him, and talked of him, if at all, and much to his relief, as if he were not there, which quite frequently he wasn't, except in body.

Stella moved in the pseudo-cosmopolitan, neo-colonial and sub-diplomatic world of large international goodwill organisations, small consulates, and companies trading in tea, cotton, oil, nuts or rum, according to the secretarial job she happened to be in. She had not married. In spite of her good looks and emphatic personality her men usually left her in the end. And as she repeated the pattern—for so Serena called it—again and again, she lost more and more of that inner confidence, as opposed to outer poise, the insufficiency of which a certain type of man can detect at once and gamble with.

And so she went restlessly about the world, lowering her sights and heightening her ladylike airs proportionately. For a while one of her favourite phrases was about top-drawers and people being not quite out of them. As she grew older she became less buoyant and more deeply unhappy, so that her superficial high spirits had something dead about them, her monologues were more repetitive and monotonous in tone, as if she were simply filling the void mechanically between herself and others. Serena had seen her equivalent a hundred times in what Rupert still liked to call *wagon-lit* society—a woman sitting at an airport bar, on the terrace of the second-costliest hotel, in a dining car, attractive but alone with a cigarette and a double martini, carefully casual and exquisitely tailored, various shades of blonde but darkly suntanned save in the never-relaxed lines of deep anxiety and the crows' feet of exaggerated laughter, a slight alcoholic blur in the eyes, a discontented droop at the corner of the mouth, and a very condescending manner of calling the waiter.

Or rather, Serena had this cruel vision in her mind's eye and had watched with horror as Stella already in her late twenties began to develop towards it. The vision and the horror were subjective, of course, and Serena was always perfectly capable of discerning not only the various shades of subjectivity, but also their cause. Oh, yes, Serena knew exactly which family traits she resented in Stella who was after all her twin, her might-have-been, her would-be, her hidden other self.

At each collapse of the latest hope, whether of married bliss or merely of the perfect job, with the perfect boss, in the perfect place, Stella would return to London penniless, or manless, or jobless, or all three, usually after a brief splash on a European holiday to look up all her scattered acquaintances. She would then either take a temporary job until the next opportunity abroad occurred, or make a sincere attempt to settle in the capital which was, after all, the nearest thing to home that was left her, even if it meant a bedsitter in Earl's Court.

But Stella never stayed long in London. As Serena said to Rupert, who explained it back to her two days later, Stella couldn't face her own reality. However that might be, she was always ready to fly off to some outlandish outfit only too grateful for a European secretary, or to join the overseas staff of some firm willing to pay artificial salaries to anyone lost or lonely enough to go so far away into such wilderness, physical, social, or cultural. She did not exactly say that travel broadens the mind, for she thought her mind extremely broad. Travel makes one more interesting, she assumed, and collected countries like achievements.

Then their relationship would settle down into that much more comfortable, because unreal, convention called correspondence: that is to say, at first, a detailed reportage on the wonderful advantages of the new place which, in her diction, sounded exactly like every other place, the skiing or sailing or riding or underwater-fishing facilities, the glorious trips and views, the delightful flat or maid she had just acquired by an absolute miracle of cleverness. Serena for her part restricted her letters as far as possible to expressions of gladness at all this joy, or formal reports on theatres and films or at most on clothes she had bought, if any. For Stella was not at all interested in her real life, that is, her work or Rupert's, and any slip of the pen into chattiness about plans, holidays, friends or, above all, minor domestic changes in the flat, provoked pages of advice, alternate plans, and expressions of Stella's absolute inability to understand why Serena did not do something completely different. After a while Stella's enthusiasm about the new place would be duly followed, as the novelty wore off, by one snag after another, accumulating into a complexity of utterly insupportable conditions. She would then arrive once again in London, on leave or job-hunting or both, and always, of course, in July.

July was Serena's busiest month, when she saw all her patients twice as often before taking a much needed holiday from their dreams, depressions, psychopathic deviations, defensive franknesses and other disguised aggressions. Rupert too, would put in an intensive spell of work so as to find a few more cheques than usual on their return.

And always, since Serena no longer put her up—indeed even if she had herself been willing, Rupert would not have her in the house—Stella would ask if she could borrow the flat while they were on holiday.

The small matter of the flat. It seemed small enough indeed, both the flat and the matter of it. Such a little thing to ask. So natural, between sisters, between twins. What had gone wrong, that it should have grown so big, as little things do between two human beings who love one another completely, with hate and envy and thick curtains of indifference?

Stella had borrowed the flat three times. Serena and Rupert were poorer then, for she was slowly building up a practice and Rupert, who had come to her as her first patient, had been rather a lost cause in those days. The flat had never been much of a flat, a rent-controlled affair in a shabby Victorian house, with a makeshift kitchen the size of a pantry and a bathroom on the landing, which they had to share with other lodgers.

Much discipline was needed to keep all their belongings in order, and much particular knowledge too—not to wrench this knob, not to open the top of that window, not to move this lamp which could fall to pieces; an endless list of avoidances. But they had got used to it, and they kept it because it was cheap and in N.W.3, and had one nice room for patients. They liked it the way they had arranged it.

Stella, however, would "improve" it out of all recognition. She even bought things, generously, extra jugs, and saucepans, better soap or a luxury towel, which Serena tried not to take as implied criticism. It wasn't in fact the improvements she minded, or even the breakages, the dents, fingermarks and drink-splashes on the walls and the stains in the carpet, it was the litter of personal possessions that Stella always left behind—clothes, shoes, cosmetics, electric irons, handbags, suitcases, oil-paints, a portable wireless, a guitar, whatever represented Stella's latest craze. Already the communal box room under the stairs was full of her belongings, and lodgers were complaining. Rupert, whose books, papers and music had all been sampled and left about or put back in the wrong order, soon put his foot down about lending Stella the flat. "You'd have thought popularised Freud had made the significance of some gestures so widely known that people would make special efforts to avoid them," he said, exasperated, and with his facile literary attitude to psychology he could, when he paid attention, wax quite eloquent on the womb-symbolism of the flat. But the request had been repeated, almost as a formality, each time for different and perfectly plausible reasons, every year or two for one and a half decades, although the flat was by no means convenient for Stella. It was not self-contained, meant a lot of housework, and was difficult of access for a businesswoman with an office job. Certainly there would always be pages or hours of criticism to face on their return, in the form, usually, of constructive suggestions such as why on earth didn't Serena have a shower put into the bedroom, or buy an espresso coffee-machine, or a home Turkish-bath, of one of those absolutely marvellous devices for electric massage of the tummy muscles and beating of the buttocks? Though sometimes her criticisms were direct, or at most disguised as personal praise of Serena's stoic courage in putting up all these years with such abominably primitive conditions.

Serena herself could analyse ruthlessly, in much more scientific terms than Rupert, but what was the use of analysis if the patient could not perform her part of it, and if the analyst were so closely involved with the patient as to become one with her, suffering each pain like a schizophrenic jab into their joint psyche? No, even the jargon of analysis failed, and they had to protect themselves with that wall of indifference that rose between them at every meeting, pierced only by chinks of irritation which so often cracked the wall and crumbled it into a dust of relentless battle between two naked, wounded lives.

"Ooh, you have got fat!" was the first thing Stella said to her when Serena came round to her digs two days after her arrival. Serena had kept the original date relatively free to meet Stella at the air-terminal, but then Stella had changed her plans at the last moment and come two days earlier, on 29th of June. When she telephoned, Serena had been unable to alter any of her appointments, which had caused a slight freeze at the time.

"Ooh, you have got thin!" Serena imitated amicably, determined not to be irritated by anything whatsoever.

Stella sat on the edge of the bed, making love to herself ceaselessly as she talked, with an elegant hand that stroked her neck, her shoulder, her underarm, under the loose silk sleeve, played with a string of beads, lifting them, twisting them, dropping them, curling them round a finger as if caressing a circle round and round over the cleft of her breasts. When she wasn't doing this she smoked, tapping a cigarette every two seconds over an ashtray. Her long legs were crossed gracefully and vanished into a pair of colourfully embroidered Sudanese slippers.

She talked of Africa, her job and why she had left it, her journey, her holiday, or rather, her sentimental sojourn in dear old Alex, so full of deliciously sad youthful memories.

But she couldn't sit still for long, and finding Serena's placid acquiescence rather dull, she jumped up to show off her latest wardrobe, since

Serena had missed the unpacking ritual. Item by item Stella brought it out, singing the praises, price and geography of each. Clothes for Stella were like her conversation, a substitute for communication. But they did more than reveal her nature, they were her nature, which was a generous one.

"Would you like this?" she said almost brusquely, holding up a pretty dress in Gaugainesque shades, cleverly cut from Sari silk. "It's much too big for me now I had it made three years ago in Bangkok, and it was loose then. Look, I'm sure it'll fit you, do try it on."

Their shared childhood was in those words. Dutifully Serena took off her cotton frock, horribly analysing the vague emotions that stirred distantly within her. 'It'll do for Serena to get dirty in,' her mother said. 'You can have it, it's nasty,' said Stella once, at seven years old, of a piece of cheese she didn't like. Serena slipped on the feathery silk. In spite of that material and the colours, which she would never have chosen, never even have spotted, in any shop, it had that classic air, and it did wonders for her, as she had known it would. Her most elegant things always came from Stella, or were bought on Stella's advice, or were made up from strange stuffs sent by Stella, by a wonderful little dressmaker Stella had discovered.

Stella was dancing around her, pinning in a dart here, adjusting the shoulder there.

"But Reeny, it's marvellous on you. Oh, I almost want to keep it, I didn't know I looked so gorgeous three years ago. No wonder the export manager of T.C.F. (Thailand) Ltd. fell in love with me. It's a wee bit too long for the present fashion, but as it's a straight skirt I won't bother to pin the hem on you. Just two inches higher. And mind you do a French hem. All the women in France do a French hem, it's just a little extra trouble but it makes all the difference the way it hangs. Look!" She lifted the hemline of her own skirt. "You just fold it like this, then fold it *back* a fraction and do a small cross-stitch backwards. You see, not a trace of stitching on the other side, it's simply marvellous."

"Yes. I see. Thank you," said Serena, who had been doing French hems all her life. The silk caressed her arms as she took off the dress. "Well, thank you very much. It'll be just the thing for Venice. Are you sure you can spare it?"

"Yes, yes, I told you, it just floats around me."

"But couldn't I pay you something for it?"

"No, really, it's terribly old."

"Well, let me give you something in exchange. I know. I've got a dress I can't get into now I've put on weight. I'm very fond of it, too, but there it is. It's a very elegant dinnerish sort of dress, most useful."

"Mmm. Which one?"

"The dark green one, you know, I was wearing it last year."

"Oh, yes. Hmm. Well, no, I don't think so. *Ce n'est pas tout à fail non affaire.*"

"Yes, all right." Now it was Serena who wore their prim look as she dressed, trying not to feel hurt.

"And oh, *Reeny*, I'm *so* glad you're going to Venice at last. It really is so beautiful you'll be left gasping, I simply can't understand *how* you could have been so stubborn as to avoid it for so long."

"Well, it was just that—"

"And if you're coming from Greece you'll see it from the *sea*, it's absolutely breathtaking, oh, I *do* so envy you. I'll give you Gina's address, she'll be enormously useful to you and of course absolutely delighted to see you if you say you're my sister. Lorenzo, her husband, is our Italian representative and he's always popping between Milano and Nairobi but they have an absolutely glorious villa just outside Venice—"

"Well, we'll only be there two days and actually—"

"Oh, and *Reeny*, if you're going to Italy you simply *must* buy yourself an Italian swimsuit, you can't go on wearing that dreadful black one that's gone all yellow with salt and sun, I *told* you it would, and besides, it's quite out of fashion now we're echoing the thirties with very wide shoulder straps and no décolletage at all. And the Italian ones are *so* much better than anything produced in this awful country."

Serena sat down again. She couldn't help smiling.

"We're going to Italy after our holiday in Greece, so I can hardly do that, unless I bathe in the nude in Lesbos."

"They are a wee bit expensive but oh, it's so worth while, they fit like a glove and they're always so beautifully finished inside too, which is so important."

"Have you seen Rusty, yet?"

Dear old Rusty, he was the subject-changer, a code, a reminder that they had at least one friend in common. Stella had brought him one day years ago, after the war, when on the whole they were closer because younger, and he would be produced as a buffer whenever in their quarrels one of them accused the other of criticising her friends.

"Yes, as a matter of fact I had lunch with him yesterday. Dear old Rusty, he just doesn't change a bit, I'm so fond of him. No analytical nonsense about *him* . . . And my *dear*," she went on in her jocular Mayfair, "we ran into some television producers! Though I must say," and her tone changed—"they were pretty ghastly people. Is Rupee's literary crowd like that? So rude! All in need of the old sickatrist I'd say. Everyone's so contorted in England these days. I must say, thank God we don't get like that abroad. You're pretty bad yourself with all your subtleties. Take life as it comes is my motto. Inch 'Allah! I'm all for the Oriental view of life. . ."

Serena knew this particular record fairly well and let it spin on the turntable without bristling to the jabs it threw out. She had also heard a different version of the lunch the evening before from her patient, Isabel Gormsley, who had been quite upset by her own rudeness to this 'neurotic woman called Stella Druid or something'. Isabel was obviously unaware of the relationship though she did mention that the woman reminded her curiously of Serena.

4

BOTH THE items of information which Isabel Gormsley had given Ted about Hughie Hill were wrong. For Hughie Hill was not only nowhere near to becoming a Catholic—that is to say he had mothed around it, fluttered to Farm Street three times for instruction from a smooth, worldly Jesuit, then found that pressure of work had somehow blown out the feeble light; but in addition, he was no use at all to Ted Baker—that is to say he blandly refused to consider introducing into his programme a documentary film made by an advertising firm, however grand, after which he skilfully took over the idea for his own team of producers, camera-men and interviewers.

Skilfully and, it must be admitted, honestly enough. "It will do just as much good," he said, "if not more, at least as far as U.V.I. is concerned."

Ted grasped the point at once and saved his persuasive powers for other businesses and other more tractable people. But he privately resolved to charge U.V.I. as much as he decently could for selling the idea to *Focus on Facts*.

Hugh Johnson-Hill—for so he had called himself at the Warmsley College of Journalism and General Culture—had quickly shrunk his name back to its more democratic diminutive when he got his first break in TV-X, so that it could more easily squeeze through the wavy lines emanating from the tiny screens and become a household word. This had certainly succeeded, and Hughie Hill had the distinction of being the only man in television whose name the public knew as well as any star's, although they never saw his face. It was the face of an apoplectic butcher in an old-fashioned comedy, red and crude with warts on his nose and networks of purple on cheeks and jowls. He looked much older than his thirty-five years, being a vast man, and as vastly powerful. For although he never appeared on either his own programme or anyone else's, and never allowed anyone to photograph him, his name filled the whole screen every night at eight-fifteen, in plain capital letters, HUGHIE HILL . . . followed at least twenty seconds later by presents for you . . . *Focus on Facts*, to a gay little tune which turned out to be, if one listened carefully, an exceedingly jingled version of *It's a Sin to Tell a Lie*. And since he employed only very handsome young men to do the presentation, who naturally were all very nearly as well-known as he was, somehow the public image of him was a vague mixture of all these handsome young men only handsomer, bigger, better.

Focus on Facts was immensely popular, because it was about everything, without ever sounding educational, that is to say, it managed to be both topical and surprisingly miscellaneous at the same time, without imparting a single viewpoint or a jot of information which anyone who had learnt to read or to argue in a pub would not already know. Play on the Pleasure of Recognition, was what he had been taught at the Warmsley College of Journalism and General Culture, and he played. Delight in Dissent, but Do Not, of course, Divide, and he did not. United his public rose to fantastic figures.

Hughie Hill was not, however, a cynic. He had learnt all these principles and more at the College and in his early days on *The Express News*, but only as one learns an elementary technique, how to apply paint on canvas, how to put words into a sentence, where to find the main chords on a guitar. The rest was art, that was to say, the genius of Hughie Hill, a peculiar combination of dynamism, quick-wittedness, genuine skill and faith. Faith in the beauty of truth and of course the truth of beauty. For Hughie Hill unquestioningly believed in the objective reality of the Facts on which he Focused. The Facts were political, industrial, commercial, agricultural, scientific, technological, economic, social and of course "human", and sometimes, in a dead season of facts, they could be cultural, in other words geographical (travelogues of various kinds), geological, archeological, botanical, zoological, astronomical; and, if the worst came to the worst, they could be musical, artistic, or even literary: interviews and/or discussions. To be fair, this actual result did not represent the order of priority in the mind of Hughie Hill, who also managed to believe, and just as unquestioningly, that his programme was the only intellectual programme watched by the wider masses of the British public. But the rationing was inevitable, due partly to the louder claims of innumerable other Facts, but also to Hughie Hill's slight sense of guilt at enjoying what he liked to call his intellectual programmes most.

So that when he had given all the preliminary study-orders for the nitron documentary to one of his producers, who then left him to brief his assistant producer on the same lines, Hughie Hill let out a heavy sigh of relief from his enormous chest, a sigh that smelt of tobacco, not just as exhaled on the tops of buses but a deep-down smell like a sweetbriar-pipe, so that his secretary's nostrils widened with pleasure. Then he turned his attention to a much more interesting matter. Lord Merseyside, an ex-Labour Cabinet Minister who had been near the Great for a lifetime, rather than among them, had written his memoirs, and had agreed, with some alacrity, to answer questions about his book on television. Hughie Hill had hit on the unusual idea of getting not only a politician to hammer at him—TV-Stevie, alias Tom Stevens, T.V. M.P., as he was also known, was the obvious choice—but also a literary critic. On the grounds that a book was a book, when all was said and done, and what had been ill done had better be well said.

Since Hughie Hill would not allow the public to see his face, he also made it a fixed rule never to meet the people who were to appear on his programme. He delegated all the preliminary discussions, the rehearsals, the camera-run-throughs, the oiling of the human machinery with drinks, all the mere technicalities in fact, to the appropriate producer. He was the brains behind the scenes and that was enough for him. But even fixed rules have exceptions that prove them, especially for their makers. As soon as he had conceived the idea of having a literary critic, Hughie Hill experienced a growingly uncontrollable desire to meet one in the flesh. But how to get one? The man who could command any number of starlets, beatniks, members of Parliament, actors, Trade Union leaders, newspaper correspondents, sports heroes and even bishops, for some reason did not know how to get hold of a literary critic. His secretary had no idea either. She rang Alby Race, the Assistant Director, and Alby Race said he didn't know where the species hung out, but the boss might try Caraway Christian Ltd., the literary agents. The voice of Hughie Hill's secretary was then tossed like a golf ball from the Fiction Department to the Magazine Section, from Foreign Rights to Drama, from Film Rights to Radio and Television. But Caraway Christian Ltd. only handled authors they could sell. She was about to pass the whole thing on to her assistant secretary, when Alby Race telephoned through again. "Just been talking to Sam Wilson, he reads all the book pages in the Sunday papers. Says you could try them."

"Get hold of some copies, and send them up."

"Yes, ma'am."

When the secretary brought them in already opened at the book pages, Hughie Hill pushed aside his other work, lit a cigar and lent his huge bulk eagerly over them. *The Sunday Times*, *The Observer*, *The Sunday Supplement*—which had been started some years before as a kind of umpire or middleman between the other two—and its latest rival *The Sunday Telegraph*. All the articles had been thoughtfully marked out with ballpoint pens by Sam Wilson, according to the office system of colour priority, red for the top-grade regulars, blue for second-grade occasionals, green for changeable nonentities who might be up-and-coming. Hughie Hill could therefore grasp the hierarchy at a glance. It was always important to grasp the hierarchy, if only to bypass it. But in fact his eye fell upon the name of Rupert Scott-Buttery, whose review of a book called *Hush! the Wind Softly* was marked out in blue. The name echoed in Hughie Hill's mind, partly because of his own one-time weakness for a double-barrelled name, but also because he had actually read a book by Rupert Scott-Buttery, a little study of Shelley's Cave Imagery which he had seen by chance, shyly bought and to his secret surprise thoroughly understood and enjoyed.

There were, of course, bigger names. Hughie Hill had no doubt at all that he could have got the great Charles Fortescue himself at the drop of a letter, or Howard Cutting, both of whom wrote the lead columns in *The*

Sunday Supplement. Howard Cutting certainly, for he now remembered that he had met him at some private dinner he couldn't avoid, and the man had seemed very anxious to please, and flattered to meet the great Hughie Hill. But Hughie Hill always acted on his hunches, and he had a hunch now about Rupert Scott-Buttery. He didn't even hesitate. *The Sunday Supplement* did not hesitate either in giving his secretary Rupert Scott-Buttery's private address and telephone number, and within four hours Rupert Scott-Buttery was waiting in the reception lounge of the X-shaped TV-X building on the heights of Parliament Hill, Hampstead Heath.

Rupert Scott-Buttery could in fact have come sooner, but made a principle of never being available on the same day, at anybody's beck. However, they had said it was very urgent, and television was television after all, so here he was.

He had to wait quite a long time.

"Look here, what is all this?" he asked the receptionist. "I'm summoned in all haste by some chap called Hill and then I'm kept waiting half an hour."

The receptionist looked shocked at his lack of respect. She agreed to ring through and find out.

"Mr. Hill is still in conference, I'm afraid, and he particularly wants to see you himself. It's a very great honour to be seen by Mr. Hill himself," she added firmly as Rupert's face began to express who-the-hell.

Ten minutes later he was sent for at last, and walked behind a black and gold messenger boy, under an arch entitled News and Documentary, into a lift and out on the fourth floor (Focus on Facts).

"Rupee!"

Stella's voice squealed excitedly from a rattle and ping of typewriters beyond a low balustrade to the right of the corridor as he passed through towards a door marked "Producers".

"What are *you* doing here?" they both said together.

Then Stella went straight on: "My marvellous Mrs. Barnsley sent me. Surely I've told you about her? I knew her in the W.A.A.F.'s—not very well, but you can imagine my surprise when I turned up at her agency, oh, ages ago, it was, when I first came back from Peru, and found we knew each other. She always gives me the best temporary jobs she's got. Holiday replacements, don't you remember? I explained to you why I like temporary work because it leaves me free to look—"

"Yes, yes," Rupert looked nervously at the messenger boy.

"So you can imagine how I jumped at THIS! Television, instead of the usual wool merchants and shipping companies. Of course this is sheer stooging, but *still*—"

"I'm afraid I must go, I have an appointment." The urgency of the telephone call and the receptionist's tone of awe had after all affected him more than the long wait, now that the wait was over.

"Who are you seeing? Are you going to APPEAR?"

"Man called Hill. A producer."

"My dear! But you're MADE. You're absolutely launched. He's the Director, not a Producer. Nobody *ever* sees Hughie Hill himself as far as I can gather. Even the *Staff* doesn't. I do believe he has his own secret lift or something. Oh *do* ask him. D'you know him well? I say, Rupee, *do* ask him if he needs a private secretary and put in a good word for *me*. I'd sure stay in England if I could hook something like that."

Rupert said, "Must go now," and waved as he moved on, half backwards, with a steady nodding of agreement that was somehow made meaningless by his over-raised eyebrows and inane smile. But as he passed the numerous doors bearing names he didn't know, and as he waited once again in the anteroom to the office of Hughie Hill's secretary, he felt swept through by one of his rare waves of genuine affection for Stella, an affection mingled with pity, but also with admiration for her resilience and courage.

Hughie Hill was a shade disappointed with his real live literary critic, in spite of the latter's artistic head, with its unruly black eyebrows and its long hair combed straight back; but this was perhaps due to the fact that Rupert Scott-Buttery seemed peculiarly unaware of Hughie Hill's importance and treated him as an equal, like a mere radio producer for instance, whereas Hughie Hill had even read a book by Rupert Scott-Buttery.

"Oh that," said Rupert Scott-Buttery with a deprecatory laugh. "The less said about that the better." And although he was pleased that a little more than less had been said, it was also quite clear to Hughie Hill that he was not going to get his discussion on The Role of Literature in Society, on which subject he had at least three ideas to air.

"Couldn't you possibly simplify your name?" he asked with a suffering face. "You see, my programme is a popular programme, and by that please don't think I mean rubbish, oh no, we simply rehandle, if you follow me, we present things, well, facts, and-er-culture, you know, in a palatable form, in a way that, well, simple people can understand and I don't mean simpletons, mind you, oh no." Rupert nodded sagely, for he had never yet refused to write any book popularising any classic, or introducing twentieth century poets to the twentieth century, or explaining the dramatists of the fifties to the sixties. "You should see some of the letters we get. Of course, some are simply moronic, but not all, oh no, not all. Ten million viewers every day, you know." Hughie Hill was about to launch on his little lecture to very important visitors when he remembered that Rupert Scott-Buttery hardly measured up to one of those and that he, Hughie Hill, had only decided to see him at all out of a private whim, which was already wearing off rather rapidly. "Rupert Scott-Buttery," he enounced elocutionally and shook his head. Then he wrote it down on his pad in block letters framed it with a rounded rectangle and cocked his red face sideways, narrowing his small eyes so that they looked like black pips in a watermelon. "Hmm. Couldn't you possibly make it Pert Scott? I say, that's rather good. You'd probably be a star interviewer overnight."

"I'm afraid not. You see, I do have some reputation, already, as a critic, not much, I know, but still, one can't very well change, well, horses in midstream."

Hughie Hill's large vague mouth pursed into a prawn-like shape and his chin jogged in and out of his fleshy neck. These casuals were all the same, they all thought of the programme primarily, no, entirely, as an unexpected means of advertising themselves; after which there was no getting rid of them—they wanted to be on every time anything to do with their silly subject cropped up. They never considered for one moment what was good for the programme. Suddenly he lost all interest.

"Right, well, one of my producers will have the book sent to you and then get in touch with you before next Monday. We'll tell you what to do. I'm glad we had this little chat. Always like to meet my performers. The personal touch, you know, that's what counts. Goodbye. And good luck on Monday. Goodbye."

Rupert was quite glad to get out of the formidable presence. "Come and have a drink," he said to Stella out of sheer relief.

"Oh, Rupee, how nice." Her smile was near to a maidenly confusion that set off her elegance to great effect. She really was pleased and surprised, for Rupert's remoteness usually frightened her. "But oh," she wailed, "my lunch hour's from one to two, they're abominably rigid here."

"My clear Stella, they won't even notice. Come on. Tell whoever it is that your brother-in-law, who's appearing on Hughie Hill's programme on Monday, is taking you to lunch."

"Yes! That's it!" She was as excited as a child, and ran to do his bidding.

"Are you really taking me to lunch?" she insisted half incredulously as they went down in the lift. "How gorgeous. Oh, and Rupee, *did* you tell him I'm looking for a job as a private secretary?" Stella tended to ask these things, partly as a joke but also in some irrational way believing in them, so that when she pressed them again she believed in them rather more.

"I'm afraid the great Mr. Hughie Hill didn't think all that much of me, let alone my relatives."

"Because it would be so marvellous, and I could get digs in Hampstead, I'm sure Margot would help me find something, and Jean Conway could put me up until I did. Then I'd be quite near you."

Rupert gave his vacantly encouraging smile. He was never quite so irritated as Serena was by Stella's apparent incapacity to take in anything one said, because he himself was often just as bad. The only difference was that he tended to hear it a few minutes later, whereas Stella didn't hear it at all. Unless it was something to her advantage, and then she would give it an unusual alertness which meant that she had taken it too literally: 'But they told me to ring them up any time,' she would say, and Rupert couldn't help sympathising. He even half expected her to reproach him with 'but you *said* you'd ask him'. But no, she really assumed that he had.

"Tell me, Stella," he asked in the pub, "do you like your rather strange life?"

"Oh, you know me. *Che sera sera*! If I were to worry all the time about whether I like it I wouldn't live at all."

"I know, I know, but are you happy?"

She made an o with her mouth.

"*No me quejo*! Don't you go all Serena on me. She's always asking, but am I happy? Why are you all so worried about happiness? One kicks along, life has its ups and downs."

"That's not quite what Serena means," said Rupert, surprised to find himself acting as middleman between them.

"Oh, I know what she means all right. Why can't I change my awful character, I'd be so much *happier*. I wish she'd change hers and let me be. Live and let live is my motto. It takes all sorts to make a world. One man's food is another man's poison. If people can't take me as I am they can lump it."

"That's just it," said Rupert very gently, "they so often have to lump it."

She shrugged again.

"Oh, I know. I've made a mess of my life, I've lost several potential husbands. I have no security. I live from job to job—what else? Oh, yes. I could have had a brilliant career in dress-designing if only I had taken up that scholarship I won at school, or in music if only I had bothered to starve in a garret and practise scales night and day. *Que veux-tu, mon vieux? C'est la vie.*"

"Yes, well, I haven't made such a startling success of my life either. We all feel that. Even Serena does at times, you'd be surprised." Rupert was suddenly moved to console her with his own sense of failure. "I wanted to write. I love literature, can you understand that? I love it as you must once have loved your music. But all I can do is to weave my commentaries out of it, thick or thin according to the level of the readers who prefer to read commentaries than the real thing, on which I feed like a parasite."

"But Rupee, you're a genius, and you write all those absolutely brilliant books I can't understand." For once, Stella answered to the point, flattered by his sudden confidence, and he was angry because of course it wasn't to the point at all. "And Serena's a genius too, though really, sometimes I can't understand a word she *says*, let alone what she writes in those learned articles. It all seems boloney to me. What was it I read somewhere in some magazine? Oh yes, I know, it did make me hoot! According to the sickatrists apparently I ought to be a gibbering neurotic because I was separated from my mama for three months at the age of one."

Rupert smiled as he took her glass to fetch her another drink. When he returned she had made a mental step back to the previous phase of the conversation, the meaning of which had just begun to percolate.

"And anyway," she went on as if there had been no break, "my music was just, just . . . interpreting too . . . I only composed one piece in my life, when I was nine. It was called *The Bumble Bee in the Garden of Allah*, it went bzzz-zzzz-zzzz-zzz-tim-poom-da-da-da-da-da-bzzz-zzzz-zzzz." She half-conducted it as she hummed and he realised, as he often had before, why men fell in love with her. He too moved back in the conversation.

"Nobody wants you to change, Stella," he said gently. "Not even Serena. One can't change radically after a certain age. It's just that, well, why don't you live and let live too?" She looked so astonished he tried another tack. "I mean, if you could only tone it all down a bit, everything in a lower gear, the aggressiveness as well as the charm. People want to take you as they find you, I assure you, but they can't. They want to, because you're attractive and unusual, and because you're warm and very affectionate and even childish, underneath all that, that—"

"Hmm. Oh, well. Yes . . . look, I'm sure you mean well, but I don't think I'll lunch with you if you're going to moralise. It was sweet of you to ask me." She had her prim look again as she put out her cigarette slowly, her long little finger at a perfect right angle with the others, pointing straight at him.

"Oh, come, Stella, don't be absurd."

"I'm not, I assure you. No offence. *Nichts für ungut!* I'd just rather not, if you don't mind. Tell me," she went on with exaggerated casualness as she picked up her bag, "when are you going on your holiday?"

"At the end of the month."

"Well, I'll probably see you before then." She smiled sweetly, "Give my love to Serena. Bye."

Rupert half got up and half bowed. He watched her walk out, head high, and reflected that although Stella spoke in clichés, proverbs and abstractions of her own choosing, she seemed quite simply not to grasp the meaning of his abstractions, or Serena's, or, probably, anyone else's. They might as well be talking Greek. Then Stella came back.

"Oh, by the way, Rupee, I forgot to ask Serena, but I'm sure you could tell me just as well. The thing is, do you think that, when you go to Greece, I could possibly borrow your flat while you're away? It would be such a saving, and of course an absolute blessing as well, and I thought—"

"As a matter of fact, Stella, well, you see, we do really prefer to lock it up, it's less work, and there are so many, things, the clutter, and my papers and—"

"Yes, yes, that's quite all right. It's of no importance, at all. I simply thought I'd ask, just in case. Well," she gave a very social smile this time —"goodbye. See you soon."

"Of course. Give us a ring. Why don't you come round to dinner?" said Rupert, desperately guilty. "On Thursday, say?"

She made a moue.

"Hmm. I think I've got something on Thursday. What about Tuesday?"

"I think it's all right. Tuesday then, unless Serena rings to say it isn't."
"All right. See you then."
"Thursday then."
"No! you said Tuesday."
"Oh, yes, sorry, Tuesday."
"Tuesday."
"Bye."
"Goodbye."

A pale young man in a grey-green checked jacket, and grey flannel trousers was sitting at the next table with a girl. He was staring at his diary with a heavy frown as if the engagements noted therein were quite incomprehensible.

"Thursday to Monday I'm in Manchester," he was saying slowly. "Tuesday I got to be in Skipton, all day, Wednesday to Thursday I'm in Loughborough, and then Nottingham—the shoe people you know—till Saturday morning. Monday I've got to be, up in Liverpool, that means travelling up on the Sunday. As a matter of fact I might as well stay the Saturday night in Nottingham and get a cross-connection. That would leave us Tuesday ... No, Tuesday I got to get down to Bristol ..."

The girl was staring at the bright bottles behind the bar as they caught a shaft of sun that made the coloured lights behind them pale. She said nothing. There was nothing for her to say.

5

"THE DISTANCE I have to walk before I remember what I've left behind increases as I get older," said Rusty to his wife. "It used to be the corner, this morning it was the Town Hall."

"Well, at least you remember it, that's the main thing."

Jean Conway was Scots to the roots of her eyelashes, and spoke in a soft burr and a gentle pitch that spread like a haze over her entire person, affecting also those around her. It was impossible to quarrel with Jean. On the other hand, it was also impossible to impose on that gentleness beyond a certain point, for at that point it would give way, not into anger but into firm common sense, quite simply, calmly, and always unnoticeably. It wasn't so much what she said, which was probably just as platitudinous as what anybody else said, Rusty would tell her in moments of marital mutual congratulation, it was a matter of tone.

"Well, I suppose we're none of us getting any younger," said Rusty, finding comfort in numbers, rather as people say 'we're *all* neurotic' and find, not only comfort but denial in the vastness of the company. Rusty had felt unaccountably sad for several weeks now. In his sessions with Serena he attributed this sadness to the hints of Harry Thorpe, the medieval fringe over Jim Fawcett's beatific face and the scientists' supreme indifference to whether the public believed in the efficacy of their new formula or not. Yet as soon as the sadness was thus attributed he knew that it was all much more ineffable.

"You know we've got company tonight?" said Jean.

"Good lord! Who? Or do you mean Guy Hart? Did I tell you? I met him at the club and asked him to drop in later."

"Oh, how nice. I haven't seen Guy for ages."

She smiled at him from the streamlined kitchen sink where she had been rinsing all the cooking utensils and placing them in the dishwasher, so as to have less to rinse after supper. Rusty had brought in his six o'clock whisky from the drawing room and sat in the breakfast-corner, sipping thoughtfully. She didn't like Guy Hart all that much, in fact, he was a little too smoothly Foreign Office for her taste, but she knew that Rusty enjoyed a chat about the old days in Tokyo, where he had represented U.V.I. interests in volcanic dust and young Guy, as he called him, had been a Third Secretary. He was now a First Secretary, waiting for his forty-second birthday which would automatically bring him the rank of Councillor, in recognition of this milestone on the path to wisdom. He had been selling the compromises of his country now for many years, in various parts of the world, but would turn up in London fairly frequently, either on leave or on his home-spell, and Rusty was always pleased to bump into him.

"Who else is coming?" he asked in vague alarm.

"Don't you remember? Stella rang up yesterday about bringing Rupert and Serena to see him on television. They haven't got it, apparently."

"Good lord," said Rusty again, partly at Serena not having a television, partly out of fear at what enormities Stella might say in front of Guy.

"Oh, it'll be all right." Jean read his thought. "Stella's met quite a few Guy Harts in her time, and he must know by now how to veer around the things said by the Stellas of this world."

"I don't know. She tends to be worse when Serena's around. Or when anyone she thinks important is there. This is a combination of both."

"Rusty, what's the matter with you? You're usually the one who defends Stella to me! Anyway, I was going to tell you, I've been thinking that Stella's much more subdued this time."

"Oh, have you?" said Rusty hopefully.

"Yes, it's even a little worrying. I hope there's nothing wrong."

"How do you mean?"

Jean was still standing by the luminous steel sink, feeding bits of bread to the waste disposal unit, as to a hungry animal. "Steady on," Rusty murmured in brackets.

"I'm not quite sure," said Jean, still pacifying the monster. "Usually Stella's brimful of her latest fad, you know, trying to force it down our throats, like when she insisted for days and weeks that I'd be able to bear children if only I'd go to that marvellous osteopath who had made all her bones feel so delicious. There's always something. But not this year."

"Perhaps she's just growing up," suggested Rusty.

"Ay, maybe. But it's more than just the fads. I can't quite put my finger on it. It's er . . . yes. You know how she likes to singularise herself by playing it very cosmopolitan when she's in England, running down everything English, and no doubt, playing it very English abroad?"

"Yes?" said Rusty dubiously, recognising with surprise the same tendency in himself, at least in the past. Though of course there were some circumstances nowadays when it was *de rigueur* to run down the English.

"Well, the things she debunks now are the same as before, the same as quite a number of befores. Usually it's new, according to the country she's been in, and probably the man she's been with. Now she seems to be, well, running out, repeating herself."

"Repeating a subconscious pattern," he said inaptly.

"Rusty, dear, where do you pick up that jargon?"

He shrugged shyly. Then, out of embarrassment or perhaps sheer melancholy, he got up and led the way back to the drawing room, still nursing his whisky. For in spite of their friendly relationship Rusty kept secret his professional visits to Serena, being rather ashamed of them. They had happened so naturally; so quietly, two years ago when he became so forgetful he thought he might well lose his job, and possibly his mind; even then analysis would never have occurred to him had he not met Stella's sister. At first he just went for reassurance. Then the visits had gone on, so naturally, so quietly, it seemed pointless to mention them now, even though Serena said it would have been better to do so.

"Most women live by their men," Jean was saying, "and those who don't have one find some other views to quote and bolster theirs with. From books, or their career, or a girl friend. It's probably most difficult for those who have many men and can't keep one."

"I suppose women were the original middlemen," said Rusty, unexpectedly inspired, and looked into his empty glass to see if the paradox had come from there. Then he cleared his throat mightily. "Hmm. We men can't create our sons without them, what."

"Rusty!"

Partly the presbyterian childhood inside her was shocked, partly the pelvic memory of enforced barrenness, suddenly aching somewhere between her hips. But Jean never felt anything unpleasant for very long and almost at once she reverted to Stella, as a woman does to a safe rival whom she admires and loves for the very rivalry, and the safety of it.

"I just wish there was something we could do to help her, Rusty. Isn't there anything?"

"I don't know, Jean, I really don't know. She couldn't stick U.V.I., after all."

"Well, but they sent her to the Persian Gulf!"

The door opened a fraction and a white-haired lady of alarming dignity peered in. "Are any of your guests coming for supper, Jeanie?"

"No, Jewel. But we'll have supper early. They're coming in at eight to watch Mr. Scott-Buttery on television."

Her real name was Maggie but Jeanie's parents had always called her Jewel, she was such a model of the old family retainer, and had refused to leave Jean after her marriage. In her eighties, the Conways supported her now even when they went abroad, and as soon as they came back, there was Jewel, ready to serve them, at least in small ways. Since Jean had got used to having servants in various parts of the globe, even the little that she allowed Jewel to do was very pleasant, but the clinging loyalty was a bit unnerving in these modern times.

"Ay, that'll be on your TV, will it, Jeanie?" The B.B.C. being to Commercial Television as Church was to Chapel in the nineteenth century.

"No, as a matter of fact it's on your TV, Jewel. TV-X. A programme called Focus on Facts."

"Ay, I know it, I know it." She didn't sound very enthusiastic about it, but Jean knew that she sat transfixed by her television set in her own sitting room from eight o'clock onwards. "Well, I'll be looking in on it, I'd like to see Mr. Rupert appear."

She certainly looked at Mr. Rupert as if he were an apparition when she showed the three of them in to the drawing room at eight o'clock. A case of bilocation, certainly.

Rupert felt unusually buoyant. It was his evening, and for once everybody would understand what he was about. Television was television. It meant, in all classes, that one spoke a common language after all, that one was accepted. Whereas books, well, yes, people knew what they were, some people even read them, but a blank look came over their faces, all over the world, from duchesses to doormen, when one said one wrote books, and they said "how interesting". It had been great fun too, and money for jam. He had even begun to toy with the idea of calling himself Pert Scott. Or Roo Buttery.

"I fear it will be a horrible experience for you all. Bad enough having me without a replica! You know, it's a devilish thing. Here am I going to say certain things and make certain gestures in about ten minutes, yet it's all decided, I can't change a single word or improve a single phrase, or a smile, or an intonation. Like predestination, brrr."

"Rusty was on television, weren't you, Rusty?" Serena tried to shift the emphasis from her family back to theirs, and from metaphysics, which had occasioned a brief pause, back to physical personalities.

"Oh, were you?" Rupert was a little peeved. "When? What programme?"

"Some weeks ago. Thing called *Public Inquisitor*. It was nothing. Just a discussion—on synthetic fibre," he added, so as not to seem rude to Rupert.

They all sat in their various armchairs and sofas, expectantly facing the set as Jean stepped round handing out coffee cups and Rusty stepped round handing out drinks. A plangent female voice from the South Midlands suddenly pattered into the room, the voice of Mrs. Barnacle, known and loved by millions, telling Mr. Barnacle that Sally had looked in for a cup of tea and had told her how she had bought a new bedside lamp, a beautiful thing it was, with a pink silk shade, but the lamp wouldn't switch on, so Sally had taken it back to the shop and the shop had looked at it and sworn it was all right, and when Sally got home, would you believe it, she found there was a fuse. The set flickered into jazzy diagonals that trembled, sank and heaved as the voice of Mrs. Barnacle rose up and down, then they changed into a music-sheet of straight blue telegraph wires on a grey-blue sky to the voice of Mr. Barnacle who said "Well I never", and almost at once the lines rippled back to the patterned diagonals of Mrs. Barnacle's voice saying what a nice girl Sally was and how she hoped their Ernie would start going steady with her soon. The patterns collapsed into a round blue face with blue hair and a blue toothy smile that gurgled its trivialities rather as a teleprinter gurgles out its tape. Then the face vanished immediately and became a whirlpool.

"Rather primitive set, isn't it?" said Rupert, a little impolitely, fearing the swirls and torrents his image might conjure upon the screen.

"It'll be all right in a minute." It was obvious that they were none of them regular viewers. Rusty and Jean had bought a small portable in the end, because one had to have one, but after the first craze had worn off they seldom watched it. Rusty usually preferred to read the rest of *The Times*, *Public Relations Review*, *The U.V.I. Monthly* or *R.A.F. News*, and Jean liked to sew or knit with the wireless. As for Rupert, he had been very superior about it in the early days, then found it hard to change when it became socially and intellectually okay. Serena was always busy with her notes on the day's patients, and Stella had lived mostly in places where it had not yet crept into every home. So that they all sat in silence, watching the monster with a fascinated horror rather than the hypnotised apathy that was required by most programmes.

T V X
(ping) (pong) (pang)

Rupert perked up as the jolly little jingle he had heard in the studio was played.

HUGHIE HILL
presents for you
FOCUS ON FACTS

"This is it."
But they had to sit through several other Facts which Hughie Hill had Focused on that day.

Rusty watched Stella in the flickering light. She had hardly spoken and was sitting quite still, almost erect on the sofa, her knees clasped in her long fingers. Her eyes were concentrated on the screen with the heavy-lidded look of puzzled distaste he knew so well, and the corners of her mouth had drooped into her disgruntled expression. She had always been thin but now he noticed for the first time that her face had lost even the flesh on her high cheekbones and had shrunk to a startling narrowness, nearer to the head of a greyhound than that of a human being. It was quite frightening. Could it be a trick of the blue light? But no, he remembered his shock on first seeing her, which he hadn't quite been able to explain. The various tropics she had lived under had long ago drunk up her strawberries-and-cream complexion, leaving an interesting desert texture, but this, this clicketed to the bawling voices from the screen like a dance of death, the skeleton of his roving life. Cairo, Kuwait, Karachi, Colombo, Kuala Lumpur, Hong-Kong, Nicaragua, Caracas, Casablanca. He suddenly wanted to marry her all over again.

"Here we are," said Rupert nonchalantly.
Three men interviewing a talkative fourth for six minutes. Himself, Tom Stevens, M.P., and Tony Black, diplomatic correspondent of *The Express News*. Rupert couldn't believe his eyes. All that rehearsing, those hot

strong lights, those cameras moving in and out, those dozen men listening to their headphones and talking in chin-cups to invisible people, that splendidly smart discussion, all this for six minutes of platitudes. And his calm, searching questions, his civilised tone of voice, his handsome, artistic head, how could they come out so inane, so pompous, so flat-faced and blotchy? He was so busy hating his own image he hardly noticed that no one else came out of it very brightly either.

"Well, that was splendid, old chap."

"Very interesting, Rupert. You were the best."

"Excellent, darling. You certainly fixed old Merseyside at the end."

"Yes," said Stella with absurd formality, "you were very good."

Then Rupert's self-hatred broke out, and he attacked Hughie Hill, as well as Sam Wilson the producer, Freddy Brown the floor-manager, the cameramen and the TV-X publicity manager, all of whom he said were spotty and about seventeen, Tom Stevens, M.P., who had only been interested in giving the viewers his own version of the internal strife in the Labour Party, Lord Merseyside, who was selling his lifetime tied up in ribbons of pink silk shot with red, when really the whole book was nothing but a spiteful postmortem in black and green, really, these politicians were worse than last war's generals the way they carried on; and above all, Tony Black, "a slimy little man with a Cupid mouth, a bow tie and blond curls that were already receding rapidly". He had been the worst. For their preliminary mock-discussion had become dead earnest, being about the Summit Collapse, of all subjects to bring up just then, and to keep on right up to the last minute, when they were having their gins and whiskies. This had led to a raising of voices that had jammed the microphones during the technical rehearsal and caused further delay. "The Supreme Soviet," Tony Black had said, and "Yes, well, my knowledge of the Supreme Society is less profound", Tom Stevens had interrupted ironically, and "When has the West ever done anything?" Rupert had asked, and Tony Black had assured them that he was in the Foreign Office at the time, and had written a memorandum, which was accepted . . . Rupert went on for some time.

Then the others joined in, if only to cheer him up, and the argument began all over again, from quip to cliché, from supposition to further supposition. In no time at all they had dealt with Suez, Israel and the Arabs, American Rocket-sites, nuclear submarines, Russian satellites, Africa, the problem of population and the Cobalt Bomb. Everyone except Stella was shouting passionately when Jewel opened the door and with a distracted stare at Rupert's flushed face, introduced Guy Hart into the room.

Their solutions to the problems of the world felt crude beneath his anglepoise look, and scurried away into dark corners.

The introductions seemed to raise Stella from the dead, but only as a medium raises a familiar spirit, at a very low level of actuality. "I used to be in the F.O.," she said in a monotone, mechanically anxious to establish the things she had in common with complete strangers, precisely because they were strangers.

"Oh, really? Whereabouts?"

"In the Consulate at Tetuán. I was keeping the Visa Index." Her voice perked up a little, as if it were a good joke compared to the previous statement, but Guy Hart only smiled wanly. "As a matter of fact it was rather hell." She still spoke in the same dead voice that set off the deadness of her ready-made phrases and the extravagance of her sentiments more unnervingly than did her usual emphases, though brevity would have been even more effective. "My boss was an absolute critter, do you know him, a man called George S. Thomas, I do think you ought to get him the sack, he wasn't even the Consul and he made my life absolute hell. The F.O. was rather beastly about it all and in the end I resigned. In fact everyone was rather ghastly out there, and if it hadn't been for the Spanish Governor and his wife who were simply charming, and those adorable Arabs, I wouldn't have stayed in the racket as long as I did. I must say, I do think you ought to look into the way the F.O. treats its staff, it's an absolute disgrace."

"Indeed," said Guy Hart nodding affably. "And how are you, Rusty, old chap?"

Then, quite suddenly, and no one knew how, they were all talking about Stella's problem, in the form of whether she should take a secretarial job which Isabel Gormsley, that peculiar woman she and Rusty had lunched with, was offering her on the Publicity side of Commercial Television. She had run into Isabel in the lift, and Isabel had been extraordinarily nice, charming, in fact, and wanted her to come and work in her department.

But Stella was snooty when she was actually offered something, especially by someone or in something she was vaguely aware of not having made a hit with. So that now she was by no means as enthusiastic about television as she had been at first—they were all such morons, she said sadly, the girls in the office where she'd been on holiday replacement for the last week didn't even know where Karachi was, and when pressed they thought it had been destroyed by the Atom Bomb. And they all wore the top button of their blouses undone, she supposed they thought it sexy or something. Besides, it meant living in London which was just so awful these days. And after all she did like living abroad. The ball was tossed back and forth, everyone was consulted for his opinion which was then not listened to. Guy Hart was asked if he couldn't get her back into the Foreign Office, something really nice this time. Rupert was asked if that M.P. on TV didn't perhaps need a secretary and couldn't Rupert ring him up and ask him, he must have got quite friendly with him surely. Rusty said desperately, what about U.V.I. and Stella made a disdainful face.

But she had woken up. And having, to her own surprise—for she was tired when she arrived—captured the attention, she suddenly played her trump card.

"Of course, if *only* Serena and Rupert would let me borrow their flat while they're away it would tip the balance and I'd certainly take the job. It's marvellous pay, for England I mean, and I'd be able to look for a small flat of my own in the meantime. But they seem quite adamant about it, so there it is."

She gave a big sigh of resignation.

The Middlemen: Chapter Five

"But Stella, you haven't even asked me!" Serena exclaimed, truthfully enough, but only just, since she knew she would have refused. Rupert hated himself all over again. Serena was genuinely astonished, as always, not so much by Stella's cunning, which she knew was totally unconscious, but by the unexpectedness with which Stella followed her expected pattern. But all this was registered by her professional mind in less than a split second of surprise, after which both she and Rupert, thus put in the pillory, said almost in unison.

"But of course you can borrow the flat."

"Oh, can I?" Stella said with supreme indifference. "Well, that's fine, then."

There was an awkward silence, and Rupert turned to Guy in sheer weariness.

"Tell me, do you know a chap called Tony Black?"

"Tony Black? No. Why?"

"I just appeared on television with him," said Rupert casually. "We all came in to watch me. Pretty awful it was, I must say. Primitive medium. Slow camera work, you know, and very confused long shots, I thought,"

"Oh, really?"

"But what I wanted to ask you was about this chap Tony Black. Said he was in the Foreign Office at the time of the Summit Collapse. He's diplomatic correspondent of *The Express News*, now, I believe."

"Tony Black . . . Oh, I think I know who you mean. Antony Black. Yes. Yes. He did his year's probation but he wasn't any good." Guy Hart sounded shocked at his own statement, and felt bound to explain it. "Some people aren't you know, even though they can get in, passing the stiffest exams, and all the country house stuff. It's rather awkward then. He was asked to go. And I can tell you, my dear sir, one has to be pretty bad for them to do that."

So Rupert was very pleased, and stopped hating himself, for several days.

6

"You SEE," said Tom Stevens, "I was taken by surprise. I had no idea he was going to be on the same programme—well, one doesn't expect that sort of thing on a political programme. And I kept feeling he must know all about me, it was most unnerving. So that I gave a very bad performance, quite unlike my usual self. It must have done my image a lot of harm, not to mention my Party."

"Well, shall we analyse it, point by point," said Serena quietly. "Why, for instance should you have experienced this loss of trust in me? That's very interesting."

"In you? But, I haven't! It's you who's going away. I don't know what I shall do without you."

"Come, no accusations, and you're going on holiday too. What I mean is, surely you must know, with your conscious mind, that I cannot and do not discuss my patients with my husband. Or with anyone else. Quite apart from etiquette my practice would collapse."

"How would it?" said Tom Stevens with a partly evasive, partly vindictive interest.

"Well, we needn't go into that. Even London is a village, professionally speaking. Or rather, the professions are a cluster of villages, each cut off from the other yet somehow linked by the odd vagabond who peddles his gossip from one to another."

"I say, that's rather good. Can I use it in the House?"

"If you like."

"I could bring it into the debate on the Professional Classes (Encouragement) Bill on Thursday. They've left it to the last minute, just before the Summer Recess—typical of them. One might, for instance, let me see, who would you say this vagabond represents?"

"How do you see him?"

"As a lawyer."

"Why?"

"No, as a matter of fact, at the moment I see him as a literary critic. As Mr. Scott-Buttery, to tell you the truth. You must admit it was pretty unnerving, I mean to say, the husband of my own analyst, Mrs. Buttery. That's why I was so rude to him afterwards. I was worried about the Party, you see, Mrs. Buttery." He had pronounced Scott-Buttery rather fast, like a machine gun, but he always lingered lovingly over "Mrs. Buttery". It made him think of the patting of butter, and the milking of swollen udders through soft, rubbery dugs, and of bosomy rink and white dairymaids, all vaguely remembered from *Tess of the d'Urbervilles* and *Adam Bede*. Serena was not exactly fat, but comfortable, and her eyelids drooped a little over a pair of placid, cowlike eyes.

"But, Mr. Stevens, my husband doesn't even know that you are one of my patients. He is either out, working in the London Library or the British Museum, or he stays in his room. It's a strict rule of the house. You have never seen him here, have you? And you know I open the door myself, unless my Mrs. Baines is here. Even my patients don't meet. That is why I ask you to come at rather odd hours, like twenty past six. I allow twenty minutes between patients, partly to jot things down but also to prevent any possible overlapping. You see, I have no waiting room here."

Serena stopped, astonished at her own talkativeness in mid-session. Pride in her system had no place here. The small matter of the flat was unsettling her.

Tom Stevens was rather surprised, too, and very ready to launch into a sympathetic discussion of the housing situation, which was all because of the Tories and their iniquitous Rent Act. But Serena managed to steer him back.

"In any case," she said, "I can assure you that my husband never even noticed that you were, or I should say, *if* you were rude to him." She was about to add "he was much too annoyed with Tony Black", but checked herself. She really was in need of that holiday. "So that the rudeness may well be an exaggeration of your own mind. Can you tell me what you think you said, and why it worries you?"

"Well, if you say he didn't notice, it doesn't matter. It's really my Party, you see, they trust me..."

When he was writing out his usual cheque—for he liked to Pay as He Earned his Peace of Mind—she said to him:

"You mentioned a lawyer, earlier on, Mr. Stevens."

"Hey! The session's over, Mrs. B. The lawyer can keep till Wednesday. Although, as an M.P. he stinks," he added viciously.

"No, no, I'm sorry, don't misunderstand me. I was only asking because I was wondering whether you could recommend a good lawyer." She smiled and added: "Evidently not."

"Don't say you're getting a divorce too, Mrs. B? Shall we get together, you and I?"

"I'm looking for a house, Mr. Stevens, a small one, to buy, I. mean."

"Ah, very wise, very wise, Mrs. B. Though you'll find the Tories have rocketed the property market with their iniquitous Rent Act, which let the speculators in. Absolutely iniquitous, that was. Of course, my Party doesn't want to nationalise everything. State Private Enterprise, that's what we stand for. It would solve everything, you know."

Tom Stevens was one of Serena's more difficult patients, for he lived, or so she repeated to him often enough, a ninety-nine percent unconscious life, active though he was. He seemed to think that analysis was just a series of cosy shop-talks, slightly more intimate, more personal and more honest than they could be in the lobby or at his club, and therefore more expensive, at the end of which the analyst would produce the explanation for his failure to reach the front bench, and of course the solution, like a rabbit out of a hat. He did, however, give her the name and address of a very good lawyer who had got him an injunction to restrain a firm from publishing a book until the author had removed a passage attacking him for some slander which had been, in fact, a case of Privilege.

In spite of all the transferred maternity she was endowed with by her patients, poor Serena was an infant-in-arms as a buyer of property. No, not even an infant-in-arms but a newborn babe, a premature piece of frailty in an oxygen tent of utter innocence.

The complexity of that innocence was colossal. It had layer after layer of illusion to be peeled off and replaced with sad knowledgeability. It was a nakedness of naïvety to be clothed leaf by leaf with the disappointment of experience.

Her first illusion consisted in the belief that all she need do was to go to an agent, visit half a dozen houses in one day, choose one, make an offer, put it in the hands of a lawyer and go away on her holiday while the whole transaction was put through. At the worst, she could postpone their holiday, if she didn't find anything she liked at once. August would after all be a little hot for Greece. All that mattered was moving. For quite suddenly she couldn't stand their flat any more. She must come back to something new, even if it meant shortening their trip abroad or taking an extra week off to get settled in.

She soon found that Tom Stevens was right about the prices, whatever their cause. The market, moreover, seemed more like one of her graph representations of a psychotic's dreamworld than a rational state of affairs carefully calculated by a handful of wicked speculators, though she supposed that these latter might well be the chosen instruments of the city's collective unconscious. For the prices of houses bore no relation whatsoever to their size, beauty, or convenience, only to some lunatic hierarchy of districts by which any area, however traffic-ridden, that could by any considerable wrench of the imagination be called a Village, was also the most plutocratic in its price-range; that is, any piece of town with one pretty street, square, corner, stretch of river, bit of heath, common or park, round which lesser, uglier streets clustered hopefully, borrowing the same name for themselves as crescents, gardens, garden-crescents, rises, hills, hill-rises, ways and ends, mewses, lanes, groves and vales, could aspire to and perhaps eventually earn the name of Village. Slum terraces and workers' cottages would be bought up, sometimes by enterprising individuals but more often by the wicked speculators for a profitable sale to less enterprising individuals, and one by one the black brick houses would turn white, or pink or blue, with bright yellow doors and flowerboxes in the windows. "This street," the agents would say, "hasn't quite come." When it did so, and several more around it, the area would at last receive by way of final decoration and of course price-promotion, the name of Village.

Second to Villages were the Best Residential Areas, where the affluent middle-class had always lived, but they were, after all, limited and unexpandable, and now that practically everyone was affluent middle-class, the Best Residential Areas were so much in demand that prices shot up well beyond the range of the affluent middle-class, and only the milk-bar millionaires lived there, expense-account experts, some of the more successful comedians, the odd reckless film star, and of course the speculators themselves. Fortunately, however, the fashion for Victorian architecture which Mr. John Betjeman had started several decades before had caught on at last and therefore saved the situation, for the affluent middle-class, who now had plenty of lovely-ugly to be coldly elegant in.

All this Serena discovered, and more, but in stages. For the first thing she did was to make an offer on a small pink terraced cottage, two beds, two inter-comm. rec., mod. k. and b., sep. w.c., small back yard, newly dec., near shops and tube in up-and-coming Camden Town Village, £6,000 Freehold.

The next thing that Serena discovered was that she could not afford to buy a house at all. And this in spite of having at last managed to save the ten percent needed. Or so she thought, being then in possession of what seemed to her the princely sum of six hundred pounds.

The lawyer said:

"Of course you must count about two hundred for legal charges and stamp duties, maybe less, depending on the price of the house, and whether it has been registered. I take it you have a mortgage lined up, then, Mrs.—er---Buttery?"

"Not yet, but the bank would give me a loan, I'm sure."

"Er, yes. You have some securities, then?"
"Well, no. Just my work. And my husband's."
"No . . . life insurance?"

Serena had more in common with Stella than she realised, for the word security had meant little to her until now, when she felt this sudden urge to buy property, paying off a mortgage like rent for twenty years and then living free of expense, she thought, when they were "old and grey and full of sleep"—though she hoped she would never be as psychologically asleep as all that. All she had ever bothered to insure was her conscious self against just such a submerging sleep.

She shook her head at Mr. Clacton, who seemed asleep enough himself, both in her terms and his, for it was a hot day and his office was stuffed to its low ceiling with undisturbed books, undisturbed files and dust from probably Dickensian times. His aspect was as dusty as his office, with scurf from dusty hair on the dusty shoulders of his black suit, cigarette ash down the front, an ashen face and yellow sleepy dust in the corners of his pale grey eyes. His fingernails were dirty, though he tried to make up for it by constantly paring them with the fingernail of the opposite hand. His voice was like his black and pinstripe, a grey superimposition of respectability over the original colour of his own natural vowels, the result being somehow as ineffective, not just dusty-grey but muddy, slimy even. His digressions too seemed to have no other purpose than the throwing of dust in his client's eyes, the dust of fake security, of the fake friend of the family, like the puffs from his Gauloises, which said 'don't you worry your fluffy little head about that, just lull back in the layers of my experience,' as he told her how he had saved one of his clients from buying a house in which he somehow owned all the bricks and mortar but not the joists, which had been omitted from the Deeds, and how he had learnt from another client who was a greengrocer that all greengrocers cheat the income tax by a complicated system of unrecorded purchases which had become the norm at Covent Garden.

"Yes, well . . ." He judged that she had been sufficiently dazzled and gave a long raucous cough. "Only cigarettes worth smoking, these. Most unhealthy, English ones. Well, now, let me see. I think I can put you onto some people who might, I say might, let you have a mortgage on this property..."

"But, they're safe, are they? I mean, they're not—moneylenders?"

"Mrs.—er—Buttery, all mortgage companies are moneylenders. That's rather the point, isn't it?"

"No, but I mean—"

"I know what you mean. You may trust me, Mrs. Buttery. I think, however, that you might have to revise your ideas about—er—the type of property you intend to purchase."

She revised them.

The little man from the Inter-Insular (British Archipelago) Insurance Company soon saw to that. He was bald and bouncy, jumping up from her sofa with each explanation, whether because of the sherry she offered him or from a passionate interest in his work she couldn't tell. When he had jumped up some twenty times, talked of premiums, policies, tax exemptions and survey fees, worked out sums rapidly on Inter-Insular Insurance Company sheets of paper which he produced from a shiny black briefcase, asked many, questions about Rupert's age, health and income, even his salesman's patter failed to smooth over the traumatic experience undergone by Serena's relatively sheltered psyche that afternoon.

Poor Serena. In spite of the good marks she had brought home from school she had never fully grasped the implications or practical application of compound interest. She used to solve all the problems set of course, but her conscious mind must have refused to accept the moral shock of it all, so that even now at the age of forty and eleven months, she still assumed that if one borrowed six thousand pounds at six per cent, one paid back, in the end, six thousand plus six per cent of six thousand, that is, six thousand three hundred and sixty pounds. The meaning of the words "per annum" had somehow got lost with the years.

Her second shock was the mortgage rating.

"You see, Mrs. Buttery," said the little man rather sadly now, but very fast, like a comic spouting gags, "the value of the policy would be worked out entirely according to your husband's earnings. I'm afraid we can't take yours into account at all. It's a rule of I.I.I. You see, you might stop work to have—well, for all sorts of reasons, or you might leave him."

"But how utterly extraordinary," said Serena angrily, "you must be living in the nineteenth century."

"Oh, but it's a very general rule, Mrs. Buttery, you'll find that no insurance companies, or building societies, for that matter, will allow for the wife's earnings. Our lawyers—"

"Who are you lawyers?"

"Clacton's."

"Well, I'm damned."

"Now, let, me see, you say your husband earns about . . . yes, that would come to . . . three, carry seven, six nines are fifty four—of course we'd have to have some sort of proof, you know, it's very difficult with self-employed persons, carry two. Yes. I'm afraid we couldn't raise this loan to more than three thousand three fifty at the most. Now you could get quite a nice little semi-detached house in Grimstead for three thousand, that's where I live, just before the green belt, lovely and modern, you know. I forgot to tell you, we don't usually laid on any house built earlier than 1918."

But Serena was not easily discouraged. She had, moreover, a reasonable endowment of intelligence and enough analytical training, specialised though it was, to get to grips with the more megalomaniac vagaries of an unfamiliar world. Within three days she had worked it all out. It was all quite clear. Houses were too expensive, at any rate for poor self-employed individualists like themselves, who nevertheless hankered for respectability and membership of the new and widespread, property-owning, affluent middle-class. Therefore they would buy part of a house. The market was flooded with long-lease flats for sale, on one and sometimes two floors of vast Victorian mansions, bought up by speculators and converted with more paint than architecture, a glass door here and there, a vine-leaf or cabbage-rose paper on one of the walls, a stainless steel kitchen-sink with perhaps a £45 waste-disposal unit to send the price up by a couple of hundred more.

"You see," she propounded to Rupert after her last patient had gone, "we can get three thousand three fifty, perhaps a little more if we can cheat your earnings a bit. I'm sure you could raise the rest from one of your publishers, get two books commissioned and write them later. I've got a bit owing too. Now, I saw some flats in Hendon for four thou, and some in West Hampstead for four two fifty, two beds, two reception, k. and b., just think, our own bathroom. Much more spacious than that poky little cottage, which wasn't a bit practical really, the reception room was too small when divided and too big when not. Waiting patients would hear everything if we used the front part as waiting-room-cum-sitting-room and the small bedroom upstairs really was rather small for your study, besides we couldn't really have got the piano in anywhere. But I'm not asking for the moon, or Hampstead Village or Chelsea, just for our own place where we can do our work and have our own baths when we like. Darling, won't you come and look at these tomorrow?"

"Hmm? Well, yes, I could. Those are the ones in Colindale, aren't they?"

"No, darling, Hendon. Two beds, two reception, k. and b., and built-in cupboards, four thousand, ninety-nine year lease."

"Ninety-nine? But we shan't live that long!"

"Doesn't matter, darling, it's like a Freehold, except that you pay Ground Rent. And Rates of course. The other flats have little balconies, which I'm rather taken with, and Ascots, but open fires, whereas these have points for oil-fired radiators..."

"Which?" said Rupert, very confused.

"These, darling, at Hendon, two beds, two reception, k. and b. and built-in cupboards, four thou, ninety-nine years. Of course it's less central then Kentish Town Village."

"I see. And Kentish Town Village had the balconies?"

"No, darling, West Hampstead."

"So what did you see in Colindale?"

"Oh, never mind, just come and see these."

Which clarified his mind just a little, and depressed him rather more. Serena was going round tapping walls and scrabbling floorboards as if she could understand their messages, and while she was explaining where her consulting room would be and what colour she would repaint the kitchen, he stood in a daze of incomprehension, unable to visualise the bareness as theirs, inhabited, intimate, alive.

"Three thousand three fifty," he chanted, standing slightly frozen on that August morning in the damp Victorian grandeur of what could surely never be their bedroom. "Where do you suppose we can lay our hands on the rest? Have you anything owing?"

"Yes, darling, I told you. About a hundred and fifty."

"I wonder if Tweedie would commission another book. I've promised him one on D. H. Lawrence. He's rather fashionable just now . . ."

"That's what I said. Oh, look, there's a broom cupboard, how splendid."

"You know what I think, Serena. If all they need is confirmation from my various publishers and editors I'm sure we could cheat my earnings a little. We might get a bigger loan that way."

"Yes, dear."

Serena was truly bitten, like a mad cow by a gadfly, and Rupert followed like a gentle ox. To save money, they cancelled their holiday altogether and decided simply to rest at home, Stella and other circumstances permitting. Stella of course would not now be able to borrow the flat.

But they did not rest. For apart from Stella's trying presence in London, Serena was soon taking on more patients, not less, and Rupert was signing his name to more reviews, more articles and more contracts for more books. Their energy came from the prospect of a new lease of life, and their minds inhabited the Hendon flat with an amazing profusion of creative adaptability. And since they were about to move, they postponed seeing their friends.

Two months after that momentous decision to put money before leisure, Serena rang up Mr. Clacton to find out what was happening.

"Ah, yes, Mrs. Buttery. Yes. I was about to write to you. I called on the Inter-Insular yesterday, and I'm afraid they cannot give you a mortgage on this property."

"But, but, but why? It's impossible."

"I'm afraid it is so, madam. The terms of the lease do not meet their requirements with regard to the Maintenance Clauses. Their solicitors have advised them—"

"But I thought you were their solicitors."

"On the conveyance side of the transaction, yes, madam, I represent both them and you. But they have to have another firm to advise them on the insurance side."

"But you told me yourself the lease was acceptable. We went through it point by point."

"Acceptable to you."

"But if you represent them you must know what their requirements are."

"I am only a middleman between, Inter-Insular and yourself, madam. If you wish to deal with them direct, you may of course do so. You will, however, require a lawyer for the conveyance."

Serena's innocence now had one protective skin, but she had not yet learnt the quality of non-attachment to property, especially property as yet unowned. Although she knew with the back of her mind that the flat was not really what they wanted, she had decorated it, furnished it and otherwise lovingly possessed it, in every detail, with her imagination, and she felt more bereftly furious than a woman scorned. Stella, who had left for Central America in the middle of September, actually received a long incoherent letter all about it, and wrote a long, sympathetic letter back, arguing that it was perhaps just as well, since this flat as far as she could gather, had no shower, and showers were so much healthier than baths, she simply couldn't understand how the English who loved to wallow in their baths really thought they could get clean that way.

And perhaps, in a way, it was just as well. The extra money was nicely trickling in and Rupert even suggested, over-imaginatively, she thought, that perhaps Mr. Clacton had done it on purpose, to make them save more and so be able to afford a much nicer flat, in a better district; this one was after all rather horrible, it had these and those snags and would really have been most inconvenient for her practice, not to mention the entertaining of his own income-sources, a politely fiscal euphemism for publishers and editors.

And so began the process by which Serena's innocence as a buyer of property slowly darkened into knowledge, cluttered into experience, painfully, relentlessly, with an obsessive quality which Rupert, silently surmised had as its driving power the small, or not so small, matter of the flat.

7

DICK BARBER, of Caraway Christian Ltd., was being lunched in the House of Commons by Tom Stevens, M.P. At least, he hoped so, but didn't feel quite sure who would be paying. Since he was the literary agent and Tom, in this instance, the author, the expense should be charged to Caraway Christian. But Tom had distinctly asked to see him, saying he was too busy to reach Soho or the West End, and although Dick felt exceedingly unlike a constituent from Dugwharton, and was pretty vague about whether such a constituent's lunch could be on the House anyway, he found it hard not to regard the summons as an invitation.

A further difficulty was that Tom Stevens was very angry, and the usual way to deal with difficult authors was to give them lunch, which mollified them both physically and emotionally. Whereas if the author, or his House, were paying, he, Dick Barber, would have to be the mollified party. As a professional and indeed skilful clarifier of situations he felt very unhappy in any situation which he could not clarify. He liked everything to be neatly tied up, like a contract, fair to all parties, with his role and his percentage clear, and all subsidiary rights reserved.

He was, therefore, getting almost as incensed as his author.

He peppered his food generously, shaking his plump, pink and blond self up and down with the pepper pot, like a baby playing with a rattle.

"All I said was that I could have got you more. But if you will go making verbal agreements behind my back—"

"I didn't. Dave Goodman was on the phone to me this morning," Tom said, meaning that he had rung Dave Goodman up, "and I simply asked him what were their usual terms for such a quick-written, quick-selling topical book. He told me and that's all. I said he must discuss it with my agent. Naturally."

"Oh, naturally. And he naturally assumed you had agreed. At least that's what he told me. And in a way he's right."

"Look, who are you representing, me or my publisher?"

"Well . . . Oh, don't be silly. But you really must leave the financial side of these transactions to me, that's what I'm there for."

"The swine. I thought publishing was a gentleman's profession."

"It is, on the whole. Dave Goodman is rather new to it, and full of his own cleverness at having got where he is so young," said Dick, who wasn't particularly old himself for where he had got. "And, I may say, he's rather unpopular among the old guard, although some of the now no longer so young publishers who were equally new and clever in the thirties feel quite fatherly towards him. The only difference is that they risked their bit of capital, whereas he's merely selling his ability for higher and higher bids. Anyway, let's face it, he's a congenital liar." Dick felt happier now that he had blamed the other side, for even blame had to be fairly shared according to the risk each party took: thirty-three per cent for the publisher, thirty-three for the booksellers, and ten for the author, rising to twelve and a half, fifteen, seventeen and a half, if he was unlucky. All the same, he remembered that Tom Stevens was always a good commercial proposition, both in print and on television, "You just stick to writing the stuff in future."

"Well, haven't I? And damn promptly too. I was working on it all night in Moscow and Peking, I could hardly keep my eyes open during the sightseeing. It was extremely important to get down exactly what Crush and Mao said—well, through their interpreters of course—before I forgot. That's what makes the book so valuable, compared, I mean, to these vagrant generals who seem merely to repeat political platitudes from the backs of their own minds. They're not politicians, you see. Whereas Crush and I understood one another at once and really got down to essentials."

"Quite," said Dick Barber, reserving all subsidiary opinions.

"And Mao, you know, I liked him even better than Crush. He's quite a charmer, quite a charmer, behind that inscrutable oriental mask. One simply has to make allowances for a different way of life, a different set of beliefs, and once one has done that, well, one discovers that we really all want the same thing, peace in our time. And in the future of course."

"You will allow me to handle *The Sunday Supplement*, won't you? I don't want to labour the point about not meddling, but I really have got Nat Warner watering at the mouth for the serial rights. Even so, they're as mean as hell, and not all that rich, so he'd pounce on any opportunity to deal with you direct and do you down."

"Okay, okay. Tom a good boy now."

He was good enough to pay the bill, too, which wasn't anything like as high as what Dick often had to spend on bigheaded authors or small-handed publishers. Nor was the lunch anything like as tasty. But Dick immediately felt a bit awful about it as he thought he remembered that Members of Parliament did not, after all, have expense accounts, or else had very mean ones or something equally peculiar, like the quainter anomalies of English Statutory Law.

Dick Barber secretly nursed an idea of himself as Monsieur de Norpois, that master of peacemaking who not only appeared to help the person soliciting his help, but also managed to represent his action to the second person as very much in his interest, rather than something, done at the first person's request; and who thus became known as the most obliging of men, this idea that others had of him in turn making his persuasions easier, so that he could play both parties and never risk any harm to his influence, since the services he rendered alienated no one, but on the contrary added to his reputation.

Proust's Monsieur de Norpois, however, was a diplomat, and from a vanished world, for even diplomacy was now reduced to babblings at the Summit and scrabblings lower down, with an occasional exchange of insults or handshakes, according to the latest scoreboard of foolhardiness on either side.

And Dick, too, found that Monsieur de Norpois remained very much a phantom figure at the back of his real behaviour, someone he thought he was when unusually elated, but knew he wasn't when he saw himself fall back on much cruder methods, such as running down one party behind its back to the other. That was the trouble with reading, it could epitomise one's ideals, crystallise one's conscience in much the same way as a film gunman could personify to an adolescent everything that he was not, strong, handsome, of few but significant words, quick on the metaphorical draw, accurate and tough. Not that Dick Barber read much literature these days, only novels for sale, indeed, his Monsieur de Norpois had numerously merged with hero after hero until he was rather closer to the film gunman than Proust himself could ever have imagined. As for the creators of these heroes, the authors, he had four hundred and seventy eight of them on his files alone, and kept them both physically and mentally indexed according to the sort of advance each was likely to get from his respective publisher, from £50 upwards; it was amazing too, how with few exceptions each author tended to remain in much the same category. But even so it was pure idealism, with such large numbers, instead of the mere occasional two parties, to emulate Monsieur de Norpois throughout.

Today, however, his real behaviour had been shaken back to the phantom figure, as violently as he had shaken himself with the pepper pot. This had not been achieved by Tom Stevens—whom he regarded as little better than the lowest member of the villain gunman's retinue, the one the villain usually calls Dope—but by the atmosphere of the House of Commons, with its murmuring of members in groups' and pairs, its measured hastening of messengers, its panelled hoarding of historical echoes, in short, the whole awe-inspiring throb in the heart of the United Kingdom and Commonwealth which had made Dick feel like a small boy on a school trip. So that when Tom had said "Tom a good boy now", he had suddenly sat up, in several senses, and made all manner of Monsieur de Norpois (approximation to) resolutions.

He nearly gave his name to the telephonist as Monsieur de Norpois. "Dave?"

"Hello, Dick, what's your line?"

"Fine," said Dick automatically, and felt a fool. Round one to Dave. Remember Monsieur de Norpois. "As fine as yours I hope."

"Don't cut it too fine."

"I'll get my cut, either way."

"Yes, Barber."

"Oh, very Good Man."

He wasn't sure whose round it was.

"Shall we get down to brass tacks?" he said.

"By all means."

"Well, look. I've seen my author," Dick said, as a lawyer says "my client". "I think there's been a misunderstanding. As I thought, he certainly never agreed to any terms with you, he leaves all that side to me. He's very busy, you know, a big television personality as well as an M.P."

"We know."

"Well, of course, he's a little vague and absentminded at times, and he may have given you the wrong impression. He was only inquiring about your usual terms for this kind of book. But he's worth considerably more than the usual terms and he won't accept a penny under two thousand advance and fifteen per cent, and I must say you're getting him cheap."

"If I'm getting him at all."

"Well, that's up to you, old man. I'm not worried because as a matter of fact, I didn't mean to tell you this, but I do have another offer. I'm giving you the first chance, naturally, as you were the first to inquire—"

"Naturally. And this other offer is, of course, as high."

"Higher, as a matter of fact."

"Oh, quite. And may one know who these mysterious rivals are, and whether they have actually and somewhat unethically been shown the great work?"

"Oh, come, Dave, there's no need to take that tone." Dick played for time. "You know me, I'm simply trying to let you have this chance of a scoop, because you were first on the ball. I've got the serialisation in the bag, your firm will be mentioned as publishing it in book form, every Sunday—"

"Which paper?"

"I'm afraid I can't tell you that yet."

"And the other offer?"

"All right." Dick chose a firm as far out of Dave's reach as he could. "But please keep it under your hat. They're the author's old publishers—he left them, you know, and now they want him back, the usual story, local boy makes good. And we have not submitted the manuscript to them. They simply heard about it, I imagine Stevens talked about it to Truelove, or something like that. To tell you the truth," Dick lied on desperately, hoping to make all the previous lies more plausible, "and very much between these two telephones, I shouldn't be surprised if he hadn't actually shown him another copy privately. They're still very good friends, you know, and the offer is *rather* too good to be a blind one."

"It must be. Why don't you take it? I'm quite willing to forfeit my claim. I should hate to stand in your way."

"Well, as I say, it's up to you," said Dick after the briefest pause to deaden the shock. "I think you'd be a fool, as it's a sure bestseller. There's not a creature in the country who isn't worried stiff about the Bomb and who won't want to read what the Communist leaders said to Stevens. He has quite a reputation as a needling interviewer, you know."

"Okay, well, I'll have to think about it."

"I'm sorry, Dave, but I really must have your decision now, I can't keep —"

"My dear Dick, I'm not the big boss, much as I'd like to be, don't force me to underline my littleness. I had Ben's okay for the other price, but I have to consult him."

Dick bit his lip. He had completely forgotten that the great Mr. Truelove, of Truelove & Thorne, who would never publish such a book anyway, was now on paternally amicable terms with Dave Goodman. It had happened so quietly, so masonic-ally, that few people had noticed, and those few, like himself, who had been told of it, wouldn't believe it or dismissed it as too unaccountable. Triple, triple fool. This was not the Norpoised way to handle things.

"I'm sure you have more power than you make out," he fawned, fearful of his own double meaning. "However, as you wish, but let me know soon. Is Ben in? Can you ask him now?"

"Ten minutes."

"Right you are."

"I'm afraid we're not interested at that price," said Dave eight minutes later. "Ben feels we shouldn't stand in the author's way."

"Tell me, Dave," said Dick who had had time to reflect, "hasn't Ben got phrases of his own to use? You see, I happen to know that he's at a Boyles Literary Luncheon, which can't possibly be over yet."

"Your point. But my game-all the same. I was only trying to save your face. We'll take him at fifteen hundred and the usual royalties, not a penny more. You wouldn't want to fall between two stools, would you?"

"It's a sharks' world," said Dick valiantly.

"I'd have done the same in your place. No ill-feelings, old boy. We'll have other business, don't forget."

"No ill-feelings."

"Return match perhaps. Let me know when you're ready."

"Bye."

How could Dave Goodman be so bloody British? You defeat the other side, a whole nation perhaps, and you say three cheers, have some oranges, hip, hip. Though Dick had to admit that the British also accepted shame with equanimity, once the fail was sufficiently *accompli*. Hip, hip.

"I'm afraid it was too late to get the terms changed," he dictated in his letter to Tom Stevens, "however, I don't think we need be at all dissatisfied as they were excellent by any standard..."

Fortunately the serial rights went as smoothly as selling soap. Nat Warner, editor of *The Sunday Supplement*, bought *A Peace of My Mind* without a murmur, for the price demanded.

Even so, Dick felt a little depressed. Whenever he had managed things in a particularly sub-Norpoised manner he was reminded of that other passage in his one and only Bible, Proust, when the boy at Balbec visits the painter, and finds him quite interesting until he discovers that the painter knows some of the young girls the boy has for so long been trying to meet; whereupon the painter loses all his intrinsic value in the boy's eyes (but only in the boy's eyes, Dick would add to himself) and becomes a mere intermediary to the young girls. That was the trouble with reading.

He felt very devoid of intrinsic value and turned with a sigh of boredom to the Willy White contract; but then read it through with a mounting relish quite unrelated to the stereotyped phrases he knew by heart, a relish which came from his memory of the novel he had enjoyed so much more than the political ineptitudes of Tom Stevens, M.P., oh, wicked Willy White.

Toni Stevens, M.P. was not, as it happened, at all dissatisfied with the terms, on the contrary, he was very pleased, for they showed that Dick was talking through the Derby hat he wore flat on his pink bald head, about being able to get him more, and that it was just as well he had had a word with Dave Goodman, or Dick might have got him less.

The reason why Tom Stevens could thus feed his vanity rather than his cupidity was fairly simple, like his conscious mind: he was quite well off. His name in print, as large and in as many places as possible but particularly on the covers of a book, was worth more to him than an extra five hundred on a contract, though naturally he couldn't sell it for anything other than a respectable sum, which was always, anyway, welcome. Even more welcome was the letter which arrived at his flat in Westminster, in the same batch as Dick Barber's letter, a letter from his German publisher's publicity department thanking him for the photograph, a letter from the Foreign Rights Department of Caraway Christian telling him that his German publisher's publicity department were very pleased with the photograph, and many other letters besides, as yet unread. The more welcome letter came from a firm of solicitors in Dugwharton, informing him that Mr. Joseph William Lake-man, J.P., of the Gables, Holly Hill, Dugwharton, had recently died. Good Lord, poor old Jo. Ah, yes, he remembered, Jo had asked him years ago if he would kindly act as his executor. Probably there'd be a small something for him. Poor old Jo. Then he read on and goggled. Poor old Jo, it seemed, had altered his Will some months before, and arranged to leave him, Thomas Wilfred Stevens, Member of Parliament for Dugwharton, the whole of his holdings in U.V.I. (United Volcanic Industries Ltd.) amounting to 1,500 (one thousand five hundred) five per cent cumulative participating Preference Shares of £ 1 (one pound) each, and 85,000 (eighty-five thousand) Ordinary Shares of 5/- (five shillings) each, in appreciation of his spirited challenge on behalf of the two ladies of Dugwharton whose unfortunate demise had been indirectly caused by the said U.V.I. (United Volcanic Industries) Ltd. A condition was attached to his acceptance of this legacy, namely, that the said Thomas Wilfred Stevens, Member of Parliament for Dugwharton, was to carry on the good work.

Tom Stevens stared at the letter with great astonishment. Still staring at it, he reached for *The Financial Times*, opened it aslant his body, then transferred his eyes with great effort to its roseate hues, travelling an angry glare up and down the columns as if it could illuminate them. It didn't. U.V.I. "A" non-voting (5/-), he read, 3/9-4/3,-3d. But the letter had said nothing about voting or non-voting shares. There had been a debate, he remembered, oh, some years back, on "company democracy" and "votes for shareholders". He had spent most of it in the smoking room, empty for once both of left-wing zealots and of the more defensive Boardroom pluralists. Voting. Non-voting. What power precisely had Jo bequeathed him?

"Mrs. Arkright," he called out.

"I'm just heating some up, Mr. Stevens."

"No, it's all right. No more coffee." He got up and walked to the kitchen door. "Would you be so kind as to come in a moment?"

"Yes, I'll come in," said Mrs. Arkright cheerily as if she'd been asked to have a go, and followed him into the dining room. Then she drew out the chair opposite his and sat down with great poise. She wore no apron, even for cooking breakfast, and he stared, at the big blue and mauve flowers on her taffeta dress. Her husband was the caretaker in the narrow Victorian block and she always liked to dress nice when she came to do for Mr. Stevens, the Member of Parliament, you know. Who went on staring so hard that she glanced down at her bosom, wondering if she were showing, or if perhaps some bacon fat had spat on her, but no. She laughed genteelly into her knuckles.

"Well, and how are you this morning, Mr. Stevens?" She had already said that earlier but still, one had to help him on, whatever he wanted.

"Thank you, thank you, Mrs. Arkright, fine. I want to ask you, tell me, what is the material of that rather splendid dress you're wearing?"

"This old thing? Go on, I've had it for years." She patted her hair, which was dyed so black that the parting looked almost indecent, like a gap at the waist between a black skirt and top.

"Have you really? Well, well. But what is it made of?"

"This? It's taffeta. Nylon taffeta, you know, non-iron, and it doesn't crease at all. Look." Suddenly she got up and turned her bottom towards him, looking over her shoulder to see his expression. The position so recalled familiar images that she put her hand on her waist, gave a small waggle of her hip, raised her eyebrows and said, "Come up and see me sometime . . . Ooh! that shook you, Mr. Stevens. Remember Mae West? Or maybe she was before your time?" Mrs. Arkright sat down again very straight, and joined her hands on the table.

"No, no, I do remember her. Tell me, Mrs. Arkright, do you ever buy a material called nitron? Or cinderella?"

"Yes, 'course I do. This is cinderella. I think. Or is it nitron? No, I think it's shanlon. Or maybe it's brincelle. They're all the same, really. Oh!" she exclaimed suddenly as she remembered, "I know what you mean, one of them got didn't it? The one you were on the telly for."

"Nitron, yes."

"That's right. No, I wouldn't buy that. Not nitron. Mrs. Ferryman-Jeeves, now, she has nitron towels in her bathroom, such beautiful colours, you know, tangerine, there's one set, with everything matching, face towels, hand towels, bath towels, and another in lemon, and another in strawberry, fair makes your mouth water, and her bathroom's painted a lovely blue. But she told me they don't dry as nice as real towels. 'Filly' she says to me, she says—she always calls me Filly just like my husband, course, my name's Felicity, really—not a bit like Mrs. Larkin at No. 2 who calls me Mrs. Ark—'Filly', she says, 'I'm going to give them to Pam,' that's her daughter, Mrs. Johnson-Peterson, the wallpaper family, you know, they've got ever so much money. Yes, that's what she says, Mrs. Ferryman-Jeeves. 'The sheets are all right,' she says, 'but them towels, you can't get the water off you.'"

Tom Stevens was nodding affably and beginning to regret his private attempt at a Gallup Poll. Mrs. Arkright was admirably discreet until one touched the spring of her ability to pass on a wealth of pointless information in a highly dramatised form. She seemed to have no private life of her own, living rather every detail in the life of Mrs. Ferryman-Jeeves with whose flat, furniture, wardrobe, family ramifications, conversation and activities he was by now—or would be if he listened—as familiar as Mrs. Ferryman-Jeeves presumably was with the colour of his own bedroom slippers. But at that moment the front door key ground in the lock and fortunately Mrs. Arkright heard it too. "Well I never, there's Miss Taylor already and here's me keeping you from your paper. I'll get you some more coffee now, shall I?" He got up and went into the study.

Miss Taylor was patently not the reason for whom Tom Stevens was getting a divorce, on the contrary, his wife being the guilty party had insisted on his not behaving like a gentleman, in view of his career, and he had not insisted very hard. He gave Miss Taylor a brisk good morning as he handed her the pile of letters.

"I've read some of these already, Miss Taylor. Would you sort the rest while I finish the morning papers? And, oh, yes, please get hold of a Mr. Conway, at U.V.I. for me, would you, in about half an hour. And ring Bill Jackson, my stockbroker, now and ask him to telephone me about eleven."

He returned to the dining room.

His secretary seemed to be having some difficulty in conveying his identity to Mr. Conway. "Mr. Tom Stevens for you," he heard her say rather loudly when he had finished his second cup of fresh coffee, so he decided to go in, and start his work proper. After a "who?"-sized pause she repeated, "Mr. Tom Stevens, M.P.". An "Oh"-sized pause followed and she said, "That is Mr. Conway, isn't it?"

"Give it to me. Mr. Conway? This is Tom Stevens. We appeared on television together, some months ago, remember? Yes, that's right. Oh, that's quite okay. Terrible memory for names myself, even in my own constituency. Still, they remember mine at election time, that's the main thing, isn't it? Look, er, are you very busy? Yes, I am, too, ah yes, we're the real working-class, aren't we? Never liked the term myself. All *travaillistes*, what! Listen, I'd like to see you, if I may, and have a chat about this, er, U.V.I. business, this, what d'you call it, nitron stuff. No, no, nothing wrong, I just want to . . . Yes, I'm on the Parliamentary Sub-Committee, you see. Well, I could come to your office, save you the trouble, this afternoon, it's Friday, isn't it, the House is dead. Three? Er, yes . . . Could you make it three-thirty? Fine. Now, tell me again, how the devil do I get there?"

8

RUSTY SOON learned from the nature of his visitor's business that it had little to do with Public Relations.

"I think you should really see one of the directors. I'm sure Mr. Harding would see you, today even. With such a large holding, and your position —" Rusty pressed the sole of his right shoe gently up and down into the nap of his blue carpet to remind himself of his own position.

"Yes, yes, naturally he could. I may see him of course. I've already spoken to him on the phone, he was most concerned. But what I'm after now, old chap, is your opinion, I mean you really have your pulse on the public reaction, don't you, and it's the public that counts, in the end, I mean isn't it? Or I wouldn't be where I am. Now you can be honest with me. I gave you a tip or two, didn't I, before our joint appearance? Speak up, I said, and don't look at the camera, unless you want the viewers really to remember something, then you gaze straight into their imagined eyes, whichever camera has the little red light on. I'm told you went down very well. Now, you don't have to give me the official U.V.I. handout. I've talked to my stockbroker. Sevenpence halfpenny tenpence halfpenny, still going easier, he said. But he told me something else. These A shares are nonvoting. And whenever anyone talks of U.V.I. it's A they mean. He hasn't dealt with voting shares for ages. There are only a couple of hundred thousand in issue. They control the whole empire and are very tightly held. The Board, he said, probably have the lot."

Rusty moved his wrist turtle-like out of his cuff, to see his watch, but Stevens went on.

"And they don't, you know. The shares I have inherited from Mr. Lakeman were a large family holding of voting shares. I rang his solicitor this morning. Old Jo, apparently, always sent in his proxy-card like a good boy, until all the fuss blew up, and then he started making a nuisance of himself. Still, he was old, and they somehow handled him. But I have to carry on the good work, remember?"

A tug on the Thames gave a hoot of derision, and Rusty too wanted to give a hoot, as the only noise adequate to express his conflict of boredom, amusement, anger and excitement.

"I see. By the way, won't you have to resign from the Parliamentary Sub-Committee now?"

"Of course, of course, if I keep the shares. That is precisely—"

"I see, yes, I see. Well, you know, it didn't make all that much difference. U.V.I's a very solid organisation and only a small percentage of the shareholders panicked. Much later, oddly enough, there was a wave of selling, a sort of delayed reaction, just after the scientists brought out their third new formula and a statement that all was well at last. People are very slow. But things always settle down. Those same people will probably start buying again just when all the curtains in a big department store catch fire."

In spite of his request for honesty, Tom Stevens didn't appreciate Rusty's unsalesmanlike brand of humour, and when he had pompously wasted his time for ten more minutes, he decided after all to let this greying ginger goof make an appointment with Mr. Harding for him. "I should have learnt by now," he thought, "one must always go straight to the summit."

He was rather chagrined therefore, after a courteous little talk which told him little more than Rusty had, to be handed back, personally, it was true, to the greying ginger goof who was requested to arrange a complete tour of the U.V.I. laboratories and factories for Mr. Stevens, at Mr. Stevens' convenience. The works, in fact, said Mr. Harding's face, with a postscript, handle with care. The face of Mr. Stevens said a good deal more, but his hand shook Rusty's as he said "goodbye, then, see you on Tuesday, sorry old boy but there it is, I must 'carry on the good work', dear old Jo, bless his memory."

Rusty felt both sad and angry after Tom Stevens had gone. He looked at his watch. Just on five. Another half hour. Although it was Friday, he was punctilious about not leaving before his staff, since he arrived after them. But he had already signed off mentally, his work was finished, all loose ends tied up till Monday, and he didn't feel like dreaming through the new catalogue for the third time. So he switched on his secretary and asked for the Press Book back, which she had removed to stick in two items out of the evening papers, sent in from the Cutting Room.

But when the Press Book lay in front of him, and his secretary had gone out again, he read the two items and some others as a dazed clerk reads his evening paper in the tube, assiduously from snippet to snippet, without a flicker of interest or amusement. He looked at his watch again, took out Stella's letter from his wallet and spread it out over the Press Book.

She was delighted with her new job. Her boss was the most charming man, and hardly ever there. She had managed to find a delicious little house with dried-up geraniums round a small terrace, all they needed was a little looking after. It was very nearly in the slum district and the English thought she was mad but it was the best house there, with running water, and the local wineshop-keeper had built her a bamboo sombra that turned the terrace into a marvellous veranda. She was going to train some vine and bougainvillea to climb up it and some promised red poinsettia to cluster down, and the wineshop-keeper had said he could fix an electric fan for her if she bought it. His daughter was keeping the place clean and doing all her washing. The country was arid and orange but very beautiful in a wild way. He would adore it, she was quite sure, since he had loved the Middle East so much, but of course, she had forgotten, he knew Central America quite well. All the same, why didn't he and Jean come out here? They had vegetated in London long enough, she felt, and, as he knew, there was a U.V.I. representative in "la capital" here. Couldn't he apply for the job? It would be such enormous fun having them around. The English Club here wasn't too awful for once, and even the English, at least those she had so far met, were quite nice types. The worst were the American oil-prospectors, who seemed to live for drink and fornication, but one could ignore them easily enough. The only people with any real dignity were, as always, the local people, but of course they were mostly extremely stupid and one had to explain six times what one wanted done and even do it oneself first to show them. As for her, she couldn't thank her lucky stars enough for having got her out of that ghastly television racket with that ghastly Gormsley woman who had offered her the job and yet for some mysterious reason which completely escaped her, taken an instant dislike to her almost from the day she started. Serena for some equally mysterious reason had been rather annoyed when she chucked it. And by the by, since he and Jean had become quite friendly with her rather peculiar sister and even more peculiar brother-in-law (who were of course both brilliant so that one had to make allowances), couldn't they ask them or rather couldn't he, Rusty, ask her, Serena, to try and understand once and for all that she, Stella, was not, repeat not, interested in making a career for herself or settling in London or, as Serena would have it, "building up her own circle of friends". She had plenty of friends, all over the world, people who were always begging her to come and stay and were always delighted to see her anyway. She was forty-one—she couldn't lie to him since he had known her so long—and surely could be assumed to know what she wanted, especially by her twin who was in fact twenty minutes younger and couldn't stand any criticism of *her* rather peculiar life.

Rusty suddenly lifted the fine pages of smooth electric typing and buried his face in it, as in a handkerchief. Not that he cried or even wanted to, but the gesture made him feel he was crying inside, tears that no handkerchief could dry anyway.

He never discussed Stella with Serena, unless she cropped up in analysis, and then of course it was his own version of Stella, not hers, or rather, it was a Stella with a contextual significance quite different even from the real Stella of his own version. Nor did he ever discuss Serena with Stella, except in the most formal way, pretending a merely distant acquaintance, which was true in one sense, and wriggling out of any diplomatic tasks proposed by Stella, or, more rarely, and in a more casually subtle way, by Serena. But he was familiar with their differences, chiefly through Stella and also, now, from his knowledge of Serena. There had been a stage in his analysis when he wanted, not only to learn all about psychology, so as to be more articulate in the correct jargon and give a name to everything, as she did, but also to learn as much as possible about her. He had browsed in a bewildered way along the appropriate shelves at Foyles, lined with tall books in cream or pale blue jackets with black or red lettering, and actually bought several, including a series of case-histories on infant twins. Jessie and Bessie he remembered most clearly, in spite of the huge diagrams of food-intake, pot-sitting and bed-wetting, because Bessie, who was the imitator and follower for their first five months of life, later caught up and became the leader, after Jessie had been removed to hospital for several weeks. But Jessie showed quite a lot of spirit nevertheless and one day when their mother was playing with Bessie, Jessie crept up from behind with her favourite doll and bashed Bessie on the head.

But Rusty was over his analyst-emulation stage now. It didn't seem to explain quite enough. What infant pattern was he repeating over and over? In the end there was Stella, who had come into his life at a particular point in a particular place, figuring no one but herself, Stella whom he had not married, who, indeed he knew would not have married him even if he had after all asked her, then or later. She had been in love with an American colonel at the time, and later, well, they had lost touch, then regained it, lost it again, he had got married, and, anyway, there had always been someone or if not, she still for a long time felt she had her life before her, until quite suddenly it was somehow surreptitiously slipping behind her, like a shadow. For although Rusty approved of the old adage that life began at forty, he knew that in its essential pattern it was not so, and he wished Stella would not so frequently, even in unknown company, draw attention to her own age with self-disparaging remarks that begged in vain for contradiction, merely in order to show how different she was from other women, who lied. And all at the same time he loved her for her sensitivity, which Serena thought was hypersensitivity, and for her toughness, which Serena called a thick skin. These two qualities he admired in Jean, also, but she wore them the right way round.

For Rusty knew that Jean had been right. There was a change in Stella, not just between the lines, but in the very tone of the letter, between the words of hope, wilting the characters of defiance into resignation. It was more than the fads and crazes that had gone. He smiled as he remembered some of them—theosophy, the correspondence course in writing, Turkish Baths. Then she had become a Catholic and they poor misguided Protestants were hopelessly hypocritical, lethargic and without the secret of existence. He'd been a bit dragged into that one, for poor Serena had written how glad she was that Stella had found peace, or some such phrase, and even sent a book about Jung and God, and Stella had scrawled great wads, not only to Serena but to Rusty for Serena, to the effect that she wanted no lectures about it, hadn't even read the books her instructor had lent her, and that she had simply woken up one morning and *known* and that was that. Last year he had received six pages on Yogi.

He understood her need to share, and more, her need to have a large correspondence, his end of which he tried his meagre best to keep up. Letters from home. One had to have letters from home, they were as much part of the local paraphernalia as mosquito-nets or electric fans. He felt reasonably certain that she wrote equally long and numerous letters to many other people, friends created with ink and airmail paper from chance acquaintances, previous colleagues, club-members and bungalow-neighbours, letters a little less personal perhaps but repeating the same phrases to each of these friends as she described the place she was in, or discussed the current political situation or imparted her latest philosophy of life.

All this he understood and loved with a love all the more exasperating because he knew he couldn't live for one moment with those aspects of Stella he most loved. It was a love, in fact, of distance. *La princesse lointaine*, he had read a title somewhere, in an advertisement column perhaps, and Stella was she. Had he failed her, after all, somewhere along the line? Could his distant princess be slowly dying?

The silence of the building roused him to a memory of closing doors and a scuffle of numerous feet that had some time ago turned the corridor into a sudden zoo of giggles, shouts, chatter and cheery male farewells. Rusty folded the letter back into his wallet and walked over to his wide glass view of the dirty river, now gold in the setting October sun. Even the wharves and warehouses on the South Bank looked romantic and the Council flats behind them winked square and scarlet. The bridge swarmed with black ants, hurrying to their daily Waterloo. "I did not know death had undone so many," Rusty murmured, with surprise at himself. He had not read any poetry since Cairo, when it had been a bit of a vogue, especially the modern stuff, among young army officers, and he would flick through the odd slim volume left around in their mess when he was on a liaison job. "I did not know death had undone so many," he repeated, and wondered why it had come into his head and who had written it.

But he wasn't the last to leave the building. As he waited for the lift to come sliding up to his summons, Harry Thorpe joined him and glared beneath his small bowler. It was difficult to avoid elevator small talk and Rusty did not try, but as he went through the friendly patter he became aware that the effort Harry Thorpe seemed to be making was out of all proportion to the difficulty of the subject-matter.

"I say, old man, is anything wrong?"

"Noothing," said Harry gruffly. His reality seemed much heavier than usual. Rusty smiled a simulation of belief and Harry added, "joos' tired, that's all."

Rusty nodded and smiled again.

"Well, I don't know about you, old man," he said when they reached the palatial exit, "but I usually have a whisky about this time. Why don't you join me? I'd like it very much," he added simply, dropping the old-man line which he suddenly realised had irritated not only Harry but himself all these years. He watched Harry weaken visibly, then tighten his lips.

"No thanks. It's very nice of you but I've got to get home. The wife is waiting."

"Surely you can catch the next train?"

"Ay, but—"

"My wife never expects me till after seven. She knows I like to drop in at the club. But I feel like the good old pub round the corner now. Come on, Harry, it'll do you good, you've been overworking."

It was the first time Rusty had ever called him Harry, just like that. It was always "Harry Thorpe" when he wasn't there, and "old man" or nothing at all when he was. Harry nodded briskly and they walked up the street in complete silence.

"Ay, it's a nice place," he said politely when Rusty brought him his drink.

"But surely you've been here before?"

"No. No, I haven't as a matter of fact."

"You're not—?"

"No, no, I'm not teetotal. I like to drop in at our local and have a drink with the lads," he said without conviction.

"Oh, good show," Rusty felt a fool again, and indeed another silence followed.

Harry did not unbend into more than a few trite remarks about his work until after the second whisky he had surprisingly and unhesitatingly accepted, making, however, not even the semblance of a move to stand the round. He sat in a dazed fatigue, staring at the lace of froth inside the nobbled glass of an empty beer mug left by a previous occupant.

"Have you heard the rumour?" he asked suddenly after gulping down his second whisky.

"What rumour?"

"You know. About U.K. Sales."

"U.K. Sales? No. What sort of rumour?"

"They say. . ." But he couldn't bring himself to utter it. "Never mind. joos' thought you might have heard something about it."

"No. Whatever it is, it's probably only a rumour. You know what big organisations are."

"Ay."

There was another silence and Harry toyed with his empty glass. Quietly Rusty took it and ordered a double.

"They say," Harry began again later, "they say that young Fawcett's in for it."

"You mean he's in trouble?"

"No." He half shouted, then his voice dropped again to the same unhealthy monotone. "In for the job. U.K. Sales."

"Jim Fawcett? U.K. Sales? I've never heard such nonsense in all my life."

"Ay, young Fawcett."

"Harry, who told you this,? Who's they?"

"I'm not one to repeat empty rumours, you know," he blurted out angrily. "Someone told me."

"But who?"

"Mr. Harding, as a matter of fact. Came to discuss it with me two weeks ago. With *me!*"

Poor Harry couldn't even thump the table or bang his glass, he was so paralysed by the horror that had been eating him up. To speak of it at all was effort enough.

"But Jim Fawcett's already in a post much too senior for his age!"

"I know."

"Harding must be out of his mind."

"Ay."

He sat there motionless as the phrase echoed between them. Rusty looked at him closely.

"Look, Harry, it's impossible. I know there are a lot of injustices in big organisations, of course, but this is beyond the wildest unlikelihood. Fawcett has no sales experience at all, except abroad, and for a very short time. How could he be put above you, in a job everyone knows you're the only man for? Anyway, Jenkins isn't eyen leaving yet."

"Due to retire next year," said Harry briefly. "Sixty-five in January."

"Is he really? Well, well, he doesn't look it."
"Harding told me."
"Harry, surely, that's *all* he told you?"
"He's taken up smoking, you know."
"Who?"
"Young Fawcett."
"What about it?"
"Cigars, you know. And a heavy signet-ring. Oh, I know the type. They're all the same."

Suddenly Rusty remembered, and knew that his intuition had been right.

"Listen, Harry. Listen to me carefully. I happen to know, and this from Jim Fawcett himself, that he has put his name down for the new job that's opening next year in the Aegean. He's dead keen, and so is his wife. He told me he loves publicity but he wants another spell abroad, especially this, because it's not too wild and remote. He was talking about it to me only the other day." Rusty watched the veil of miserable incredulity fade from Harry's face like daybreak as he spoke. And to prevent any objections like "but Harding said", he went on for a long time about the new development on some of the smaller volcanic islands in the Aegean, over which U.V.I. had signed a trade agreement with Greece, all of which Harry knew perfectly well; and how Jim Fawcett wanted to go to Greece to get his hair nice and blond like his friend Ted Baker; and how Mrs. Fawcett would be worse than most English wives abroad for she really was unusually ugly, and nobody could understand why Jim Fawcett was always so unbelievably happy with a thing like that to trail around. But trail he would, for he wanted to go. Not a flicker of amusement lit Harry's expression, only a pale exhausted look, almost green, but relaxed, like a devastated face after a lifted fever. The locusts had flown away. "So you see," Rusty explained charitably, "it was a complete misunderstanding. Whatever Harding said to you it certainly can't have been that."

Rusty felt, extraordinarily elated on his way home, partly as a good scout, for the good deed done, but mostly because his ancient and secret envy of Harry Thorpe had dropped from him like an infatuation; he had been allowed to relive his lost moment of group captaincy over Harry's colonelship, as a hangdog lover is sometimes allowed his moment of indifferent refusal, and it had not mattered a jot. When he became aware of the reason for his elation he felt slightly ashamed, but still elated nevertheless. Then suddenly his mood changed in reaction, and he began to wonder whether he too wasn't going a little screwy at U.V.I. Perhaps Stella was right. Perhaps he should apply for a transfer to Central America. Or perhaps not Central America, precisely. West Africa, anywhere really. Japan, he had liked Japan, and so had Jean. It wasn't at all like American guilt-films, heroic marines versus horrific monsters or, alternatively, life is just one big bowl of cherry blossom. There was more to Japan than that. There was Hiroshima for one thing. Yes, perhaps he would apply for a transfer, even though it meant giving up being Chief Public Relations Officer and a London Head of Department. They couldn't demote him financially, anyway, and he could do with the extra allowances. It was time he saved properly for his retirement. Their old age. He felt tired at the very words, tired of London, tired of Serena and his analysis, tired of being Chief Public Relations Officer at U.V.I. Headquarters. Joos' tired, as Harry Thorpe had said. Joos' tired.

9

DICK BARBER experienced more than an agent's professional disappointment when Tweedie and Tweedie returned a novel he had been trying to sell for some months. He felt peeved and personally slighted, almost as if he had written it himself. For he believed in it, more, in fact, than if he had written it himself. Not that he knew the author, who seemed too busy even to drop in and see him or have lunch. "Just sell it," the author had said in his letter, "and don't let me hear a word until you have. I'm not interested in rejection slips." Very businesslike, cynical or modest, whichever way one preferred to take it, cool, real cool. This had impressed Dick no end, for most authors had a morbid desire to analyse, weigh, comment on and refute the details of such letters of refusal publishers deigned to write. This time there wasn't even a letter, which annoyed Dick even more. The manuscript had been to nine publishers, from Truelove & Thorne down, and he really had thought that it would appeal, if not to Mr. Tweedie himself, that dour Scotsman, then at least to Justin Jacob, who was a smooth exquisite, and nothing if not sophisticated. Evidently he was nothing.

The novel, hopefully entitled *Mass Medium*, was by one Ted Baker, and all about television advertising. It was wickedly funny, as smart as a Schweppes campaign, and the characters were vividly real. There was a good plot, too, about a young man who makes television ad films and tries to sell a brilliant new idea for a documentary to a big television boss, who turns it down out of hand and then pinches the idea for one of his own units. The whole thing ended hilariously on location with everyone behaving outrageously and the hero, who by then was on his honeymoon with a famous film star, looking casually on and surreptitiously sabotaging the proceedings. This chap had genuine imagination, no doubt about that. As for the big television boss, whose name was Hal Williams and who was called Hill Billy by most of the other characters, he was a positively Dickensian creation, massive of course, grotesque, ruthless yet oddly likeable. For despite his bedside reading of Proust, which like most Bibles was more often than not set aside for the latest thriller, Dick's mind worked in biurbish grooves, but without a blurb-writer's cheek to put his tongue into.

Dick Barber was not perhaps temperamentally suited to the life of a Literary Agent, for besides his Norpoisean ideals he had a tendency to get emotionally involved, not with his authors, who were on the whole an unlovable lot, nor with their books as books, but with their books as commodities which he, Dick Barber, was trying to sell and which, therefore, acquired a very personal relationship to himself, being symbols of his success or otherwise, and moreover, visible, tangible, conveyable expressions of his intelligence, his good taste, his sophistication, in short, his personality. Sometimes they even seemed to prove his own existence. He could therefore get quite offended even when he merely lent or privately recommended a book he had much enjoyed, to a friend who then thought little of it, and actual criticism made him get pinker and pinker, like a string of insults. His work was made unnecessarily complicated by these unpractical subtleties.

The printed rejection slip from Tweedie & Tweedie reminded him of numerous other such insults, which he began to list in his mind according to which publishers had thus insulted him most frequently. Then he remembered his recent defeat by Dave Goodman over the Stevens book. He thought of all this with a relish that was only half revengeful. And suddenly he knew that he would submit *Mass Medium* to Dave Goodman. Of course, why hadn't he thought of it before? Yes, well it *was* a small firm, but then none of the bigger ones wanted it. Dave had an eye for new talent. Especially clever talent. He was, in publishing, prince of the wide-boys.

Again, as when he had said that Dave Goodman was too young for where he had got, and was viewed with suspicion by the elders of his profession, so now Dick was partly reflecting his own position. But this time he rather flattered himself. Their names were linked, it was true, as the coming men, but the contrast between them lingered in people's minds, emphasised by the strong physical differences—Dave dark and slight, almost sinister, Dick blondly bald, round and baby-faced. Dick and Dave, Queen and Knave, someone had coined, a little unfairly, for Dick was not particularly potent either way, except in rather special circumstances. But the phrase had stuck, like a joke pinned upon their backs without their knowledge, though recently the Knave had risen much faster, from one of several bright young men at Tweedie's to Chief Literary Editor at Ben Clef, a newish firm that had done well on beatnik howls of protest, the new school of Nuclear Fiction, and the reaction against it, the Antinuclear Novel.

Dave Goodman was not in fact as sinisterly intelligent as Dick in his desire for punishment made him out. He had his weaknesses, as any sharp observer of his pretty mouth and soft dark eyes could tell. He created enemies, or rather, indifferences, foolishly, by inviting married women to lunch or to first nights, for instance, rather persistently and without their husbands, not for any particular reason except to be seen with them, as variously and as often as possible; and by fibbing carelessly, pretending to have met all sorts of aristocrats and famous foreign writers, or telling an author that a decision to publish him had been chiefly due to him, when perhaps his had been the only voice against.

Such streaks of silliness were bound to affect even a clever man's judgement, and to Dick's surprise and very slight chagrin—soon drowned in triumph and professional joy—Dave made quite a reasonable offer for *Mass Medium*, "this unusual novel by a clearly very promising writer". To Ben Clef he raved about it for hours, talking of Satire and the New Social Realism, so that when Ben Clef read it he was privately rather disappointed, thinking the book mildly amusing, personally vitriolic and even more shoddily written than most of the stuff one saw around. But then Dave was his bright young man, with his pulse on the new generation, it didn't do to put spokes in his wheel. Or just a little spoke perhaps.

"Promising exactly what, Dave? A bit old-fashioned, I thought. One of those professional jokes novels, the lid off the law and all that. Still, they usually sell a bit. To the profession anyway."

Dave politely protested that although he knew it had a good chance of selling there was a good deal more to it than that.

"Yes, well," said Ben Clef when he had finished, "we'll take it, don't worry. The boy's obviously in the racket himself. A copywriter no doubt." He laughed asthmatically at his little joke. "They say publishers are all frustrated writers, but I can tell you one thing, the lowest rung in the ladder of literary frustration is entirely occupied by copywriters."

It was true that Ted had started as a copywriter and had indeed been a very good one. It was not true that he was frustrated, except perhaps as regards his profession, through which he had risen so rapidly as to miss much of the scope it might have given to his creative ability. He consequently despised it, and led a richly unfrustrated life as regards his private person. There was no play or foreign film, fashionable restaurant, no socialite party, and, for that matter few model girls and London hostesses, that had not been however briefly, visited by him. Such promiscuousness of mind and body could hardly be called frustration, literary or otherwise, and it had in fact produced, like the painted lips of the women he kissed, a thing full of empty promise, here entitled, rather deliciously, he thought, *Mass Medium*.

So he was extremely pleased when he heard from Caraway Christian that they had sold the novel to a firm called Ben Clef. He knew little of the publishing world, but as a top salesman of top publicity he appreciated the difficulties any agent for anything must experience, and had an absolute trust in their judgement, efficiency and—even though he would never so have named it—magic powers, that would have nonplussed Caraway Christian himself.

He looked at the name at the bottom of the letter, rang it up and invited it to a party. Together with the name mentioned in the letter, by proxy as it were, if its owner so wished.

The Middlemen: Chapter Nine

The TV-X biannuals were famous all over London, especially among people who were not asked, but read, about them in the Press. They usually occupied the largest reception suite at the Ritz or the Dorchester, and sometimes the vast hall or even an interlinked set of studios at TV-X House in Hampstead. But this one, just to be different, was being given in the palace of polaroid glass itself, for TV-X was proud both of its commercial basis and of its connection with Screen Persuaders Ltd., who were the best, the biggest, the brightest in the business. The best and the biggest boys of Screen Persuaders therefore, including Ted Baker, had each been sent several invitations to dispose of at their discretion, and Ted Baker's discretion included his brand new publisher, his brand new agent, and his momentary mistress, an Honourable fish-faced girl reputed to have once belonged to the Princess Margaret set, from which relationship, together with his skill for manoeuvring the right weekends, Ted Baker had secretly screen-persuaded himself that there was no reason why he should not marry Princess Alexandra if he tried—or even Princess Anne when she grew up. But Ted never liked trying. He was convinced that the introduction and its inevitable consequence would come his way quite naturally, without effort, like everything else. In the meantime, all he had to do was to keep his thick wavy hair from going grey.

The Greek sun had renewed its wonders the previous summer and both Dick Barber and Dave Goodman were suitably impressed when Ted and his Honourable Fishface met them at The York Minster and drove them in his lilac and skyblue Ford Consul to them palace of polaroid glass. This unusual author was promising indeed.

It was not so much a party as a symbolic representation of the Christmas rush in the chasm of London's main shopping street, performed as it were by crabs, limpets, jellyfish, squids and sea-urchins, sea-anemones and hundreds of smaller fry at the bottom of a huge aquarium. Tall plants, artificial palms, streamers and decorations, floated in the gentle breeze of numerous ventilators, which hardly relieved the crowds below as well as wide banners bearing the firm's modest motto: TV-Xtra, TV-Xellent, TV-Xtraordinary.

Everyone raved about the parrot, and the parrot raved loudly against everybody, loyally squawking Squeak Persuaders at them, for he disapproved of this invasion, even by the mass medium itself. So he bit the finger of a gushing girl who tried to stroke his beautiful scarlet and crimson feathers. And later he bit several more.

The great Hughie Hill was of course, as always, present in absentia. Sam Wilson was talking about him to a willowing bunch of algae, and all his other producers were talking about him to each other. Isabel Gormsley was talking about him to Jim Fawcett, who wore a glaucous grin, and more particularly to his wife, one of the numerous sea-horses swimming about hunch-necked. Tom Stevens was talking about him to Tony Black, who pouted and wriggled like a goldfish at 'being remembered' by Tom Stevens. Simply everyone was there who had had anything to do with television, either permanently or in the six months since the last biannual in June. And beautiful girls wearing TV-X badges just above the point of their right breast moved smilingly among them all, trying more in vain than not to introduce some of these variously celebrated souls to one another.

TV-X, moreover, used these opportunities to launch such new programmes or personalities as were planned for the next six months or the immediate future, so that the whole of the Press from "quality" TV critics to "quantity" gossip columnists was also invited. The Press, of course, made straight for the bars and buffet tables, leaving the artistes to talk to each other in programmatic groups. Several launchings were taking place this time. In one corner a new sports' commentator scheduled for stardom was being splendidly pally with a long-distance runner, a lady showjumper, the last Cup Finalists, a huge Sudanese channel swimmer, a Wimbledon player who never quite made it but was at least British, and three leading South African cricketers who were being purposely confronted with the visiting West Indian eleven. Further along was *Teenage Time*, a new programme which was launching itself there and then to some rival pop from the B.B.C. that was jolting out of somebody's jeans-back-pocket, from a miniature transistor-set with a tall silver aerial like a

The Middlemen: Chapter Nine

very proud tail, until Danny (Hip) Dago himself arrived and, rhythmically accompanied by squeals of delight, gave a free performance with his guitar, his larynx, his eyes and of course his famous hip. These tender-aged guests looked less like fish than the others and rather spoilt the aquarium illusion: for as the couples swung each other around in their broad leather jackets, narrowing then widening the distance between their four gangling legs and between the lank or stiffly brushed up hair, of the boys and the tossing ponytails of the girls, they reminded one more of awkwardly prancing colts trying their limbs not long after being born. On the opposite side of the enormous hall every passerby was being asked to vote for the new TV-hostess they preferred, out of seven lovelies who sat in a pink glow on low and cushioned couches, each in a low and cushioned teledecolletage, being stared at, mentally undressed and otherwise celebrated rather than launched. Finally, a *Woman's Weekly* had recently been started, to tell the housewife all she didn't need to know but liked to hear about and see. It stood a little primly in a corner by itself, and no one from the milling masses came to speak with it.

Dick Barber felt exceedingly lost in this vast vanity fair, for Ted, after, introducing them to several producers of publicity films and a few big financiers, had drifted off with his Honourable and forgotten all about them. Dave Goodman immediately struck up a friendship for life with one of the financiers, and Dick disentangled himself and shuffled about in zig-zags like a crab, cooked pink yet alive somehow.

He was relieved to see a face vaguely familiar from literary parties, domed and aureoled with straightly combed black hair, but receding below like a rather squashed Beethoven. He walked up to it and smiled pleasantly.

"Haven't we met somewhere? I'm Dick Barber. From Caraway Christian."

"Rupert Scott-Buttery."

"Oh, yes."

It was so pleasant when one's name evoked an "Oh, yes," instead of the usual deaf look. Rupert's had in fact become quite well-known since the small matter of the flat and the large matter of the mortgage had galvanised him into success, and even his television appearance had been repeated, first on *Public Inquisitor* (about library royalties for authors), then on *Watch Others Work* (about being a literary critic), and finally on *The Brains Trust* (about everything), inflating the value of the name he signed until he was forced to raise the Bank Rate with a spell on the B.B.C. Critics.

"Crowded, isn't it?" said Dick.

"Yes," said Rupert, looking round a little wildly for Serena, who was better at small talk than he was.

"To tell you the truth I feel a little lost in all this lot," Dick went on with a slight whine. Clearly he was going to cling.

"Prefer our own crowd."

"Ah, yes. You're in—er—the city?'"

"No, I'm an agent. Literary agent. Carway Christian, you know."

"Oh, yes, so you said, sorry."

"Are you Hughie Hill?" said a man with a pasty face and a pasty voice jolting Rupert's drink over his suit. "Because I think your programme's sordid. Absolutely sordid." He goggled at them then moved off.

"Who was that?"

"No idea. Could be Wall Wootton. I'm not too sure."

"Oh."

"To tell you the truth I feel a little lost in all this lot. Prefer our own crowd."

"Yes . . . Well, actually there are a few publishers around. You might even find one if you look hard enough."

"Oh, really?" Dick brightened. "Who?"

"I admit they're like needles in a haystack. I saw Geoff Brandon earlier, talking to Howard Cutting." Rupert said this cuttingly, because Howard Cutting still appeared in bigger letters than he on the book page of *The Sunday Supplement*. "And Tweedie's here."

"Good heavens, why?"

"I expect some book of theirs was 'done' on *Woman's Weekly* or something. Truelove's here too, who published Lord Merseyside's book, you may remember, I interviewed him, Lord Merseyside I mean. I was talking to him just now."

"I'm so sorry," said the pasty voice as its owner emerged once again from behind a voluminous dress of aquamarine cinderella, "someone has just told me you're not Hughie Hill after all. Have a drink on me." He snatched two glasses of champagne from a passing tray and handed one to Rupert, who now had one in each hand, and felt like half-filling the empty one and giving it to Dick Barber, who had no glass at all. But then he was afraid of offending him so he didn't.

"I'm Cliff Morrison, journalist. Who are you?"

"Rupert Scott-Buttery."

"Oh, so *you're* Rupert Scott-Buttery? *The Sunday Supplement*, eh? Rudest paper in the world."

"This from a journalist."

"Oh, don't give me that. I mean manners, dear boy, not matter. Or are you part of *The Sunday Supplement* mystique?"

"Is there one?"

"Very rude people, very rude indeed. They don't send proofs of letters. And if one insists they take no notice of one's corrections. I was on the phone only this morning to some chit of a girl who asked me whether I really meant to spell Krafft-Ebbing with two f's. 'Yes, dear,' I said, and—"

"Oh, I see." Rupert blanked his mind and emptied his second glass.

"Still, I suppose one has to make allowances. The mind of the petty clerk is less fathomable than that of the rarest mystic. No adventure in their lives, no searing of the psyche. Even so, there is a way of returning articles. To people well known in the trade, so to speak. Tell me, what are Tweedie & Tweedie like as publishers? I'm thinking of joining their list. Do they promote you properly? Put you on television? That sort of thing?"

He went on in this vein for some time and Dick Barber realised why he had been uncertain of the identity. He had met Clifford Morrison some years ago, when he was a rather bad translator of rather bad Italian novels, proud, Dick remembered, of his ability to talk in complete sentences, with long subordinate clauses and parentheses that followed on from each other with a rolling rhythm. Now he still spoke much but clipped his phrases short, as if he were trying at all costs to keep up with the times. Or perhaps he was just drunk.

Drink was certainly flowing in the aquarium, and as usual at English parties, groups of men clustered together, reverting to nature after the second or third glass had relieved them of the pretence that they enjoyed being polite to women. One of the many multicoloured bouquets of silk, satin, muslin and cinderella consisted of Isabel Gormsley, who had found Serena and was almost having a free session with her, until they were joined by Sonya Dandridge, editor of *Elegance*, and Maryon Farquharson, a matronly author of a family saga in twelve volumes and generations, who had been appearing on *Woman's Weekly*.

"I thought we were going to be launched," Maryon said in a jolly voice. "Nobody's launched me yet." So Isabel like a wicked little girl threw the luckily small remnants of her champagne on the lady's noble prow. Sonya Dandridge decided this was terribly funny and linked arms with Isabel suddenly as everyone laughed. They were both almost as elegant as the vacuous figurines of metropolitan saints in Sonya's magazine, but older, and Isabel was more fussily elegant; Sonya had kept a much better figure, looking almost boyish in a pure silk coral shirt and cropped silvering hair, Isabel was pleased but disentangled herself, ostensibly to wipe Maryon Farquharson's dress, but really because Serena was present.

"Thank you, thank you, Miss Gormley," said Maryon good-naturedly. "I feel well and truly launched now, sliding off into a sunblue bay."

"I'm terribly sorry. I don't know what came over me."

"But it was no worse mischief than my youngest son would have done." In anyone else's voice this could have sounded vicious but not in Maryon Farquharson's, and this made Isabel even more unnecessarily gushing.

"I do hope it won't stain."

"No, my dear, it's nitron, washes like a dream."

Serena gave a horribly professional laugh.

"What a huge place this is," she said to change the subject and added, conscious of being obsessive as she uttered the words: "One could make at least fifty fair-sized flats out of the ground floor alone."

She seemed drawn and pale, even in the flattering tinted mirrors of the polaroid glass palace. She had lost weight, too, and Rupert, who had sidled up with moving-off signs to his wife, thought she was looking remarkably like Stella at this moment.

"Hello, girls," said another voice, belonging to a head of almost Prussian hair, which in turn belonged to Nat Warner, editor of *The Sunday Supplement*. He had met Rupert, and Serena once only, but was an old friend of both Maryon Farquharson and Sonya, nodding to the one and patting the other familiarly on the bottom. "Fancy seeing you here."

"Small world," said Maryon Farquharson.

"Closed worlds," said Rupert. "All the literary crowd seek each other out like amoebae. Met a chap earlier on who felt quite lost because he couldn't find any publishers. I finally palmed him off on an American rubber tycoon who was suffering from post-jet fatigue. Do you know that apart from that American I haven't met anyone from big business? Or from the advertising world. Or the teenage world, or the football world, or the city, no moneylenders, for instance."

"What do you want to meet moneylenders for?"

"I don't know. They might be interesting people. It's not impossible."

"My dear Scott-Buttery, are you trying to become a journalist? Perhaps you're bellyaching to spill over to my side of the paper?"

"No, no, sir. But look at this madhouse. I haven't even met anyone from television for that matter."

"I'm in television," said Isabel.

"How do you do?"

"And I've met simply dozens of people tonight, it's my job. I'm Director of Advertising Time, you see. Only just now I was talking to the head of a big travel agency that takes a full half minute every Friday night—good psychological time that. *Winged Chariots Ltd.* Do you know them?"

"Travel agents, how fascinating." Clearly Rupert was a little tipsy.

"Any news?" said the pasty voice again over Rupert's shoulder. Cliff Morrison had edged his way into the group, obviously hoping for an introduction to the editor of *The Sunday Supplement*. Rupert obliged, charitably, then moved off with Serena after saying they really must go.

But they met, suddenly, many people from television. And Tom Stevens. And Tony Black. So they stayed.

Much later Rupert tripped over the legs of Cliff Morrison, who was sitting on a low couch with one of the no longer merely viewable lovelies who had competed as a future television hostess. The winner had been promoted out of familiarity's way into some more central group, at some producer's right hand.

"Sorry. Oh, hello. I hope you repeated all your complaints about *The Sunday Supplement* to Nat Warner?"

"Some," said Cliff Morrison, with a glare that meant 'not quite, if at all', and turned with fantastic optimism to his nineteen-year-old lovely, who thought that a journalist might with careful handling be almost as useful as a television producer.

She must have been soon disillusioned however, because when Rupert and Serena got away at last there was Cliff Morrison in the pink porch of the glass palace, like a footman waiting to hand Cinderella into her crystal coach. He was unaccompanied and indeed insisted on giving them a lift home to Finchley Road, as he lived in St. John's Wood.

His crystal coach was a very large station wagon with a bunk and a dinette at the back, into which he pressed them to enter although the front seat was more than wide enough to take the three of them.

"Do all my work in here," he shouted, for the engine was very noisy. "Africa, overland to India, Asia, the lot. Special correspondent you know. None of this topical stuff for me. Interviewed Pasternak in it, he sat just where you are."

He drove, indeed, as if North London were the Gobi Desert, and as he bumped and swerved and screeched to a stop at the pedantic red lights of the empty city, Serena and Rupert clutched the table round which they were idiotically sitting, and which fairly soon came off its peg so that they were thrown down on top of it, Cliff Morrison yelling his more successful articles and assignations the while. Rupert managed to haul himself into the bunk at the back, clutching its edges for dear life, and Serena remained on the floor, firmly wedged at last, between the front seat and a small refrigerator, holding the table's one leg away from herself.

"This is it," said Rupert weakly, some three roads before theirs. He has been sobered back into his usual caution. "Thanks a lot."

"Hope to see you again."

"Yes."

"You can always get me through *The Express News*. If I'm in the country, that is."

"Good, splendid."

"And you, where can I get hold of you?"

"Oh, just, my publisher," said Rupert desperately.

"Okay, fine, I will, very soon. I expect you're in the book, anyway. Cheerio."

"Good God, do you think he knows my name or who my publisher is?" said Rupert as they walked home.

"He'll find out if he wants to. If he doesn't, he won't. Depends what impression you made on him, not, unfortunately, vice versa."

"His car certainly made an impression on me," said Rupert furiously. "Look, my fly-zip's broken. At least, I hope to God it *was* in the car, not earlier."

10

CLIFF MORRISON was soon spending regular Sunday evenings and sometimes others with the Scott-Butterys. His paper had allowed him a spell in London, and he was using the opportunity to widen the bridgehead afforded by his introduction to Nat Warner, for his greatest next ambition was to work for a Sunday paper, which he had convinced himself put less pressure on its correspondents and was also more rewarding, since one was read by the top people, yet without the galling anonymity of The Times. But Nat Warner was not so easy of re-access, and in the meantime it would not hurt to cultivate Rupert Scott-Buttery, for although he was only a book page reviewer on Warner's paper, his name was going steadily up in the non-literary stockmarket, indeed, he was well on the way to becoming a personality, Cliff thought. In no time at all he would have to have a publicity agent. Then Nat Warner would listen to him, a word in his ear perhaps, about Cliff Morrison, or a little dinner engineered. And besides, Cliff really liked Rupert.

Curiously enough, Rupert rather liked Cliff too, after a while. Serena teased him and said it was connected in his subconscious with the breaking down of the armour over his masculinity, and Rupert got quite annoyed. Of course he hadn't been firm enough at first; but soon he was intrigued by Cliff's very persistence, envying his confidence and his thick skin. And then he found there was more to Cliff than a thick skin, there was a soft mush under the hair-shirt that made him shudder and yet want more, like an old maid listening to gossip. It wasn't the sentimental mush of the tabloids, nor was it their muck-raking. Cliff was better educated than that, but only just. He mixed his ingredients more minutely, however, more subtly even, presenting them, like a slightly backward child of his time, as depth psychology, on which subject his clipped syntax could grow as flowery as a herbaceous border.

One of his basic assumptions in life, Serena soon found out, was that all married couples were straining at the leash to leave each other, and that only by a constant dosage of love affairs on both sides could a marriage survive. "How do you manage, with Rupert here all the time?" he asked her as he carried the coffee tray into the kitchen on his second visit. "Ah, but of course, you have your consulting room. Still it's not quite the same. Can't let yourself go. Tell me, do you scream at the climax? I knew a woman who passed right out, every time. I was terrified at first. Thought she was dead. Have you ever fainted?"

"I prefer my knitting," said Serena, who couldn't tell purl from plain.

"Ah . . . yes, very significant, knitting." He shook his head and gave a sad sad sigh, followed by a lascivious giggle suggesting, she realised with distaste, a leering familiarity with the cruder aspects of her profession.

He seemed to think that all people, especially women, who did not respond to his luringly fascinated questions and impart to him all the details of their private life, were rather prim and stuffy. So much so that when they did not do so he imagined that they had, hinting, for lack of knowledge, not at dark secrets, which anyone could do, but at dark unreleased passions hidden even from the conscious selves of those he was talking about. This had the double virtue of making quite dull persons sound rather interesting, and Cliff himself unusually perceptive; especially since, when pressed, he would pretend to a sudden renewal of a discretion that had very slightly lapsed in the presence of such amiable and trustworthy friends, among whom he felt so very much at home.

All these principles he also applied successfully in his articles and interviews with the great, but they did not give him so much scope as private relationships. He preyed on marriages and wherever he appeared as a family friend, there, sooner or later, an emotional crisis would arise, not with him as the third man, though this too would be attempted as a matter of course, but simply out of his innumerable suggestions that emotional crisis was the desirable norm in life. "Any news?" he would ask on arrival or on the telephone, meaning news of just such crises. He was a vampire of other people's emotions, a middleman of sex urges, a pandar of possibilities, indeed, Serena automatically supposed he must be impotent.

Rupert, however, who did not see quite so much of Cliff's prying side as Serena did, found him more and more entertaining, and had no objection at all to his questions, in or out of her presence, like "Are you often unfaithful to each other?" or "How far do you repress your homosexual tendencies?" Unlike Serena, he felt a rinsing quality in such disarming frankness, as if Cliff were scooping up his words in mid-air, his thoughts even, and reshaping them, retransmitting them with different meanings, more real meanings, back to him, or to Serena, or to some invisible world at large.

Since Rupert liked him, Serena humoured Cliff, reflecting that he would probably be sent abroad soon and that anyway Rupert's sudden and over-intimate friendships never lasted very long. They were too unlike him, his vagueness, his idealism and his caution. All the same, he had changed a bit since his success and she found that she was not so much humouring Cliff as bearing him with mounting irritation.

She did in fact very nearly lose her temper one evening when he was putting Tom Stevens through the Cliff Morrison treatment. They had been discussing the second series of articles by Tom Stevens in *The Sunday Supplement*, on State Private Enterprise.

"Ah yes," Cliff said with a sigh. "Poor man, there's a fundamental dichotomy there. Yes, indeed. A fundamental dichotomy. Great turmoils deep down below, dear me."

"Really, Cliff, how on earth can you know?"

"Ah my dear Serena, it's written in his every phrase, his very syntax."

"What is? The deep turmoils?"

"Serena my dear, you're a very clever woman. Very clever. And attractive, if I may say so. Oh, yes. The White Goddess and all that. You understand life and its dark ancient rituals, buried deep down in the collective —"

"For Christ's sake."

"But, my dear Serena, *but*: you are not a stylist. Rupert will understand me there. How do young lovers in their first speechless discovery of the flowery paths that wind their scented, colourful, enchanting ways to the deep abyss, try helplessly to cover their inarticulateness, their verbal nakedness, how? By copying out poetry, quoting half-remembered lines they learnt at school perhaps and will doubtless never quote again, using our poets as messengers and heralds, interpreters if you like, translators —I began as a translator, so I understand the problems, no, more, as communicators, in an agreed code, of those ineffable, inexpressible—"

"Turmoils," put in Serena.

"You may laugh. But the English language—"

"Phooey!"

She went out and slammed the door.

Rupert was very surprised, for Serena the equable, the unruffled, the serene, hardly ever lost her temper except, once a year or so, with Stella. But he turned back to Cliff with the shrug of a patient husband and they got down to some real man-to-man stuff.

Serena had been particularly angry because that morning, for the first time, she felt she was getting somewhere with Tom Stevens. He had actually brought her a dream. "No, I'm afraid I never dream," he had said from the very beginning. "Most unusual, isn't it? I sleep like a log." But now he had dreamt about a pair of red shoes. He couldn't be sure whether he was supposed to be a ballet dancer or not—rather rum, really—and he couldn't remember much about it, except that instead of not being able to get the shoes off, as in that film, you know, he couldn't get them on; he kept losing them, and yet he had to have them, for his travels, which were terribly important but on which he couldn't even set out without the red shoes. Extraordinary, wasn't it? So that's what it was like to dream? Well, well, what a rum thing. And he had seemed so pleased about it all that Serena expected quite a few more dreams, from now on.

But the anger about Cliff and Tom Stevens was only a symptom. Serena was quite simply exhausted. In their scramble to make more money she had been taking too many patients, imbibing their aggressions all day to a point of surfeit. And although she was naturally delighted by Rupert's success, the fact that he was now making more money than she was, instead of less, hurt her feelings more than it reasonably should, indeed she soon analysed that out of existence as unworthy of her nobler self.

The real trouble, she knew, was the small matter of the flat, which was clogging the machinery of her mind with an obsessiveness that blocked the obsessions of her patients out of her concentration. It had by now loomed into a quiet but steady loathing of every present inconvenience, every load of coal to be dragged up the stairs, every ill-fitting window and squeaking floor-board, every tidemark left in the bath by other lodgers, every pull of the chain that flushed nothing at all with an agonised croak. And she would soothe or perhaps feed the nagging with perpetual adoration of the glossy coloured pictures in the smart magazines, of dream-kitchens in mulberry and tomato, duck-egg and pineapple, lined with every labour-saving device and designed to the very latest and minutely worked out time-and-motion planning which made the previous year's kitchens hopelessly unpractical and, worse still, out of date; or feminine bedrooms with cinderella gauze curtains and fluffy nitron rugs; or gracious drawing rooms in deep startling colours, with early Victorian chairs upholstered in silk the colour of unhealthy urine, which the magazine caption called chartreuse.

Serena had now mentally furnished and decorated three entire flats over a period of about two months each before each had fallen through, and she was becoming quite an expert, albeit interiorly.

The last loss had been a restatement of the original theme, with coda variation. Assuming that all was at last proceeding smoothly she rang up Inter-Insular Insurance, some five weeks after making her application for a mortgage, to ask them whether they had surveyed the property yet.

"Which property is that, madam? Fifty-seven. . . Yes, I've got it, and your name . . . u, double t, e, double r, y. Just hang on a minute, will you?"

She hung on for five. "Hello? Yes, here we are. But there must be a mistake, madam. We turned down your application at last week's board meeting ... I'm afraid so, madam ... Well, I can't help that, we informed Clacton's on the 22nd, the copy of our letter's here in the file ... Pardon? Oh, the lease was not satisfactory, that is to say, the maintenance clause did not meet with our requirement 2B7a that the lessor should grant the lessee ... Pardon? Oh, right-ho, madam then, cheerio."

She rushed to Mr. Clacton, who because she had no appointment let her know that he couldn't see her for twenty minutes and kept her waiting for an hour and a half.

"Good afternoon, Mrs. Buttery," he said, rising to meet her with outstretched hand. "I was about to write to you."

"I've just heard from Inter-Insular."

"Yes. Yes. I'm very sorry this little deal fell through, Mrs. B., but there's plenty of fish in the sea, you know—"

"But why, Mr. Clacton, why?" Serena echoed her earlier self, but with renewed passion.

"I think they're right, you know, Mrs. B., they're only protecting you. So many speculators on the market, out for quick profit, capital gains, you know, untaxed, they don't want to spend rising cash looking after a place for ninety-nine years, so they get some shady lawyer to draw up a nice loosely worded lease. I remember a case—"

"Yes, but you yourself passed it, you said the maintenance—"

"Tell me, Mrs. B., how badly did you want this particular property?"

"Very badly."

He still pared his nails with his other nails and they were still dirty. He looked at her over the rimless halved spectacles half way down his nose and she still felt like dusting them off him with a feather mop, and all the spilt ash down his suit as well.

"Because you see, we could argue. Oh, not with Inter-Insular, of course, but with the Vendor's Solicitors. They drew up the lease, after all, and I still say it's a very reasonable lease indeed. Only a very small point needs changing, it's a question of wording you know."

"Then why didn't—" She stopped. There was a very long silence as she tried to widen the glimmer of light she had just glimpsed through Mr. Clacton's bland expression. "You mean," she said slowly, "that this phrase, which is in the Inter-Insular form, about their requirement on maintenance, must be in the lease?"

"Yes, that's all. I can get them to put it in. Nothing to it."

Serena for good measure went to see the house agent, and he, a thin bald young man like those one sees in mock Tudor pubs was delighted to act as a more efficient go-between than her solicitor. He rang up the owner, talked to her, dictated the phrase which Serena had brought—it's very reasonable, he said to her, very reasonable—and hey presto, all was arranged, the owner promised to instruct her solicitors accordingly. Much relieved, and feeling very clever, Serena went home and waited.

She waited three weeks. For the owner's solicitors would not be so instructed. It was in their client's interest, they said, not to change the lease which they, thinking of those same interests, had carefully drafted, and so forth, thus delaying the payment of the capital their client badly needed. Letters passed between the two firms of solicitors, repeating the formula required by Inter-Insular, with slightly different trimmings according to whether the formula was being insisted upon or refused. Every now and again Serena received copies of these missives, with a covering letter at a guinea a time, drawing her attention to the enclosed, and finally suggesting that she might perhaps achieve more by approaching the Vendor direct. Serena, who by then had become wary, if not wise, carefully repeated Mr. Clacton's own admission of failure word for word in her letter of acknowledgement. One found oneself using their own weapons.

"You want to sell, I want to buy," she said to the weak-willed woman whose telephone number the agent had given her in despair, "what is all this?"

"Well, you see, it's so difficult, they tell me it's in my interests. And the other two flats are sold, you see, and we already had to change the maintenance clause for those tenants..."

"Ah," said Serena. "I'm beginning to understand. So you don't really *want* to add this phrase?"

"Well I do, but you see, it's so difficult..."

"Yes, well, of course, they're taking advantage of her," said the agent, "she's not used to the property market, you see, a bit unpractical if you know what I mean. She just bought this house, lovely house it is, and spent far more on the conversions than she bargained for, they're lovely conversions, you know, architect-designed, oh yes, she got an architect to do it, real beautiful job, but of course she doesn't understand these things herself, and I can't do anything, can I? Had just the same trouble before with this flat, last February it was—"

"Do you mean to say that this flat has been on the market a whole year? And her lawyers—?"

"Well, yes, but I've never had anything like this sort of trouble and of course, they're right in a way, you know, I mean to say your people are being a little unreasonable. Still, we're not worried, they all go in the end, the top one went six months ago and the people have only just moved in, yesterday, as a matter of fact. Oh, they're very pleased. Lovely conversion." Serena gave the owner and her solicitors a three day ultimatum to make up their minds one way or the other. It stretched, with a promise of a suitable compromise, at the end of which Serena renewed her ultimatum for one more day, then withdrew her offer when they said, after all that, no.

Mr. Clacton still had her deposit on the previous flat, which he had insisted she should pay to him and not to any agent, much to the agent's annoyance. He had never returned it, despite repeated requests throughout the negotiations for the next flat, and she quite thought she would never see it again.

"But why didn't you ask me, Mrs. Buttery?" Philip Hayley exclaimed when he had told her the right sort of phrase to use in demanding her money back. "I would have been delighted to act for you."

"Oh, but I can't have professional relationships with my patients, it would be impossible. As it is I shouldn't have spoken to you about it."

"Oh come, Mrs. Buttery, you said nothing till I was about to leave. But at least I could have put you on to an excellent firm, with their own sources of mortgage as a matter of fact."

"Oh no, not that."

"But really—"

"It's very kind of you, Mr. Hayley. But I've got someone now, on very good recommendation."

"May one ask who?"

"Farnham & Co."

"Oh dear, oh dear, they're the most expensive West End lawyers, oh dear, oh dear, I wish you'd asked me."

"If they're expensive they should at least be good," said Serena naïvely.

"Look, I have to go now, but why don't we talk about it, say tomorrow, it's Saturday, you might just as well have the name of another firm in case you change your mind."

"All right. Thank you." She broke her rule and said, "Why don't you come to lunch tomorrow?"

But, as Serena half expected from this particular patient, he forgot all about it. The letter he had helped her to write to Mr. Clacton, however, did produce, somewhat grumpily, the return of her deposit, from which Mr. Clacton's fees for doing nothing at all had been deducted. So Serena was grateful to Philip Hayley, and went to Farnham & Co.

She did not see Mr. Farnham himself, it was too grand a firm. She saw Mr. Parkinson, the Conveyance Manager, and was by then cowed enough to be unduly frightened by him, considering her profession. He had a slight stoop, and smooth ivory hair, a smooth ivory face and smooth ivory smile, but she did not feel the shock until he let his right hand rest casually upon his papers, minus three fingers, the index, the annular and the little finger, and picked each form carefully between the third and thumb. This aggressive use of mutilation belied his saintly manner and in anyone else she would have allowed for it accordingly. But professional relationships tend to impose their own rigidity of pattern over the ebbs and flows of human feelings, and like a pupil, however recalcitrant, with a master,

Serena sat meekly and looked at the man with awe. He was so calm and sat so still, apart from the occasional gesture through the air with his maimed hand, that it seemed not him but rather his fixed smile that spoke, slowly and pedantically:

"Yes, well, now, I don't think we'll bother with these—erm—Inter-Insular people, shall we?"

"Oh? . . . Well, I don't know. As fax as I can gather they're the only firm willing to consider freelance earnings, and—"

"I don't think you need listen to everything these little insurance salesmen tell you. They're very good at spinning it out, you know, about income tax rebates and so forth. But I rather feel that if you go and talk to your Tax Inspector about that, you'll see it all in a very different light. No, no, it won't do. It won't do at all. A Building Society's the thing for you, I think."

"But I rang up dozens. Hardly any will consider flats at all, and if they do they have all sorts of conditions, it must be 'purpose-built' as they call it, and in a post-1918 house, or they won't consider—"

"You leave it to me, Mrs. Buttery, we have our ways and means."

He repeated almost the very phrase when Rupert rang him two days later. They had found a flat, or rather it was on two floors of a tallish Victorian house, and consequently was called a maisonnette, which word Rupert could hardly bring himself to utter, though Serena, who by then was immune to the horrors of property parlance, happily pronounced it maze-net, just like a house agent. But it was much larger, more elegant and more expensive than any of their previous mishaps, and now that they had turned misers and money-makers they felt they could afford a much bigger difference between the mortgage they had not yet got and the actual price.

"It was all meant," Rupert kept saying. "I now shudder to think of those other places we nearly got. That last one, facing North, brrr. Oh, yes, it was all meant. We were being protected."

"Whoever by?"

"I'd have turned into a damp cluster of moss in next to no time. What? Oh, I don't know. The saints or something. Saint Antony, isn't he something to do with property?"

"Lost property."

"Well, there you are."

And since Cliff had also seen the maze-net and approved of it, Rupert's interest in it perked up considerably. The maze-net, however, was a Freehold.

"I'm busy all tomorrow morning, darling, could you ring up Mr. Parkinson and ask him yourself, before we make the offer?"

"Ask him what?"

"Oh, darling, I told you. Why don't you ever listen? I *think* it ought to be all right, even *better* than a Leasehold, judging by all the trouble we've been having with leases. But there is some complication about Freehold Flats, I can't remember what it is, something to do with being on top of each other."

"Ah, yes," said Cliff knowledgeably, "you see, in theory, a Freehold goes all the way down to the centre of the earth, deep, oh very deep, to the collective unconscious, one might say, and all the way up to—"

"*Law makes long spokes of the short stakes of men*," Rupert quoted with a happy smile.

"Anyway, some firms won't lend on Freehold Flats. I know I.I.I. won't 'cos I asked them. Houses, yes, but not flats, and of course we can't afford a house, at least not yet, though if this goes on much longer we may. So have you got that straight?"

"I think so," said Rupert.

"*Your rights extend*," said Rupert down the telephone to Mr. Parkinson, "*under and above your claim Without rebound; you own land in Heaven and Hell*." Mr. Parkinson did not exactly appreciate Rupert's recitation of Empson or his painstaking explanation of the Freehold legal fiction and the problem it raised as regards mortgages, but he did ask a few questions about the age of the house and the type of conversion and said, "You go ahead and make your offer, Mr. Scott-Buttery, and leave the rest to me. Of course you will need to have a survey done. It shouldn't cost you more than about £40. Would you like me to put this in hand?"

"Forty pounds!" What was it Serena had said? Had she mentioned surveys at all? "I think we'd better wait a little, don't you, Mr. Parkinson?"

"As you wish."

"You're sure it's all right about the Freehold, with your mortgage people, I mean?"

"You leave it to me, Mr. Buttery."

"I'm awfully sorry Mrs—er—Buttery," said the agent, on the telephone three days later, a different agent of course, for the bald young man had lost all interest in her, "but I've had another offer of five five on this property, and unless you're prepared to raise your offer—"

"But surely my offer, was accepted, legally? You can't show the place to other people and let them make offers."

"Oh, no, madam, it's not like that at all. Until you have your mortgage secured we have to consider the property as on the open market—"

"I raise my offer," said Serena briefly. Then she knew she had played into his hands.

"To do old Parkinson justice," Rupert said some two weeks after that, "he doesn't take quite so long to muck things up as your other chap did." The news had just come through that Mr. Parkinson's mysteriously generous mortgage source, which was really nothing more mysterious than the Peak Building Society, had turned down the application because the house was built upward of eighty years ago, the flat was not purpose-built and, moreover, was a Freehold. Mr. Parkinson had, however, found another source willing to lend on such a property, but at a higher percentage, and was waiting to hear from them, etc.

The row was tremendous. Though Rupert had to hand it to Serena that it was Mr. Parkinson's temper that let fly, not hers. They went to see him together this time, and Rupert was so fascinated by the Captain Hook behaviour that he felt like the crocodile who'd swallowed the clock and just sat there grinning, looking alternately at his watch and at Mr. Parkinson's waving hand.

"You keep criticising me!" Mr. Parkinson hissed when Serena, without a word of reproach on the previous application, quietly said she wasn't very happy about a firm that charged a higher percentage than any other, and, moreover, didn't belong to the Building Society Association. "I spent the entire morning trying to find you a mortgage source and not a single one is willing to lend on a Freehold Flat. Not a single one except this. You should be grateful to me, instead of criticising me at every stage." His smooth ivory face was even paler than that with rage, and a nervous trembling of the skin under the eyes belied the smoothness. His right hand rested rigid on his desk.

"D'you know, I met an insurance-broker at a party the other day," said Rupert brightly. "I wonder if he'd help. He was enormously interested in astrology and I told him he would be going to China in May. It really shook him, and he gave me his card. Now where did I put it?" He patted his breast-pockets with both hands as if to make the card come out of his own accord. Serena by now felt quite astrological herself about the whole business. Within ten minutes, they had made peace, filled and signed the application forms of the Torch Building Society, shaken Mr. Parkinson's left hand and withdrawn. And when, five weeks later, almost out of spite, she rang the Torch Building Society direct, and was told that they had no application, no letters from Farnham & Co. and no file on her whatsoever; and when she rang Mr. Parkinson and he said that this was nonsense, he had just heard from them that they could not give a mortgage on this property because it was a Freehold Flat, she said: "The fault, dear Mr. Parkinson, lies not in ourselves, but in our stars." And he said, "I beg your pardon?" And she said, "I said, I think I had better instruct you to withdraw my offer." And he said, "I think you're very wise, Mrs. Buttery. Very wise."

11

"**W**HAT I simply can't understand," wrote Stella from Buen Punto, "is why you are having such absolutely unheard of difficulties in getting your flat. I told Molly Hardways about it and she simply can't understand it either as she got an extremely nice flat for herself and her mother last year, for which she pays just under £500 a year, maybe even less, but whatever it is she just sailed into it with the *greatest* of ease. I simply refuse to believe you're not making more than that between the two of you, especially now that Rupert is so famous (I saw his name in *The Times* the other day, I was tremendously thrilled!) Now *don't* jump down my throat but Molly tells me that there are a few other flats going in the same block (it's in Chelsea, my *dear!* Or as near as makes no difference), and believe me hers really is most comfortable. She is one of my oldest friends and would consider it an honour to do *anything* to help me *or* my sister, and I feel sure that if I asked her she would put in a good word for you with the porter. Moreover, she tells me that she got it from Harrod's Agency, who are absolutely *marvellous*, so that if you don't tumble to the idea of those particular flats, she says they had simply dozens on their list, though of course at higher rents. So please, please do try Harrods Agency, they really are absolutely marvellous. I do hope you will get one with a shower, and of course a bidet, I simply can't understand how the English..." And so on and so forth.

Serena lifted each of the six electrically typed airmail sheets, skipped through a political discussion of the situation in Israel, a harangue about the superiority of the Central American way of life to anything else, especially English, and a dissertation on a new wonder-tonic which was injected into the buttock and made one feel marvellous for three days and which, of course, Serena really must try since she felt so depressed. She read mechanically and very fast, only to see if Stella wanted anything sent or done, then folded the letter and went to put it away in a large cardboard box marked "Stella", which sat behind her shoes at the back of the wardrobe.

"Come to think of it, why *do* you want to buy?" Cliff asked them that evening when the problem like a post-prandial rumble returned with obsessive inevitability. "Most of us pay rent and taxes like good ordinary citizens that we are."

"You're not married."

"My dear Serena, I'm more married than any man I know."

"That's good," chuckled Rupert, who believed Cliff's stories, "what's all the sparkle for, have you just sold something, or what?"

"Come, come, if my wit depended solely on my sales, I'd be a very poor companion," Cliff said, roaring with laughter at his own modesty.

Serena said: "There comes a time in life when the desire to possess must after all be satisfied if possible. I'm forty-one, you know."

"Gorgeous," said Cliff as expected.

"And then we're both freelancing in a way, there's the question of our old age . . ."

"They tell me it's marvellous after the menopause."

Serena shrugged her scorn and said nothing.

"Say no more, I understand. Never mind, Serena, something else will turn up. I'll carry these for you, always the gentleman, that's me. Rupert, I'm going to rape your wife on the kitchen table."

"There isn't one."

"What's wrong with the floor?"

But in the kitchen he said:

"You know, Serena, when you do find your flat, you should keep this one as well. Be businesslike. Its property, after all, and everyone else makes a profit on their slightest foothold."

"But it's rent-controlled."

"Precisely! You say yourself you hardly notice the rent. Just think if you sublet it furnished."

"It's not allowed. Only the sitting-tenant—"

"Proof of habitation, that's all. A chair or two, a bed. What's to prevent you having a nephew staying, in the form of a lodger?"

"Called, I suppose, Cliff Morrison?"

"My dear Serena, you malign me. I was only suggesting ways of making a little more money to pay your outgoings in the new place. You'll find they shoot up, you know, quite apart from your mortgage repayments there'll be rates, ground rent, maintenance, property tax, it's no fun at all being a property-owner. No, no, I prefer to be free. I have my wagon—"

"Yes, I know."

"Well, of course, it's up to you. But I think you'd be a fool to let it go. It's a pied-à-terre and you of all people should have your two feet firmly planted ha-ha. It could be useful, even without profits, for profits of another kind, perhaps?"

"Since you made exactly the same suggestion to Rupert yesterday it might be rather awkward, might it not?"

"Serena, you're marvellous. Oh let me touch those antique breasts of yours, that mother-earth belly—"

"For heaven's sake, Cliff, I don't need reassurance. You really are an unutterable bore."

"Bad luck," Rupert called from the sitting room. "Come back here, Cliff, I'm lonely."

Cliff certainly clave. Serena thought she would never be rid of him, and even when Jean and Rusty came to dinner Rupert insisted on inviting Cliff too, indeed, inviting was hardly the word, he seemed so much part of the family. Besides, and here she knew she was being rather nasty, it might be just as well to provide a replacement couple for Cliff to barter his second-hand emotions with, just in case he was getting tired of themselves but had no one else to turn to. It wouldn't do Rusty any harm, he needed something really ghastly to cope with.

She miscalculated, though, not only about Rusty's needs, but about Cliff's reserve of married couples to prey on, which was greater than she knew. Nor was he by any means tired of them yet, at least as a reintroduction to Nat Warner.

His interest in Rusty was therefore a much more professional affair, for he had heard curious rumours, and indeed, Rusty had had plenty of ghastliness to face in the last twenty-four hours.

"Is everything all right at U.V.I., Mr. Conway?" Cliff probed at what he judged to be the right psychological moment alter a good dinner, and Jean looked anxiously at Rusty, who sat gulping down a whisky as fast as he politely could.

"Yes, yes, of course. Still going, you know."

"I'm sure. But there were rumours in Fleet Street, we sent a man down —"

"Fleet Street never sends a man, it sends a regiment."

"The paper, I mean, of course."

"I hope someone or other was courteous to him," said Rusty, who had been seeing the Press all afternoon and felt nothing remotely resembling courtesy towards it.

"I wouldn't know. I only heard the rumour."

"What rumour?" Serena asked impatiently.

"You know Fleet Street," said Rusty quickly. "Just can't wait for an official announcement, which would make their work so much easier. There always is one, after all, if anything real happens. But no, some poor director only has to take two lumps of sugar in his morning coffee instead of three and Fleet Street is seething with rumours, the city barometer falls and everybody's hammering on our doors."

"Come, my dear sir, that's a very picturesque way of putting it, but slightly exaggerated, no? We have our ear to the ground, that's all."

"And your nose at every lamppost."

"It's the lamps that illuminate the shady streets."

"Sophist," said Rusty, so crossly that Cliff decided to leave it alone for the night.

But he was hammering on the U.V.I. doors at ten the next morning. Metaphorically speaking, that is, for the golden gates of the big portal were open and Cliff went straight to the lift like a man with an appointment, carrying a bulging briefcase and ordering the eighth floor with a weary familiarity.

It wasn't Public Relations but the Laboratories. Even better, he thought and walked straight along the corridor. When he got to the end without finding what he wanted he looked out of the window, up at the sky and down at his watch, just in case he was being observed, then walked back with slow deliberation to the far end. Ah, yes, there it was. Gentlemen, it said, and without a moment's doubt he swung in, locked himself into one of the cubicles, put the lid down, took out *The Times* from his briefcase and settled to the City columns.

After an hour and a half, he discovered to his disappointment the otherwise interesting fact that scientists, although they washed their hands frequently and long, did not talk much, and only in a Utopian language of letters and numbers which he tried to jot down on his *Times* but lost count of, scrappy though it was, too scrappy, certainly for decoding. So in a clear moment he left his hiding-place and made for the floor below. The geography was of course geological.

"Bloody scientists," was the first thing he heard after a patient ten minutes, and he rather agreed. "It's all their fault."

"It was well and truly named the gunpowder plot. They'll blow us up sky-high."

"Yes, we do our bit. What the hell do they expect?"

The expectations were lost in a generous flush, then a door banged, steps thudded on the tiled floor, the outer door swung back and forth like the wind, and all was quiet again.

Forty minutes of tricklings, gurglings, gushings, sighings and coughings, counterpointed with snippets of sometimes trivial, sometimes personal but sometimes tantalising information, had got Cliff into a state of extraordinary excitement which was just nearing a soggy climax, when he suddenly heard Rusty's voice. "Oh, hello, Jim. How are things your end?"

"Fine, thanks. And you?"

"Murder."

"Ah, yes, of course, nitron. Poor Rusty. Doesn't affect me at all, really. We just cut one campaign and intensify the other. As a matter of fact it's quite a nice coincidence because Hughie Hill's at last finished that documentary on cinderella. Twenty minute job, most unusual on his programme, though he said it might have to be cut. I'm going to the preview this afternoon, like to come?"

"What I can't understand," said Rusty's voice to a squelching noise of soap, "is why they have to withdraw nitron now. Why couldn't they have done it then, when all the trouble began, instead of fiddling with their filthy formulas and making life a merry hell for all of us."

Cliff's satisfaction was complete.

When they left, he washed as discreetly as possible, tidied himself up and walked along to Rusty's office, which he found without difficulty. It was an unpleasant half-hour for Rusty.

"Now come on Mr. Conway, you might just as well cooperate with me. It's no use crying over spilt beans, you know."

"Sniffing at lampposts was putting it mildly."

"Listen, Conway, I'll be frank. You're in my hands but I'm in yours too. I can't just print a bald item of information like that. Well, I can, in my own paper tomorrow, Friday, and that would simply set the pack of them on to you by Monday, and more, during the weekend at your private home, not to mention those of all the directors. Now why not give me the full facts, soberly, presented your own way and to your best advantage?"

"But we're going to do that. We're preparing a full statement for Tuesday. For the whole of the Press."

"Precisely. I want to write my sober, factual and, if I may say so, helpful article for *The Sunday Supplement*."

"No, I'm afraid we can't let you do that."

"I'm afraid you'll have to. Unless you prefer it the vulgar way."

Miserably Rusty rang Mr. Harding and took Cliff to see him. Cliff was the perfect gentleman.

"I'm sorry, sir, I can't divulge my source of information. I wouldn't want to get anyone into trouble. But I can assure you Mr. Conway didn't breathe a word to me about it, and I tried to pump him, mind you, but he was beautifully evasive—quite put me off the scent in fact. No, no, rest assured, Mr. Harding, no one on your staff betrayed you. It's simply that, well, you remember those notices during the war, walls have ears, the enemy is listening...."

"You mean you snooped."

"Come, Mr. Harding, I have my job, you have yours. And, if I may remind you, yours now consists of helping me as best you can to help you."

"On one condition."

"Which is?"

"That you let Conway here go through the final version with you."

"I don't see that you're in any position to make such a condition, but O.K., fair's fair, I'll be generous."

"I'm not interested in your generosity, but in the quality of your mind, sir. You might as well get the bloody thing accurate. It's a complex business."

"But of course. Delighted. I never was much good at chemistry anyway. And then there's the financial situation. I assume the nitron shares will be converted into cinderella shares, like pumpkins into coaches?"

An emergency meeting took place in everybody's lunch hour, much to everybody's annoyance. Finance were detailed to get a personal-looking letter sent off to every single nitron shareholder to explain the situation. Sales, who had held back the week's nitron consignments on some substandard excuse, now undertook to step cinderella to top priority as from that afternoon, instead of the following week, and to persuade as many of the nitron buyers to take cinderella instead, just for this week, they were to say. Publicity was to launch their Fairy Godmother Campaign now, rather than on Monday week, after the announcement, which would have had the double advantage of looking, to the general public, like a rival cashing in, and at the same time appearing more gentlemanly, that is to say, decently paused, to the trade, the city and all who knew perfectly well that U.V.I. were responsible for both nitron and cinderella. Now this latter advantage was forfeited, with little regret, for the Fairy Godmother

Campaign, subtle child of Jim Fawcett's imagination, somehow managed to imply, without saying so, that all other synthetic fibres except cinderella were nothing more than Ugly Sisters. The plans had been much admired in embryo and looked forward to at birth. But now the Ugly Sister suggestion could be slightly more underlined as nitron. For as Mr. Harding wisely remarked, the only people one could safely libel were one's various selves. Half a page in Saturday's *Times*, a full page in each of the Sunday papers, well, no, not *The Supplement*, naturally. And television, of course, double-time Friday and Saturday, urgency rates.

"But F.G.C. isn't ready!" Jim Fawcett yelped, monitoring a fat cigar with a fatuous grin.

"You'll 'ave to make it ready, lad," said Harry Thorpe.

It was then that Rusty suddenly woke up. Woke them all up. "What's the matter with us all," he said, "are we hypnotised? If we're going to be up all night, Statistics, Consumer Research, Finance, Public Relations and all, working out a statement for this bloody man, who'll probably twist it all round anyway, what's to prevent us from giving the same statement to the other Sundays? I know their city correspondents well."

"What's the difference?" said U.K. Sales and Harry Thorpe together, with Mr. Jenkins' Kentish voice a shade higher. So Harry Thorpe elaborated: "Only does him out of his scoop, and who cares about that? Doesn't affect Sales whatever the bloody paper."

"Something in that," said Finance.

"I don't agree," said Harding. "Conway's right. It would look much better, whatever the Sales position. Sales and Publicity have their marching orders, as have Finance. But there is the question of etiquette. And I've got an even more brilliant idea—" it was only an elaboration of Rusty's, but Mr. Harding looked as eurekish as Archimedes. "We won't let any of the Sundays have the statement. We'll work even harder and give it to *The Times* for the Saturday edition. What could look more gentlemanly than that, gentlemen," he said to the gasp of amazement at his genius, "indeed, more governmental? more royal? Gentlemen, the Queen."

They all scrambled to their feet, clutching their now empty sherry glasses, assuming in their confusion that Harding had simply got intoxicated by fear, relief or his own brilliance, and toasted the monarch by way of adjourning the meeting. And there was something in that, Rusty thought as they shuffled out, for really, everyone must have been panicked into a state of idiocy, including himself. What was so extraordinary about giving their statement to *The Times*? They always gave their statements to *The Times*. Their complex ones anyway. The other papers then condensed and simplified them, or sent for a simplified version, or ignored it, according to their degree of interest. Really. They must have all gone mad. Or been mad to start with. Everyone had been more or less hysterical for three days.

As it happened, Nat Warner, editor of *The Sunday Supplement*, was not in the least interested in Cliff Morrison's proposal. Not personally anyway. He was a squat, elderly man, with a Prussian head, who had been chosen by the proprietor for quick efficiency and lack of impressionability, rather than for brains, as ideal to edit a paper originally launched as a sort of umpire between the then two other Sundays, whose commentators on any subject whatsoever had always flatly disagreed. In recent years, however, the two Sundays in question were so busy turning themselves into magazines for the millions that, as with the two main political parties, there was little to distinguish them from either the middle paper or its latest rival *The Sunday Telegraph*, except perhaps age and tradition. Indeed, most people who took one took all four, the whole point being to skip everybody on everything. The early rivalry had therefore lapsed a little, and in any case, Nat Warner knew very well that it wasn't old-fashioned scoops of this kind that sent circulation up but the true-life stories of generals, lion-lovers, peeraged politicians, speleologists and other public heroes. However, just to be on the safe side, he sent Cliff Morrison to the City Section.

The City Section was slightly more interested but told Cliff Morrison that they had their own expert correspondents and their own ways of getting the detailed information needed for such an article. They were of course grateful for the tip which, however, was no news to them, in fact, one of their best men was working on it at this very moment. So then Cliff threatened to let *The Express News* print the whole story the next day. The City Section shrugged and said they didn't mind, he hadn't got the details yet, had he, and wasn't expert enough to suggest them convincingly either. They would be printing a sober report, not a scarifying sensation. Still, in view of the pointless panic an ignorant article might cause, and for that reason only, they were prepared to let him collaborate with their expert. Yes, that did mean, in other words, supply him with the detailed information. The signature? Well if he absolutely insisted, his name could appear as well. Only his? They'd have to consult their expert about that. He might not mind, he was a modest fellow and after all his name appeared every week. And would continue to do so. He was their expert after all, wasn't he?

The result of Cliff's little session in the seventh floor lavatory of the U.V.I. building was quite simply that everyone concerned worked for forty-eight hours non-stop, whereupon there appeared a brief, succinct report low down in the financial columns of *The Times* on Saturday, and a longer, less succinct but similar report in *The Financial Times* of the same day; the city columns of the three Sunday papers mentioned the bare facts, either as part of their usual reports or, in the case of *The Sunday Supplement*, as part of a short optimistic article on the state of synthetic fibres in general, signed by their regular correspondent. The other two Sunday papers, however, had each an entire page taken up, most attractively, by the newly launched Fairy Godmother Campaign.

12

MIDDLEMEN HAVE one thing in common with souls in hell, which is that for the most part they do not know that they are middlemen, any more than the souls in hell know that they are in hell, hell being a mere negation of heaven, of which they catch occasional glimpses, too agonising in their positiveness to be borne or remembered for more than a flash of eternity.

One says, for the most part, because there are in fact two kinds of middlemen, as there are two kinds of sinners, the self-confessed and the unaware. The self-confessed are at least formally aware of their middlemanship, which is usually hallowed by long tradition, so that even the awareness has often become a little fossilised. These include lawyers and diplomats, whose middlemanship is not officially concerned with sellable commodities but rather with abstractions such as peace and understanding which, however, they naturally have to transform into concrete paper, lots of it, and paper always means money. In spite of this formal recognition of their own nature therefore, these middlemen are in a way less honest about it than other self-confessed middlemen like merchants and shopkeepers, or their modern extensions, agents and salesmen, who take their percentage on the way, frankly for being there.

Most other middlemen, however, of the kind who have clustered round and clambered over the original merchant, changing his aspect—at his own demand, it is true—into a sprawling shapeless monster, most of these are as unaware of their own cell-like growth, as of the primary organism that feeds them.

Biologically speaking, one might compare the first kind, the formally self-confessed, to the dead matter that often protects life, the bark, the wood of a plant, the feathers of a bird, the shell of a snail, the fossils, which frequently survive, though dead, long after the living cells have vanished; lawyers and diplomats, who are our protective shells and also our burdens, will still be arguing over formulae on the Day of Judgment, and merchants will still be selling their nice clean shrouds, non-iron and sin-repelling. And although it will do them little good, it will probably do them little harm either. But the second kind is cancerous, and kills what it pretends to increase.

In spite of these varying degrees of unawareness, middlemen have one invariable quality in common. They always recognise each other, if not as middlemen, at least as belonging to their own species. "People like us", they say, not quite knowing what that means, and of course the species is innumerably subdivided, and each subdivision says of itself, "people like us", and of all the other subdivisions merely "they". So, no doubt, the plasmodium thinks of the liver fluke.

Consequently, Jim Fawcett said one evening to his wife, whose name was Virginia, and whom he called Gee-Gee, which suited her, for she had the teeth of a healthy horse:

"You know, Gee-Gee, Isabel was quite marvellous over all that extra time I wanted. I think we ought to ask her down for a weekend."

Thus an ancient Greek might have spoken of a courtesan to another ancient Greek. But Gee-Gee was much too public-school-spirited to notice the way mere words were used.

"It's okay by me. Which is Isabel?"

"You remember, you met her at the TV-X do."

"Shoals of them, darling."

"Little woman, about fifty, bulging eyes and belly."

"Oh, yes, the pekinese woman. Advertising time, and would she let me forget it."

"Oh, Isabel's all right. She's jolly decent actually."

"Darling, I'm sure she is. Nothing wrong with keen types, I used to be one myself."

"You still are, Gee-Gee, my love."

"Oh, how sweet of you, Jim."

"Mium-mium." Which was Jim's way of rendering homage to one who had, after all come out top of all England in cookery at the Surrey Ladies' School of Domestic Science, and who had already entered their daughter aged nine, an image of her mother, for the same noble institution. Gee-Gee stroked Jim's Henry-the-Fifth fringe with two fingers, as one strokes the nose of a pony.

"Isabel what was it? Gormsley. Yes, I remember her eyes. She stared at me like a form-mistress at prayers. I felt like chanting the ninety-ninth psalm on top of my voice, to show I was attending."

"Oh, the occasional *adsum* would have been enough for Isabel."

Several more names soon clustered in their minds round that of Isabel, and the single invitation, as often happens when the guest is not a close enough friend to offer certainty of a whole weekend's entertainment, soon became a small dinner party; that is to say, from a list of various social creditors, three were picked to drive out to Esher and help the hosts with the original guest in exchange for a truly excellent meal from the culinary curriculum of the Surrey Ladies' School of Domestic Science, or, in more domestically scientific language, several birds were killed with one stone.

Jim did not exactly owe Tom Stevens anything, on the contrary, Tom Stevens had been making an infernal nuisance of himself from the top of U.V.I. down, in a no doubt praiseworthy effort to carry out the terms of that unfortunate Will. He had been handed from department to department like a fire-bucket, and indeed he was now convinced that the quenching of nitron was entirely his own achievement. "I got them to withdraw it at last," he had said to *The Express News*, implying a personal scoop over the Parliamentary Sub-Committee from which, as a voting shareholder in U.V.I., he had uprightly resigned. He was consequently a little calmer now, presumably for the time being, but Jim had received the brunt of him, not because Stevens was more interested in Publicity than in any other aspect of U.V.I., for he wasn't, but simply because everybody else, including Rusty, thought that good old Jim would best be able to choke him off with sheer cordiality, as one kills With kindness. There was certainly something deadening about Jim's jovial spirits. And although this did not mean he did not find Tom Stevens as much of an infernal nuisance as anyone else; his only method of self-defence, by a process alas not Christian but as instinctive as the chameleon's change of colour, was to be more kind. So he asked him to dinner. Besides, he needed an unattached man to balance Isabel. The other two guests were Ted and his Honourable Fishface, whose not particularly Honourable name was Fiona Clark. And Fiona Clark was talking about retailer-passivity.

"Billy says he's going to vanish altogether."

"Who, Billy?"

"Who is Billy, anyway?" Tom Stevens asked on a point of order.

"Billy Carmichael, you know, the Market Research man. I work there, it's terribly interesting. Billy says the consumer has taken over all the salesman's burdens, he just rushes out, the consumer I mean, not Billy, to buy what he's seen advertised and if the retailer hasn't got it he orders it, in fact he's just a sort of mail-order firm and only stocks things for show. Most ads nowadays even make the consumer work, you know, 'Write and ask for your nearest stockist,' and all that. Billy says the retailer might just as well be cut out. He's passive, you see, the retailer I mean."

"I'm all for cutting out the middleman," said Isabel and the other middlemen agreed. "Advertising is much the best shop window."

"It would certainly solve the traffic problem," Tom Stevens murmured with the glint of a Private Member's Bill in his eye.

"Except," said Gee-Gee, "that one can't get what one orders. Especially furniture, and such. I had to wait weeks for, my new fridge. And clothes too, if you want anything unusual. I ordered a Butiform bra from Peter Jones two months ago, 34A, you see, they didn't have it, and they still haven't. They say that's quite normal with Butiform."

Isabel looked at Gee-Gee's long neck and the wide stretch of patchy white flesh before her breasts began, rather flatly, and she thought what a horrible name, Gee-Gee.

"I imagined," she said to Fiona, "one had to have all sorts of degrees in social science to be in that racket."

"Oh, no," Fiona answered amiably. "Market Research is all the rage among ex-debs. That and Interior Designing."

"Do you mean to tell me, Miss Clark," said Tom Stevens, who sat next to her, "that rows of débutantes queue up to hold the paint pots of interior decorators?"

"Designers. Designers don't paint, Mr. Stevens. They visualise. And they do need someone to make their appointments and type their bills. One of my best friends is secretary to Paul Partridge and she adores it. After all any old do-it-yourself maniac can *paint*."

The middlemen all defended Do-it-yourself schemes in general, on the grounds that they always found they did things much better themselves than anyone else. Especially Isabel. And Tom Stevens agreed with her vehemently.

"Nothing gets done at all unless I do it myself," said Tom Stevens, "and I don't just mean in Parliament. Look at that nitron affair at U.V.I. They had to listen to me, you know."

"Well, I assure you it's not so in designing," said Fiona firmly. "People think they can do it themselves, and of course they can hold a roller and perhaps hang paper. They can even dream-of-a-scheme, or pinch one from the law-laying glossies. But you only have to go into most people's homes to see the result. Who did yours?" she turned politely to Gee-Gee, "it's rather darling."

"I did," said Gee-Gee, pleased and taken in. "With my two strong arms, and my own wee brain."

"So you see?" said Isabel, for the sake of winning the argument rather than out of genuine admiration for the Fawcett dining room. She was sitting opposite Fiona at Jim's end, which annoyed her as she would have liked to be in Ted's place, next to Gee-Gee.

"I think I'll write a Do-It-Yourself book on sex," said Ted to steer the conversation out of Isabel's vexation, and everyone laughed, and Fiona exclaimed "darling!" to show that she had every right to appear in its index.

"As a matter of fact," Fiona said in a conciliatory tone to Isabel, "you're perfectly right about degrees and things in Market Research. I slipped in through the back door because I knew Billy personally, but most of the girls have been up. As a matter of fact Mummy says it's cheaper to send one's daughters to University these days, instead of coming-out, I mean. One apparently meets lots of people there, future prime ministers and all that sort of thing."

"The question is," Ted put in, "how to distinguish the future prime ministers from the future makers of advertising films."

"I'm not too fussy." Whenever he spoke, she accorded him the exaggerated attention of a woman trying to catch her man, and after such an unusually personal allusion she shot him an adoring, possessive glance which Isabel knew was enough to send Ted scurrying out of her life forever, if repeated more then twice in one evening. Indeed Ted excluded her at once by talking straight to Tom Stevens, who was opposite him, about their mutual publisher, Ben Clef, whom she didn't know; then quickly, in case she brought that down to Dave Goodman, whom she had met, he switched over to Tom Stevens' last television appearance which he was sure she had not seen. Nor, for that matter, had he, but he read more papers than she did. Gee-Gee sat between them at the head of the table and was willy-nilly brought into it. Isabel was left with Jim and Fiona and, hearing television talked of, was furious at missing it, and rather than listen to Fiona again on retailer passivity, interior designers or the activity of designing mothers, she lobbied Jim mercilessly on the technical intricacies of the Fairy Godmother Campaign, referred to throughout as F.G.C. Jim thought the party was going splendidly, and Fiona, who was a well-brought up girl, just sat gazing across at Ted with a word-drinking look in her eyes.

And even as Isabel talked, mechanically, to Jim, she kept a corner of her eye on Gee-Gee, the permed colourless hair, the small colourless eyes, long teeth, long neck, long arms, long everything. No, she couldn't stand the type, which the British so generously distributed all over the world in a class-hierarchy that varied with the importance of the area and job in question, though admittedly it became silvery-distinguished when it got older. But always it was clumsy; unappetising, and of course married. Gee-Gee's teeth flashed again down the table. Isabel gently clicketed her own front-teeth against the rim of her wineglass as she drank, and determined to call Gee-Gee Virginia.

"She's in Birmingham with her schoolmaster husband," Gee-Gee was saying to Tom about somebody or other.

"I suppose they do have schoolmasters in Birmingham?" Fiona queried airily, determined to get back into the conversation at the other end, and the other end laughed dutifully. Gratified, Fiona went on with her eye on Ted: "Tell me, Mr. Stevens, do you get a lot of fan mail, as a TV personality? I mean do you feel that you do after all get something across?"

"Of course he gets something across," said Isabel. "You said yourself that the consumer rushes out to order what he's seen advertised on the screen. My char, for instance—"

"That's all very well, but Mr. Stevens isn't selling ideas like detergents which the housewife can trot out and buy."

"You'd be surprised," murmured Ted, "the housewife can trot out and vote."

"I know what Fiona means," said Gee-Gee. "It's this business of the visual medium, whether it has more effect than pure sound. I remember at school, for Current Events, we'd—"

"Yes, that's what I meant," said Fiona, who hadn't, but was now reminded of something she had heard at a party. "Pure sound. It ought to be more effective, not less, you know, as in Huxley—was it Huxley, or was it Angus Wilson? But the people have lost the oral tradition—"

"How's Cambridge?" Isabel turned to Ted with deliberation, and at once they were each penetrated with a sense of *déjà-vu* which paralysed them both for a full two seconds, while the rest al the table was stunned by her rudeness, except for Jim, who thought it was a joke and giggled. She turned to him gratefully and plunged once more into technicalities and personalities, for Ted had refused her gambit and was talking once more to Tom Stevens, this time kindly including Fiona. Later, Isabel tried to explain quietly to Fiona, without precisely apologising:

"It's rather difficult, being an expert. You see, we were arguing about pure sound already in the thirties."

"In the thirties I wasn't even born," said Fiona, goaded at last, and with a deadly barb in her eye.

At coffee Isabel firmly sat on the sofa with Gee-Gee, and talked about holidays, a subject so safe one suspects people of going on them purely to replenish it.

"Are you going anywhere this year, Virginia?"

"I've no idea. It's a bit early."

"Well, yes, it depends when one goes. I take my holidays in May, usually, before the rush. One has to these days, now that abroad has gone all democratic. And I work so hard of course, I'm always a wreck by March, and start booking feverishly to cheer myself up."

"Yes, I see. Jolly good idea. Actually we don't quite know where, we'll be. Jim may be sent abroad soon."

"Oh? Where?"

"He put in for a new job in the Aegean but knowing U.V.I. he may be sent—"

"Greece, but how simply wonderful!"

"Jolly d, yes, but of course nothing may happen at all and we're just waiting. We're awful, actually, even for normal hots I mean, we always leave it to the last minute."

"Well, that too depends where you go. Spain and Italy are absolutely ruined by English greengrocers and other such riff-raff. Even my hairdresser went to Sorrento last year, it's ridiculous. One has to go much further afield to meet reasonably nice people."

"And very far indeed to get away from them," said Fiona, who had politely come up for more coffee so as not to disturb Gee-Gee. Then she went back to Ted and Jim on the other side of the room.

"I suppose I deserved that," said Isabel meekly, but querying Gee-Gee with a coy demand for denial, as a dog looks to his mistress for sugar with a tilt of the head.

"A bit below the belt perhaps, but not to worry," said Gee-Gee with a laugh that started as a neigh and turned abruptly into a snort, like a horse sneezing. Isabel had noticed it before with irritation but now found it strangely gratifying.

"Not at all, not at all," said Tom, who was so used to being polite to committee-type women that he did it automatically. He had little use for the Fionas of this world until they too started serving on committees.

"Where are you going, Mr. Stevens?"

"Going? My party—"

"No, I mean, for your holidays?"

"Oh. Well, I seldom take any, you know. Always something to see to. But I'm hoping to do a fact-finding and goodwill tour of Africa during the Easter recess. I've been invited here and there, you know."

"The Easter recess? But isn't Africa rather large for that?"

"Well, by plane, of course. Facts always stare one in the face, but I like to see for myself, you know. As for good will, it doesn't take long to establish, really."

"I should have thought it was exactly the other way about, in either case," said Isabel sharply, "facts disappear or change their shape as soon as you go and look for them, and as for good will, well, it takes an awfully long time to establish and no time at all to disestablish."

"Oh, jolly good, well clone," said Gee-Gee.

"I say, I've just had a wonderful idea," Isabel exclaimed after that score. "One of my clearest friends runs a travel agency called *Winged Chariots*, I daresay you've heard of it. Stan Barker, he's been enormously successful."

"Oh, yes, I've seen it on television. The Golden Road to Samarkand or something."

"Yes, that's the one. And they do take you really miles, Hawaii, Japan, or the Caucasus, for instance, three weeks in all for hardly more than the normal return fare. But of course, they are tours, that's the whole point, and one does get landed with the most ghastly people. Now I thought, if one got up a party oneself, with one's own friends, carefully chosen, one could have a wonderful package holiday without tears. What do you think?"

"Yes, I suppose one could," said Jim brightly, for Isabel had spoken so loudly that the whole room was listening now.

"Carefully chosen is the operative word," said Ted and Fiona underlined it with an ironic laugh. "Where were you thinking of going?"

"Oh, I don't know. I've only just had the idea. Greece, for instance."

"Bit of a come down after Samarkand, isn't it? Famagusta and the hidden sun's not all that much cop." Ted rose, determined to keep Greece as his own preserve, to which he was planning to take not Fiona but another young lady much more difficult to impress—for why waste his casual familiarity and his fluency in demotic Greek on someone who admired him anyway? "Well, I'm afraid we must be going, Fiona and I," he said, pulling her up by her index finger then moving his hand up and down her bottom to make it quite clear just where they were going. "We're supposed to look in on another party, and it's quite a drive back to London. Erm . . . can we give anyone a lift? No? Well, thank you, Mrs. Fawcett, it's been a delightful evening."

"No, but seriously," Isabel returned to the charge after they had gone, "why don't we make up a party?"

"I think it's a splendid idea."

"Okay by me."

"What about you, Mr. Stevens?"

"Count me out, I'm afraid, Miss Gormsley, I have my own Party to think of. The African tour may be in the summer recess after all, you see."

"Golly," said Gee-Gee, "how hot for you."

"All in a good cause."

"Well, what a shame. Who else can we have? I can think of dozens of simply charming people."

"So can I."

"So can I."

"Well, let's first decide where to. What do you think of Greece, actually?"

"The glory that was," said Jim. "Ted's always raving about it, though, so it must be all right. I may even be sent there in September."

"September. Oh, well, that's fine, you might as well see it first, and if you're sent somewhere else you might as well see it period."

Jim grinned at her enthusiasm. He had never seen Isabel like this except over her work.

"I might be sent there earlier, of course, though I doubt it, the job isn't ready."

"Well! Even better! If you're going in May for instance, why not drop *Winged Chariots* altogether and come with me in my car, overland?"

"Shocking waste of our paid fares."

"Well, you could keep them in reserve, and just send your main luggage on. Anyway, we can cross that bridge when we come to it. I've always longed, to see, the isles of Greece, the isles of Greece . . . Corfu, Kythera, Melos, Khios, Lesbos . . . Lemnos," Isabel breathed and looked hard at Gee-see.

"I'm sure it's jolly marvellous," said Gee-Gee.

Driving back to London with Tom Stevens, Isabel talked about the techniques of television all the way, in the elated tones a woman used who had just fallen in love. The stars were out, faintly beyond the neon glow of London. Sometimes the car stopped at the traffic lights in a suburban High Street, and as she talked she stared bright-eyed at the bright-lit shops full of clothes, mass-made and mass-displayed, or at a pinkly translucent column of provocative plastic bosoms in tight white brassieres, which was leaning out of a window's side-wall like the tower of Pisa. She said, what a pity Tom Stevens couldn't come with them on their tour, but of course he had his own Tour to think of. They had compiled a list of ninety people, to be lengthened or shortened according to the number required on Stan's planes, she wasn't quite sure. It was going to be wonderful, "jolly marvellous," she quoted to herself and felt as excited as a schoolgirl. She saw a blue sky propped by golden caryatids. Melos, Khios,

Lemnos. Fly Bovril, said an optical illusion of night-signs over Trafalgar Square. Jolly marvellous.

"*Winged Chariots*," said Tom Stevens, "Aren't they connected with some sort of high-powered pressure group?"

13

SERENA SAT on a half-hexagonal window-seat in a turret at the top of a large Hampstead house, gazing out at the trees, rooftops and chimney pots of the gently descending road. It was a good residential area. The turret was really a corner of a long drawing room, from the other windows of which one could see over a series of pleasant gardens and more rooftops and catch a glimpse of the Heath between a filigree elm and a tall plane tree with its round black pods dangling like tiny baubles in the distance. That was an even better view than the one from the turret, but Serena sat in the built-in window-seat because there was nowhere else to sit.

The house was built at an angle of about thirty degrees to the road, not quite facing it with its elegant late Victorian breadth behind the short drive, so that all its windows faced south at the back, and the turret window faced West. Serena gave another jolt to the pocket-compass which lay on the seat beside her, and it dutifully repeated the same information. Besides, the wintry March sun was there, poorly trying to advertise its promised glory before darkening away.

The flat occupied the whole length of the top floor, except for some attics full of pipes and metres in the front of the house, which was just as well since the front faced North. The top floor moreover was in the roof. This was a disadvantage if the roof was bad, but made the place look very romantic. One looked out of dormer windows framed in red tiles, and the rooms, though not low, were not too high either, and all had slightly odd shapes. The kitchen was a large trapeze and the top branches of a chestnut tree outside touched the window, their buds glistening golden in the late February sun. When the leaves came out it would be like living in the treetops.

But Serena no longer said things like that to herself. She could look at the dusty floorboards and the dazzling white walls and woodwork, without once dreaming up colour-schemes for carpets, walls and curtains, without once placing a single item of their own or as yet unbought furniture in any corner, without growing a single rubber plant or Philodendron Scandens or Hedera Helix anywhere. Her thoughts did not move one inch beyond mere gratitude that the Vendors, as she had got used to calling them, had not tried to raise the value with some paint and paper she would have to remove—ready-to-walk-into, such places were usually called, as if walking in depended on a few repetitive rose garlands or landscape motifs. Serena, in short had reached about the halfway rung in the property-buyer's ladder of perfection, that is to say, she was now able, and more or less automatically, to size up all the snags and advantages of a place, even with regard to their most personal tastes and habits, without in any degree becoming attached to it. She had learnt, also, that the differences between places consist of little more than a varying combination of advantages and snags. Such a flat had a garden, but faced North, and a terrible little kitchen, but an elegant drawing room. The permutations were endless. One merely chose the combination of snags one minded least, or persuaded oneself one minded least. She felt quite sure, too, that this principle applied all the way, even for the rich. The prices were of fantasy but the dream-house did not exist. Serena was fast becoming a businesswoman.

She had almost turned Quietist, too, without knowing it. A house or flat, like a hotel room, was a dead thing until one had moved in, not only with one's belongings but with one's spirit; and when the move was done, even out of one room to another in the same hotel, the first room seemed alien and unknown when glimpsed through a momentarily open door. But the impatient spirit, she had learnt, could go ahead disguised as imagination, and occupy a place, fondling a view, a fireside, a streamlined kitchen sink, so that when one lost it one lost part of oneself. Attachment to property was bad enough when the property was one's own, but when it wasn't . . . "Thou shalt not covet," she murmured aloud at the white walls, and then felt quite surprised. "Or his house, or his ox."

His ox she did not care for, and she found it remarkably easy not to covet either her neighbour or his wife. But his house was a different matter. Every one of her friends and acquaintances had a house. She had always taken this curious fact completely for granted, but in the last few months she had begun to wonder about it, and the more she wondered, the more the sin of envy ate into her heart. She didn't call it envy, however, but deprivation. Which hardly explained the mysterious and, it seemed, underground ramifications of the English capitalist system. For whereas in every other country worldly success was something one wore on the crest of one's Cadillac, so that all one's neighbours could calculate one's income to the last half dollar, franc or duro, in England the decent thing to do was to pretend one had no income at all. But when an Englishman said he was flat broke, he merely meant that he had forgotten his chequebook, or at most that he was living on his overdraft, well backed by securities, which of course was very advantageous with regard to income-tax. "We've just bought a house," a friend would say casually, "I don't know how we're going to pay for it, the price is astronomical." But then it would turn out that they had sold another, and borrowed the difference of three thousand at no interest from their mother/mother-in-law. And if one rudely inquired how, as a young married couple, with the husband only an apprentice underwriter at Lloyds at the time, they had been able to buy their first house, they would explain, with coyness or perhaps distaste, that it has been a wedding-present from their father/father-in-law, but of course it was much too small now.

Neither Rupert nor Serena seemed to have any parents/parents-in-law, and although they had always regarded this as an unusual bit of luck, she was beginning to wonder whether the luck wasn't perhaps double-edged.

Stella and Serena had always laughed at this aspect of middle class life, for being broke to them meant not eating till the end of the month, or week, according to their time of life, and losing or giving up a job did not mean going home to mummy and daddy until a new one turned up on a plate held by a family friend. The Druins were what is usually called impoverished gentility, the word gentility having become so impoverished since the twelfth century as to mean its exact opposite, so that both the twins in their different ways had been not only glad but determined to escape from its blackmailing niceness. The war had helped them both, for they were both self-supporting at sixteen and took it completely for granted that they should be so. The Druin family were no doubt equally glad of their escape. The links therefore were tenuous on Serena's part, and nonexistent on Stella's, who had stayed with and exasperated every branch of it to breaking point. In both cases they were unfinancial. Serena had benefited from post-war schemes to get her training free, living the while on deprivation in yet another form, which secretly she had rather enjoyed; and Stella had managed to prolong those artificial wartime conditions for over fifteen years by the simple expedient of selling for a high price her willingness to work away from home, far, far away, from a home she did not possess.

Serena lit a cigarette. She had started smoking again in the last few months, after three years of having given it up. Most of her patients smoked, it was very difficult not to, she said, but she was annoyed nevertheless, as it was nearly two pounds a week steadily burnt to ashes, whatever it meant in *Brust-Psychologie*. To hell, however, she thought at the same time, with all this miserliness. Since that miserable six hundred pounds with which they had so confidently approached their first flat the year before, they had saved over two thousand that was mounting up in their deposit accounts, and every now and again she would examine her balance with a mixture of irony, pleasure and disgust. They were becoming inhuman. Even Rupert, the Shelleyan idealist, had become famous now as "the man who's two topics behind". She had begun to notice during the Cliff episode, which thank goodness, had quietly petered out, that Rupert was perfectly capable of keeping up with what Cliff said, or indeed anyone else. It had never occurred to her that she was the only person he blocked off, except perhaps for Stella, but then everyone had to block off Stella. She had always supposed he was simply slow, but profound when he got there, just as in his criticism he would toy with a poem for three days before producing his magic web of ambiguities, ironies, paradoxes, fulcrums and objective correlatives. When she realised that this wasn't the case at all, she was hurt at first, but later appropriated his inattention as something particularly applicable to herself, individual, and therefore flattering. She had asked him jocularly whether his first lapse on television had been a *lapsus linguae* or an intentional fallacy, but he had only said, rather crossly for him, that she didn't know what she was talking about. Whatever it was, it had been an instantaneous hit, and he now exploited it like a master. It had become his gimmick. Rupert (all behind) Scott-Buttery, the columnists called him now. And she, what had she sold? Perhaps only someone else could tell her, one of her patients, or some other buyer. Had they both sold their souls to the devil?

She was surprised at the old-fashioned images her thoughts were using, for she had no formal religion, only an acceptance of formal religion in others as a symptom of buried confusion, piled high over some lost mandalian goddess called reality, with which the modern world was all so signally failing to relate.

What then did she want? Serena asked herself that question for the first time since the beginning of their mortgage machinations. It amazed her now that she had not considered it before. She knew well enough that the urgency and pressure of her desire to move was connected with Stella and the small matter of the flat. But how, exactly? Did she want a larger, more comfortable, more private place, in which she could invite Stella to stay whenever she liked and for as long as she liked without suffering the inconveniences which soured her hospitality and corked up all their mutually generous instincts? Did she want, in fact, to provide Stella with a home, just as Stella was always inviting her to come and visit her in Kenya, Copenhagen or Caracas? Or did she, on the contrary, want a smaller, more comfortable, more private place without, most definitely without, a spare room in any shape or form of studio couch?

Serena looked down the long stretch of white corridor and dazzling doors. This was the largest, pleasantest and oddly enough not the most expensive flat she had so far seen. It had a small dining room hatched from the kitchen and opening into the long low drawing room where she now sat; the corridor then led along and into three more rooms; another large reception room which would be her consulting room, and two bedrooms, one of which would be the waiting room. Or, maybe, a spare room.

A car gravelled up the drive and she peered out of the turret window, extinguishing her cigarette stub with her foot on the chalky floorboards. The car, which was purple shot with green, like an exotic insect, pulled up, opened its four doors like wings, and four slugs came out.

Who could they be? Prospective rival buyers? The owners, or, probably, the speculators? The architects? The water-inspectors? The rate-assessors? They vanished into the house. She waited for them to come up, but they didn't. If they were prospective buyers, then they, were only interested in the ground floor or first-floor flats. She heard voices, and someone being called. The workers were still busy below, so perhaps the men wanted to see the foreman. That was it. They were there so short a time she decided they must be speculators, so she raised the newly-painted window with a great rattle and screech to lean out and see whether the speculators belonged to the human species. Of one accord, all four of them, each with one hand on a door handle, looked up suddenly, as if alarmed that one of the chimneys might be cracking. The quadruple stare from under their three felt hats and one bowler lasted about ten seconds. Then the man in the bowler raised it slightly, bowed his bald head and the four doors of the car opened in unison to swallow them up. The exotic beetle crunched off, turned into the road and smoothly vanished. Serena's impression of the type was slight, for she could only reflect that whereas one can usually guess, even today, the class and probably the profession of any Englishman by his haircut, baldness was a much more thorough democratic leveller than super-tax.

"I'm very interested in this flat," she said to the agent, who didn't seem to care. "But I'm afraid I shall have to see the lease before I make a formal offer."

"Well, that's a bit unusual, you know," the agent said, in a louder, franker cockney than she had heard so far among agents, who mostly used a prim suburban veneer. The wooden name on his desk was Mr. Pratt, and her mind nursery-rhymed as he was talking—Jack Spratt had a flat, But he wouldn't give no lease—"We don't have anything to do with a sale after we put the lawyers in touch, you know, they're the chappies who look at the lease for you."

"Quite. That's precisely why I want to cut them out of the preliminary stages. I have a good mortgage source, but they're rightly very particular about the maintenance clauses in the lease and—"

"Oh, the maintenance is all right here," Mr. Pratt shouted, "you know, all flats have the same arrangement these days, let me see, I've got it down here, yes, you contribute—"

"I know. But my mortgage people want to see the exact wording first. It will save time all round. They have put me in touch with their own lawyers who have promised to look at it on the spot if I bring a copy myself. It's a matter of one morning."

"Well, as you wish, madam, I'll have a word with the owner about it, but it's very unusual, you know. And I don't think the lease is ready—Hey, Nobby, is the lease drawn up for 28 Carrington Road?—No, you see, I was right. There's been a lot of complication with this property, you see—"

"Complication? You mean legal complication?"

"Oh, it's all right now, they're disentangling it. The owner went and bought the Freehold and started to convert without permission from the lord-of-the-manor or whoever it is, anyway the deeds didn't allow for it."

"But goodness, why didn't you tell me? I'm not touching anything with legal complications."

"Oh, it's all right now, as I say, they're disentangling it." Serena wished she could block her ears and listen to him through her fingers. "The owner was in here only this morning. Nice chappie, you'll like him, he's going to live on the ground floor, himself. Good taste, you know, he's done a lovely job. This is one of the best properties we've had on our books, and if it hadn't been for this legal hold-up those flats would have gone like hot cakes. We've had enquiries about them by the dozen, every day, all this time, oh, it's well over six months now, no, nearly a year, but we couldn't put them on the market proper until this other business was sorted out. The other flat's sold of course, to a girl who's dead keen on it, well, when I say girl I mean a lady about your age, if you know what I mean. She was so keen she preferred to wait for it. But you're lucky, you've just come at the right moment, as I say, they're sorting it out now. But there's been people after them by the dozen every, day—"

"I can pay a nominal deposit while you get me the lease, if you like," said Serena, so weary of his loud sales talk she forgot her alarm at the legal entanglement.

"Oh no, madam, we can't do that, but don't worry, I'll have a word with the owner, and I'm sure he'll agree. Nice chappie, he, is, not a bit like most of them."

The owner was so much like most of them that the lease, which had been promised for two days later, had not yet arrived after two weeks. Then three. Then four. And Serena realised what Mr. Pratt meant by "not a bit like most of them". For Mr. Pratt was the lowest form of human agency she had yet encountered, and was soon spinning a very different side of the yarn.

"You're telling me, Mrs.—er—, I can tell you, I'm a bit fed up meself, as I say, I've phoned the gentleman in question every day since you came in here, and he keeps promising it for Tuesday, then Friday, then Monday, and the weeks keep going by, as I say—"

"I know, but what's happening?"

"Well, I don't think he's got this other thing sorted out yet, Mrs.—er—. It's been going on for over a year and I can tell you, we're all sick to death of the gentleman in question here in the office. If you ask me—"

"But surely he can get his lawyer to draw up a draft lease on the assumption that this permission thing will be settled? Hang it all, he's *done* the conversions, it's got to be settled."

"That's what I told him, I said, you can go and buy them in Fleet Street, I said, I could go and buy a lease meself and give it to the lady with the necessary local adjustments, I said. And then there's the other girl who's bought the flat below, been waiting a whole year—well, when I say girl I mean a woman your age, really. She's sold her house and she's boarding in her own house, waiting to buy this flat, you see. But he's having some difficulty or other with his accountant, who wants the Ground Rent to vary with the Cost of Living Index, or something like that, I've never heard of such a thing meself, and I said to him, we don't do that sort of thing here, I said, he's a foreign gentleman you see, and he doesn't know our English law if you ask me—"

"But who is the owner, then? I mean why can't he cope with his own lawyers and accountant?"

"Don't ask me, madam, we get all sorts here. He's an ostipat, and if you ask me he needs a bit of ostipatting himself, he's not quite all there—I beg your pardon?"

"I said, good God."

"Yes, well, that's how it is. I don't know if you want us to go on with it, I've explained to this Dr. Funk, if you ask me he's in a blue funk about the whole business, and as I told him you can buy a copy of a lease in Fleet Street any day, I could do it meself. But anyway he's promised to have the lease here on my desk by Friday morning, so if you'd like to phone me then I'll be there. All right, Mrs.—er.... Thank you."

The Pratt-flat, as she called it to Rupert, who had lost interest in the whole affair and hadn't even found a moment to go and see it with her, became quite a joke. Serena herself didn't take it at all seriously, although, paradoxically, it was the nicest one of the lot. She regarded it as her last gesture to property ownership. If it fell though like all the others, they would simply rent a new flat, although rents were getting higher and higher; or else they would go on saving, under a miser's mattress, until they had enough to pay the difference on a house, on which Inter-Insular or anyone else made few difficulties as regards loans, but houses too were getting higher and higher in price. One never quite caught up with the cost of living. And then of course, she didn't want a house, she wanted a flat.

The cost of living. What on earth was this Cost of Living Index with which the Ground Rent was supposed to vary? She had always assumed that a flat or house was either rented, in which case the rent could be put up according to some mutual agreement every so often; or sold on a long lease, in which case the owner benefited from the capital and the Ground Rent was fixed, sometimes for nine hundred and ninety nine years, however absurd it might become. This owner was trying to have it both ways.

He wasn't in the Medical Directory but he was in the telephone book, so she rang him up, careless by now of middlemen's etiquette, and asked him, in suitable code, what the devil he thought he was doing about that lease, for which she had now been waiting six weeks.

It wasn't "ostipatting" he needed but analysing. However, she couldn't very well do it there and then on the telephone. Instead, she extracted yet another promise—and, unlike an agent, he used the word faithfully as if he meant it—that the lease would be ready on the following Tuesday, his lawyer had faithfully promised him, and he himself would faithfully take it to Mr. Pratt's office by eleven o'clock. She also expressed her strong disapproval of the Ground Rent scheme, on behalf of herself and her mortgagors, and he faithfully promised to see what he could do, but of course he was in the hands of his lawyers, but yes, no, yes, of course, yes, he agreed, he wanted to settle the business too, it had been dragging on for a year.

"Stella's coming," said Serena to Rupert in the middle of May. "But only for a few days in July."

"I could go and see it, I suppose, but it's sure to fall through. And I'm so busy these clays. Hello, here's a letter from Cliff. He's in Bombay."

"She's coming in late July. I think she's giving up her job, but she doesn't say."

"I don't think so, he's still on *The Express News* as far as I know." Then he saw her face. "Oh, you mean Stella? Is she coming back?"

"Yes."

"In July, I suppose?"

"Yes."

"Not that it makes much odds these days, we're always working double-time. What about the small matter of—"

"Not mentioned. She says she'll only be passing through on her way to a new job in Paris."

"Ah. Well. Cliff sends his love."

"Is it Tuesday today?"

Rupert looked hard out of the window and said, "I don't think so. It doesn't look like it."

But it was. And to her surprise Mr. Pratt rang her up at eleven o'clock sharp.

"Morning, Mrs.—er, well, you'll be glad to hear it's all settled, but not quite in the way we expected, though that Ground Rent nonsense has been dropped. I've got the lease here on my desk and I don't know what's been holding them up because as I say you can buy them in Fleet Street any day. Now do you want me to send it on? Because the point is, the owner's accountant decided that all the flats were underpriced, well, and it's true in a way, they were going at last year's prices, you know, and I went to see them meself yesterday and I must admit I was most pleasantly surprised, they're very much nicer than I expected, well, I hadn't seen them since they've been finished and I must say, they've done a fine—"

"Mr. Pratt, would you please come to the point."

"Yes, well, I'm trying to tell you, as I say, the Ground Rent will be fixed, but they've put it up to fifty pounds a year and they've knocked the price up by a thousand. Now do you want me to send the lease on to you at once?"

"You mean, the price is now six thousand pounds?"

"Yes, that's right, Mrs. er— and the flat below is now seven five, that was six thou. And as a matter of fact I'd rather like to know how you feel about it because I've got a firm offer here for six thousand—"

"Of course."

"I beg your pardon?"

"Nothing."

"And they're waiting for your decision as I told them you had first refusal."

"Them being the girl—you-mean-to-say—a woman-of-my-age?"

"I don't follow you."

"Never mind." Serena felt completely reckless and refused to bargain or call his bluff. "I will fetch the lease in half an hour and take it to my mortgagors' lawyers this afternoon. If it meets their own conditions I will make an offer of six thousand pounds by, telephone, before four o'clock and put a letter in the post for you tonight. You will kindly ask the other party to wait until four. I have waited nearly seven weeks, so it isn't too much to ask if they have only just appeared on the scene, is it?"

"Well, as I say, all right, Mrs. er . . . I'll hold it here for you."

Inter-Insular's "other" lawyers vetted the lease, by appointment, in ten minutes. "Are you sure?" said Serena, "I don't want the same trouble as before." But no, it really was entirely acceptable. So Serena made her offer, and gave Mr. Pratt the name of her solicitor, Mr. Philip Hayley.

"I don't quite believe it yet," she said to Rupert that evening, "but I think this one may come off."

"Unless old Parkinson bungles it again."

"Darling, Parkinson gave us the brushoff ages ago, don't you remember, I wrote to say I'd let him know when we found something else, and he wrote back a primadonna two-line note to say Farnham & Co. would have too much on hand to undertake any conveyance in the near future."

"So he did. Damn funny, that was. Who will you go to?"

"Philip Hayley."

"Where do you dig up these people?"

"He's a patient of mine."

"Ho-ho? Tit-for-tat. I hope his tat is bigger than your—"

"Really, Rupert, what has Cliff done to you? Anyway, he's no longer my patient. He's had five years, and in view of everything we both thought that was enough."

"Mother-figure knows best," said Rupert, and thought, she's losing her sense of humour; or perhaps she never had any.

Mother-figure did not know all, though, all being inexhaustible. It was the following week when Philip Hayley rang her up to say that apparently the draft lease she had given him was not the real lease. The owner's lawyers had only let the owner have it because he had promised them that the prospective buyer was only interested in the maintenance clauses. The real lease was still to be drafted, and was to contain a scheme for varying the Ground Rent according to the Cost of Living Index. They were still waiting for their client's instructions. What sort of scheme, Philip Hayley had asked, how on earth does it work? That's our headache, they had replied, and between him and them, they thought their client more than a little batty.

"I don't care," Serena exploded to Dr. Funk when he pleaded that he was with a patient. "I've waited for nearly nine weeks now and I still haven't got the lease. You're going to ring your lawyers and tell them that the first lease is the valid one. You already put up the Ground Rent by twenty pounds a year, and the price by a thousand, and you distinctly told Mr. Pratt and myself later, that this was instead of your mad Ground Rent scheme. You got an offer out of me on completely false pretences, and you're going to put that right today, patient or no patient."

He blamed his lawyers, in a thick foreign accent, and when she wouldn't buy that one, he blamed his accountant. "But who's the boss, you or your accountant?" she asked, and he said that in fact the transaction was in his mother's name, and that his accountant kept reminding him that he was in charge of his mother's income, that it was in her interest, and anyway it had been the agents who had first given him the idea, he would never have thought of it himself. She couldn't understand a word of his broken explanation about fifty real pounds as opposed to just fifty pounds. "And what if fifty real pounds come to mean five hundred?" she asked. "Haven't you heard of peppercorn rents? That's the whole point." But it was no use. Having come so far, she had to agree to wait for the new lease and see the thing in writing.

To her utter astonishment the mortgagors' lawyers raised no objection at all to the added clause. "But are you sure?" she asked once again. "Do please read it carefully." For it was a jibberish of calculators and numerators and denominators which Philip Hayley had frankly admitted was incomprehensible to him. "Oh, it's a bit odd," they said, "but it shouldn't affect Inter-Insular at all."

Inter-Insular was indeed little affected, for on the 8th June they wrote to say that according to their lawyers, who had now had time to examine the new lease, it was perfectly acceptable provided the clause about the Ground Rent rising according to the Cost of Living Index was removed, since they were not at all clear as to what the numerator and denominator referred to. The application could, however, be forwarded to their surveyors on the assumption that the clause would be removed. Six days later they wrote to say that their surveyors could not proceed with their survey since the clause about the rising Ground Rent would effect to its detriment the value of the property. When Serena made Rupert protest in writing that they themselves had suggested proceeding with the survey on the assumption that the Ground Rent would be fixed at £50, they wrote back to say this was the first they had heard about a fixed Ground Rent of £50.

"The mind of the petty clerk," said Rupert, echoing Cliff, "is as unfathomable as that of the rarest mystic."

Serena had allowed this idiocy to go on while the owner or his lawyers or his accountant made up their communal little mind. But now she instructed Philip Hayley to give them until the 1st of July.

"He says you can't withdraw now," said Mr. Pratt when she told him what was happening.

"Oh, but I can, you know."

"Yes, well of course, it's not a bad scheme, you know, I hear it's quite usual nowadays, quite usual, you know. We agents can't go around giving ultimations and things, or we wouldn't stay in business you know."

"I'm not an agent," said Serena acidly, and put down the receiver.

When her ultimatum expired Serena knew it was she who had capitulated, unconditionally, to the property world. She gave up all idea of ever owning the smallest patch of ground and snapped up the very first rented flat she saw on the very same morning. "Renting's easy," Cliff had urged, "the market's flooded with flats now, at a price of course. They get it out of you somewhere. I did an enquiry for my paper, you know. Either rents are fabulous, or there's a premium of say £1,500 for filthy carpets and curtains, which would cost at most £300 new. Divide that by the five or so years in the lease and the rent's fabulous again. But the legal side is simple and at least you can keep away from the mortgage morons."

The flat was in Primrose. Hill, on the fourth floor above a branch of Farley's Bank, the agents were very suave, the rent was £675 per annum exclusive of rates and Serena didn't care. She was in a hurry, she said. So much so that she would not take the flat if the owners were going to do anything about the reception room floor which was sagging visibly in the middle. As long as it was safe. Would the agents please find out. She wanted to be in legal possession by the first of August, so that the decorators could go in and prepare it before she went abroad. She was leaving on the 15th. Surely the legalities could be done in a month?

"Oh, certainly, Mrs. Buttery," said the smooth young man with the Third Programme voice. "Of course we must wait for your references and forward them to our clients, but after that, it needn't take more than a week?'

The owners, a letter said three days later, had no intention of, doing anything about the reception room floor, which they were satisfied was perfectly safe for normal purposes.

After two weeks she rang up the agents again.

"We're not in a position to say," said the smooth young man with, the Third Programme voice. "We haven't heard of any hitch. Your references were all right. It shouldn't take more than a week, unless of course you bandy the lease back and forth."

"Look, blame me when I've had a chance to bandy it back and forth, will you. I haven't seen the thing yet."

"Yes, well, solicitors are solicitors."

"If they are at all. Who are your client's solicitors? There has been no contact whatsoever."

"We're not in a position to say," said the smooth young man with the Third Programme voice.

"I want to speak to the Senior Partner."

"I'm afraid he's out, madam."

"Any partner, then."

"They're all out, I'm afraid. We're very busy, you see."

A week later she insisted on speaking to someone responsible. "Oh, lord," she heard, by mistake, a male voice say, followed by the telephonist's diagnosis, "she's a bitisterical, sir". The responsible person, however, turned out to be still no more than the Senior Partner's Secretary, who didn't know anything about it except that the clients had been hesitating whether to let the flat or keep it for themselves.

Serena called on the agents that afternoon.

The smooth young man said "You see, your bank manager's reference hasn't come in yet." His voice was almost for announcing early Greek music in the Dorian mode.

"My bank manager sent his reference on July 3rd. I know, because he asked to see me. And then put over all the tycoonery he could think up. Just like your Senior Partner. But he did, perhaps to make up for it, show me the letter. Now will you please let me see Mr. Barnes or make some effort to tell the truth."

The smooth young man lifted his eyebrows and his telephone.

"I have Mrs. Buttery' here, sir. About—ah, thank you, yes . . . The matter can proceed? Good. Thank you, sir. The matter can proceed," he said to Serena as he put his telephone and his eyebrows down. "Our clients are instructing their solicitors tomorrow."

Philip Hayley managed to put enough pressure on the Bank's solicitors, a large firm he knew well, to get a lease out of them within three days. He went through it with her and returned it the same afternoon. Serena was astonished.

"We may just make it," she said to Rupert three weeks before they were due to leave. "I've got permission to put the decorators in on Monday, before we actually sign. That'll give me more time to supervise them."

"Is that wise?"

"I really can't think what can possibly go wrong now."

"Let's rack our brains."

They couldn't think of anything.

It was, however, the reception room floor, which the owners had decided was not really safe. The District Surveyor had estimated that the work would take approximately a month.

"But why didn't you see to it when I raised the question on 1st July? You assured me in writing..."

"Oh, we didn't say exactly that..."

"We never said..."

"You know, this sort of thing is perfectly normal, Mrs. Buttery, it happens every day..."

"If we said your bank manager's reference hadn't arrived then it hadn't..."

"You really can't reckon to get a flat in a month..."

"You'll feel much safer..."

"In other words," Serena said to the frock-coated gentleman from the Premises Department in the Head Office of Farley's Bank in the City, "your agents were perfectly prepared to assure you the floor was safe as regards mere tenants, but they were not prepared to certify it as safe to an Insurance Company once you started having doubts."

The frock-coated gentleman spoke to her with closed eyelids and an exquisite smile.

They were sitting at a mahogany table in the middle of the Bank, in line with many other mahogany tables, and by-passed continually by scarlet messengers and more frock-coated gentlemen.

Very occasionally, he opened his eyes but immediately looked beyond her. She wondered, since he evidently could not see her, why he nevertheless had the power to make her wish that she had worn a hat, or might melt into the rubber tiled floor and vanish. He held his own fingers very tight and explained, with great delicacy, that she should not have come here.

"I am very dissatisfied with the way your agents have handled this affair."

But her voice was wavering, and as his eyes were still closed she knew he couldn't see the firm look on her face. Soon she was being grateful. Apologising. They had summoned their own contractors, he said, who would be much more expensive, in order to get the job done quickly. He gathered it was not a very extensive job. Now what did she want him to do, exactly? Of course he would have to let the agents know that she had called. Well, naturally. What else could he do? He could only ring up the agents, with whom they had been dealing for many years, and ask them to put the matter in hand as quickly as possible. Yes. Oh, that's quite all right. Certainly. Not at all. Goodbye.

Presumably he opened his eyes again to walk back to his office.

Three days after Stella was due to arrive, later than usual, by air from Buen Punto, and hadn't, Serena went to the flat and talked to the foreman. The workers had only just moved in that morning. The centre beam was full of dry rot, the foreman said. The job would take well over six weeks, if, that was, they could get the necessary steel in a fortnight, which was doubtful. The worker's were sitting on the piled-up floorboards, drinking tea and morosely gazing through the gap at the ruined flat below. And suddenly they were not workers at all but she and Rupert, staring at a whole party of sixty guests, including literary giants, TV personalities and all her patients, who had fallen through the floor while Rupert was in the kitchen fetching ice and she was at the door seeing someone off. The moment passed.

"It seems every place I touch has a jinx on it," Serena said sadly to Rupert that evening.

"It's quite evident," she said very humbly two hours later, "that the powers that be want us to stay where we are."

"What powers?" Rupert asked, puzzled.

"Oh, I don't know. Saint Antony. And people like that."

The next day Rupert received a letter from the Life Insurance Department of Inter-Insular, drawing his attention, with tender concern, he thought, to the fact that his weight, which he had given as thirteen stone three on his application form of the previous year, was now given as only twelve stone two. Could he give any explanation? "My loss of weight," he typed on two fingers, "was no doubt due to the worry as to whether I would ever get a mortgage out of the Inter-Insular (British Archipelago) Insurance Company Ltd."

14

For some weeks now, Rusty had been in that peculiarly unreal state when words leap out from pages, voices or one's own thoughts, and rudely rattle their bones about, or shove their meanings under one's nose like exhibitionists until the meanings themselves vanish in a dance of death. Cinderella mutated from rinsedella to rinse-a-leader and denser-liar, nitron became non-try, then trianon, U.V.I. kept changing into I-view-you, and synthetic fibre had long completed its various transitions from thin fetid cider to fist ethic neighbour and finally to thigh fetish sabre, where it looked like getting stuck for quite some time.

He was consequently neither pleased nor frightened when Mr. Harding rang through to say he would like to have a word with him, as if a word were a glass of wine, or a loaf of bread.

"I see you've put your name down for a transfer, Conway," said Mr. Harding, after the entering-and-sit-you-down formalities were done. "Any particular reason, compassionate, or ... otherwise?"

Rusty felt a great urge to talk about passion and compassion, for the word "compassionate" evoked swift images of Christ leaning down from the Cross, fading rapidly into preachers thundering from pulpits, politicians yelling down from platforms, and Screen-Persuaders persuading from the screen. But they were gone in a flash and he said simply:

"No, sir, just restlessness, you know how it is."

"Yes. Yes. It's always the same with you foreign representatives, you get it in the blood. Still, can't say I blame you. Wouldn't mind a spell abroad myself, for that matter. Last time I went it was such a swift round trip I came back quite a wreck. However, let me see. Yes, you've been here some time, haven't you. And you handled that nitron affair extremely well, yes indeed, extremely well."

"Oh, Thank you, sir."

"Yes. Most gratifying, everything. Cinderella's doing splendidly, as you know. Haven't had such a boom for years."

"I always felt, sir, that nitron was rather spoiling cinderella's chances, as soon as we put it on the market it started affecting cinderella sales. We were sort of cutting our nose to spite our face, in a way."

"Could be, could be. Though we didn't do too badly with it, you, know, and everything came out in the wash. However, that's not the point at issue. Tell me, Conway, how would you like to take over the Aegean job?"

"But, I thought Fawcett—"

"He put in for it, yes. Yes, indeed. But I had a chat with him and, well, people are funny. They don't always know the reasons for their own actions. One has to allow for rashness and that sort of thing. Probe a little, you know, probe a little. It turned out that he didn't want to go to Greece at all, he was merely going through the usual spell of disgust with publicity. A bit, slow, as a matter of fact, was Fawcett, most of our publicity boys go through that stage much sooner. Much sooner. He waited till he reached the top, and it's more serious then. In any case the directors have decided we need a rather more subtle line in advertising. More . . . subliminal, you know. Got a new man coming in, but that's between these four walls, of course. Good chap, Fawcett. So I'm transferring him to Sales. Said he wanted something more real. More directly connected with, the product, you know. Hence the volcanic island. But he'll be quite happy in. Sales. Thorpe's job, you know, Southern Division. Thorpe will train him."

"And Thorpe?" Rusty asked anxiously.

"U.K. Sales, of course. He was always marked out for it. Jenkins is retiring, you know."

"I'm very glad," said Rusty with sincerity. "I mean, about Harry Thorpe."

"Yes. Good man, Thorpe. Absolutely reliable. Hard worker. Great common sense."

"Yes," said Rusty, fervently.

"The Aegean job is not exactly a promotion for you, as it would have been for Fawcett, I hope you realise. But it's no step down either. And of course, the usual allowances. You'll be completely in charge and directly responsible to us here, to me in fact. It's a job, if I may say so, Conway, which needs imagination, initiative, and of course tact. The Greek Government is being co-operative, for the moment anyway, but of course the people of the island depend on lava-dust for their crops, they get no rain you see, so we don't want any resentment and so forth. No local trouble, you know, or any of that sort of thing. You'll have to study the whole layout. I think you're just the man, but before I recommended you to the other directors and put it through Personnel; I wanted to, well, have a word with you. Probe a little, you know probe a little. Who, for instance, among your own boys could in your opinion best step into your shoes? At least temporarily. You can always come back to them, you know, they are yours."

When Rusty got back to his office, he found Stella sitting in his chair.

She looked, as usual, stupendous. Thin still but healthier than the year before, suntanned without that dried-up look. It was only later that he noticed the glazed light in her eyes and the increased droop of her mouth. She wore a dress of a fashionable cut, which he couldn't name or take in the details of, neither could he grasp just what combination of *dernier cri* and traditional elegances, what variations of flesh and colour, silk, and crocodile and straw made up that general impression of something fabulous yet warm and real, something not icily *outré*, stepped from a glossy page, but human, astonishing and desirable.

"Stella!"

"*Hombre, cómo está?*" Rusty knew that she spoke a foreign language, or mock-Mayfair, or mock-Cockney, when she felt moved or affectionate. He felt moved and affectionate too. Especially when she added shyly, "nice to see you".

She was full of the revolution. It had been quite terrible. Manolo had been absolutely ruined and his finca destroyed by tanks. Bombs fell in every street and even if one took a taxi home the driver would stop suddenly and pull the whole vehicle to pieces if he thought he heard something ticking. It was far more serious than just a local business because it had been a world trouble-spot for years and was now completely infiltrated with Communists. She had been glad to get out, though really, she had no idea what she was going to do, she had left all her things and furniture in her casita there and given the key to Manolo.

"Was that wise?" Rusty asked.

"Oh, Manolo's all right. He still wants to marry me, apparently." Rusty's disbelief scooped the uncertainty behind her trust, and he suddenly felt sad. "I hope it was all right my barging up here unannounced," she went on. "I can't stand the man downstairs, he has such ugly ears, have you noticed? So I just hoped you wouldn't have some tremendous vip here and I came straight in. What a gorgeous view, Rusty, it's pure Canaletto with a breath of Whistler, at least if you very nearly shut your eyes."

She sat on the corner of his desk, puffing the smoke of her cigarette at the view on the river.

"I'm going to Greece, Stella, for U.V.I. A posting to the Aegean, I mean. In September."

"Rusty! How absolutely marvellous. Oh, how I envy you, I did so adore the Acropolis. And you simply must visit—"

"Stella, will you come and help me buy a tropical-weight suit? I need a new one. Now, I mean?" The urge to pretend that she was his wife was so strong that he decided there and then to take the morning off, even though he wouldn't need his suit till September. "There are still some sales on," he added, surprised at himself. "I thought I might pick up something in Shaftesbury Avenue. Then we could have lunch."

Stella made a disapproving face, not about the invitation but about Shaftesbury Avenue. "Don't go there," she said, "you'll look like all those awful Englishmen one is so ashamed of abroad. You know, in shapeless dark grey trousers and bright red cotton shirts with little yellow windmills or something, they think they're being frightfully gay and continental and they wear the same shirt every single day of their holiday, without, of course, a vest to absorb the sweat and change. I really don't know who's worse, the men or the women."

"That's precisely why I need your help," said Rusty amicably, though he would never have worn a red cotton shirt with yellow windmills; in fact he usually went to Saville Row for his suits, where women were distinctly unwelcome, and had only mentioned Shaftesbury Avenue so as to go with Stella.

"And then there are those shabby student types," Stella went on as if he had said nothing, "one can spot their nationality a mile away. Scruffy hair, belted trousers and tucked in shirts so creased and dirty they look as if they'd been worn for a month. I do believe the English just hang out their shirts on a chair at night and think that's the equivalent of washing it. Ugh!" She stubbed out her cigarette with a disgusted look.

"Now blue's a very popular colour this year," said the first salesman, "and white's lovely for the tropics."

"I said light grey."

"Light grey's very difficult, sir, very difficult," he said, as if it were ancient Greek.

"Why?"

"Rusty, for heaven's sake don't argue with a salesman!"

The man's look said he would gladly have sold her to the white slave traffic, then it ignored her pointedly as he turned to Rusty.

"I have a light grey one, sir, in cinderella linen, but it comes slightly more expensive, if you'd like to step this way."

"*Not* synthetic fibre, Rusty, you'll die. You know that."

"What part of the world was the gentleman going to?"

"Greece."

"Oh, that's not tropical, sir, come and look at this map, sir, you'll see—"

"Goodness! Let's get out of here, he'll be trying to tell us where Africa lies in a minute."

"We're selling a lot of these, sir, even for the real tropics. You'll find it's quite comfortable, really—"

"If I ask for a light grey suit in specially treated linen or cotton, it's because I don't want a dark blue one in cinderella, nitron, shanlon, brincelle or any other fibre, whether I'm going to Iceland or Timbuktu," said Rusty, very red in the face and more angry than he would have got had Stella not been there. "Are you able to grasp such a simple fact about serving a customer?"

"Good-day, sir."

The salesman pursed his lips and turned his back on them as he put the cinderella linen suit back among its numerous companions on the rung.

"Rusty, you really must not quarrel with tradesmen and servants," said Stella as they went downstairs and out into the street. "Surely you know that by now?"

"What's the difference between your insulting the man to me in front of him and my insulting him to his face?"

"*Me*, insulting? *He* was insulting!" Stella was genuinely astonished.

"My, dear Stella, you're living in the past. There are no servants any more, except in underdeveloped countries and the bedraggled remains of the British Empire. And they're all being given progress on a plate. In England we're all very prosperous and very equal, and everybody's as good as everybody else however bad everybody may be."

"Oh dear, how awful." Stella was genuinely shocked. "I thought it was only like that during the war."

The next shop had no light grey suits at all.

"No, I'm afraid not," said the salesman. "Light grey is very difficult, sir."

"What's that then?"

"What? Oh, that. Yes, that's light grey. Yes. Funny that. Non-iron cotton that is, specially treated. And it's your size too. Would you like to slip it on, sir? Very lightweight it is, this, lovely and light."

The salesman busied himself with counting shirts so as not to talk to Stella, who was sitting near the counter smoking and looking round the shop like a grand duchess. When Rusty peered out of the cubicle he bustled up to him, looking over his shoulder as if to dare Stella to follow him, which she did. The suit looked terrible.

"Now that's a perfect fit, sir, could have been made to measure. Just a little long in the leg, perhaps, but our tailor can soon fix that, a matter of a couple of days, you're not in any hurry, are you sir?"

"It's quite hopeless," said Rusty, "and you know it."

"Yes, well, of course, it's a standard size, sir, you can't expect it to fit bespoke, your being rather wide in the rear, and a little spread out here in front, that's what does it, you know."

"What charming salesmanship," said Stella addressing him direct this time. "It's the customer who doesn't fit the suit now, is it?"

"It's a very good suit, we sell a lot of these," said the salesman at a loss.

"Take it off, Rusty, we'll go elsewhere."

The salesman retired, fuming with delayed anger. He was nowhere to be seen when they left the shop.

"I think it'll have to be Saville Row after all," said Rusty sadly. "I rather wanted to avoid it because they have their own deadly brand of salesmanship there too. They quite simply, refuse to believe that a sleeve has been put in wrong, or a shoulder cut too sloping, and of course one has to take it as it is in the end. I was hoping to be able to step into something, modern style."

"I told you so," said Stella.

"Ah, well, let's forget it and have a drink. I'm whacked. I hope that one day we shall all be buying our suits from slot-machines."

Stella didn't bother to ring Serena until a week after her arrival, days which Serena had kept as free of engagement as possible, since Stella was supposed to go on to Paris shortly after. But when the days had passed Serena was obliged once again to plunge into intensive work before she and Rupert were due to leave for their much needed holiday. There were only a few days to go when Stella rang up.

"Oh, yes, I arrived last Friday, but I just felt so depressed about the revolution, I simply didn't want to inflict myself on anyone."

"Is it so serious?"

"Oh, Reeny, you just can't imagine. Manolo is absolutely ruined and everything's just going to be awful for years. I had so hoped that here at last was a country I could make my home in and everyone says it's just going to be a world trouble-spot for years. Far more than local politics is involved..."

The flow was unlocked. Serena listened with both genuine sympathy and professional patience, though her professional self couldn't help reflecting once again how external circumstances were always on the side of the unconscious patterns.

"Well, look, Stella, I'd like to see you, even if you don't want to see me." She was full of good resolutions. "When can we meet?"

"I don't really know," Stella drawled, "let me see. Tomorrow I'm booked for lunch and dinner. How about Saturday?"

"But I thought you were only passing through London?"

"Oh, well, no. I've changed my plans. I'm staying until September."

"I see." She did, too. "Well, then, there's the whole weekend. Come to lunch."

"Oh, all right."

The next day, Friday, Stella rang up in the middle of Serena's session with Tom Stevens. It was very urgent. Oh, well, would Serena ring her back at the following office number as soon as she could?

"The thing is," she said when Serena did so, "I've found some marvellous digs I'm moving into on Monday, and the woman is a *writer*, called Daisy Linda, and I thought that perhaps if Rupee could put in a good word for me—"

"What do you mean, put in a good word? He doesn't know her."

"Oh but she'll know *him*, she'll be terribly impressed."

"But Stella, I don't understand. Since when does one have to impress landladies with one's connections?"

"Oh, but then she'll give me particular treatment, and her best room, and so forth."

Serena was beginning to seethe. Quite apart from the unmentionable fact that Rupert would certainly not feel inclined to recommend Stella to anyone at all as a pleasant person to have in one's house, did Stella really suppose that he would want to communicate with a total stranger, merely because—but there was no point in arguing, even to herself.

"Your attitude is very oriental," she merely said.

"Yes, it is," said Stella proudly. "That's how things get done in all parts of the world. *And* in England, but nobody admits it. Especially in literary circles."

"Oh, come off it, Stella."

"But it's true. I met a woman in Buen Punto who was once married to a critic called Howard Cutting, and she told me it was all 'Larry this' and 'Johnny that' and 'we must get Freddy a good review'."

"Howard Cutting is Howard Cutting," said Serena wearily. "You are coming on Saturday, aren't you?"

"Yes, all right. Bye."

Later that afternoon there was another urgent message, this time while Isabel was relating a complicated dream. But urgency to Stella simply meant something she herself had just thought of. Was Serena still looking for a house, she wanted to know, because a friend of hers had a cottage in Sussex which she was thinking of selling the following winter, and as Stella was going to see her next week she would mention it because this friend in fact would prefer a private sale and so on and so forth.

"Really, Stella, couldn't it have kept till tomorrow?"

"Well, you see, she rang me this morning and I thought it would be exactly right for you and Rupee, it's got about ten rooms, I believe, and I think Sussex is simply enchanting. I can't understand why you and Rupee never go to the country, instead of—"

"I don't like cottagey rooms."

"Oh, don't you? I think they're *far* nicer, I'd far rather have lots of small rooms than these huge big ones the English go for, no privacy, and of course they're always freezing, really, the English will pretend they've got a mild—"

"Thank you, Stella, it's very nice of you. We'll talk about it tomorrow, shall we?"

But on Saturday morning Molly Hardways rang up to say that Stella was terribly sorry, she had decided to go to the country for the weekend, she had been invited by her girlfriend in Sussex, and felt so very exhausted, she had particularly asked her, Molly Hardways, to apologise for any inconvenience caused, and Serena thought Molly Hardways would never ring off, she took so long to say so little. By Monday evening, when Stella returned, Serena was so tied up with last-minute arrangements before their departure on Wednesday morning that she couldn't, with the best will in the world and no doubt a little latent annoyance, find a moment.

"What, not even for a drink?"

"I can't, Stella. I've got eight patients tomorrow, and I have to be alone at lunchtime when I see so many, and it means working all evening on my notes. Not to mention clearing-up and packing. Look, why don't you come round now?"

"Well . . . it's rather late."

"That's all right." Serena gaily took the remark as a considerate one, but her gaiety was horribly forced. "I'm sorry, Stella," she couldn't resist, "but I kept all those days free for you and you never rang me, then you couldn't see me on Friday, and you cancelled the weekend."

"I could come tomorrow night, though, and moreover I'll help you pack. Then you'll finish in next to no time and we can sit and talk. I'll bring some sewing."

"Come to dinner, then," said Serena weakly.

"Yes, all right. Look, Reeny, there's just one thing I wanted to ask you, and it's a matter of *complete* indifference to me what your answer is."

"Yes?" said Serena with as much curiosity of tone as she was capable of enacting, which wasn't much.

"Well, you see, I have to stay here till September, that is, I'm going back to Buen Punto then, I hope, but I'm extending my leave, unpaid, and so

I've decided to do temporary work during my leave, so as not to spend my savings..."

There followed a complexity of plans during which Serena could only think, it's not just the revolution, something's gone wrong about Manolo, but she's hoping he will beg her to come back. At last, however, Stella came to the long-awaited point.

"And it occurred to me this morning, well I mean I thought to myself, a real business proposition, I mean, which would help *you*, and I could pay you in cash now, before you go, in dollars moreover, which would simply unroll the red carpet for you everywhere in Europe, I mean, *if* you could see your way to *letting* me your flat, for rent I mean, not a lot of course, less than I pay here, but for you it would be sheer profit since you always say you hardly notice the rent, well I mean it would help me considerably, and you too, since dollars simply unroll the red carpet everywhere in Europe these days..."

Serena wanted to cry.

"No, Stella, it's impossible, I'm sorry." She foolishly sought authority. "I knew you'd ask and I discussed it with Rupert during the weekend."

Stella was extremely vexed.

"I don't know why you talk as if I'd been hatching a sinister plot or something. It literally only occurred to me this morning, in the train up as a matter of fact, I thought to myself well, it would be so helpful to *both* of us, and since I have dollars, which simply unroll the red carpet everywhere in Europe... But it doesn't matter *in* the least."—Her tone resumed its casual drawl—"I simply wanted to know one way or the other, because the digs I've just moved into, well—" she lowered her voice and broke into French—"*ce n'est pas tout à fait mon affaire*, and I only wanted to know, just in case, but it's of no consequence."

Serena carefully did all the packing before Stella arrived on Tuesday evening, to avoid a critical commentary on her wardrobe. As her last patient had left at five, and she had managed to finish all her notes between five and half past six, she was in a state of complete exhaustion by eight, when Stella arrived and said, "Ooh! you're a fat little thing, now, Reeny," which annoyed her very much because, although she knew that she had indeed been getting more middle-aged looking in the past few years, she had in fact lost weight, just like Rupert, during the episode of the flat fantasies.

She hardly said a word while Stella toyed with the cold dinner, leaving most of it distastefully on her plate as she talked. There was a long story about a French girl of eighteen she had met at her digs, who had agreed to move out and share a room with her elsewhere, borrowed money from her and disappeared, leaving her to pay the double rent. Fortunately Rupert was making the right sympathetic noises and after a while Stella turned to her usual tirades of advice about the place they were going to and the clothes they must not wear in order not to appear too English ("but I am English," Rupert feebly protested); though of course she simply couldn't understand why they didn't take weekends in the country more often, or even live there, instead of killing themselves all the year round then going to bake for three weeks on some European beach. Most unhealthy . . . Now if only Serena would take up riding, as she had in Buen Punto . . .

It was then that Serena knew she must break the pattern. For once she did not bother to analyse the why, the wherefore or the wisdom of this aggressive instinct. The calmness of her certitude excited her, as such calmness had no doubt excited other aggressors. She and Stella had quarrelled before, but somehow Stella had always started writing again a few months later as if nothing had happened, or else she, Serena, had written to try and explain—"one of your awful letters telling me my character," Stella called them—This time she wanted peace for several years, real peace, even from letters.

Rupert had a last article to finish and vanished after supper. Serena insisted she would wash up herself later. "Let's go and sit quietly," she said, "and do our sewing."

Stella had not, of course, brought her sewing, which was only an excuse, and she sat as usual on the sofa, stroking her neck and shoulders as she talked. The quarrel began quite late, at eleven fifteen, in fact, just as

Serena was beginning to think she would never engineer it. But at last it happened, and went on for sometime.

Like most quarrels, it was pointless, not because they said things they didn't mean but because they said things they did mean: Serena, who had decided, smugly, to buy her years of peace by giving Stella the comfort of righteousness, put herself completely in the wrong and hit Stella, who stood stock still, said something quasi-manic about changing her Will so that Serena would now *not* be troubled with it after all, and walked out of her life for ever with enormous dignity, on the stroke of midnight.

Or a few years, Serena reflected as she washed up for the last time before their holiday. It would do them good. Both of them. Twenty years even. They would meet again in old age, she a widow and Stella a tired old maid, and share a little house . . .

The next morning she received a hand-delivered note from Molly Hardways, who "took it upon herself to suggest" that in view of what had happened all communications should cease, as if that had not been decided without her, and who "further advised" Serena not to attempt writing to her, Molly Hardways. Poor Stella, Serena thought as they sped through London in a taxi. Poor Molly Hardways for that matter. Poor everybody.

One of the Siamese twins who had been operated on last week, she read in the plane, had died. Serena looked down over the Channel. Until seventy times she murmured. And she knew she had no excuse.

15

"THE ISLAND of Hephaestos is the most fantastical in the world that will furnish you with most incredible dining conversation for many years back home. In two hours of one another you can indulge in spearing numerous big fish beneath its sapphire waters (bring your gear!) or lolling on its two white sandy beaches one over 2 km. long which are extremely rare on a volcanic island, then visiting the most horrific landscape like the moon, a petrified foretaste of our immediate future perhaps, but certainly also of cataclysmic events aeons gone by as well as the last eruption of 1836, almost within living memory of our own grand greatmothers."

Serena was lolling, not on the white sandy beach 2 km. long, which was about 40 km. away, but on the sun-terrace of Lord Byron Hotel in the town of Thermos, capital of the island.

"Thermos," she read in the pamphlet from *Alpha Excursions*, "was once an ordinary fishing village and you can still see the little boats dotting the wine-dark sea with their lanterns at night like stars for squids, returning at dawn to the picturesque little harbour, or some sailing off by day to catch the more quotidian fry like pollock and sardines, and special expeditions for tuna, merlin, hake. But after ,the eruption of 1856, which destroyed the old capital of Kytheropolis, where the Phrygian king Mydas is reputed to have once held court, Thermos grew in importance, chiefly on account of the travellers who came to see the famous point outside the city where the lava-stream stopped before a Byzantine statue of the Virgin Theoticos, now venerated with great celebrations on her feast-day the 8th of September, which is extremely picturesque on account of the unique costumes worn by the folk from all over the island."

Serena felt very smart in her new Italian swimsuit, which flattered her figure, an achievement worth the high price she had paid for it in an expensive London shop. For once she felt really at ease on a beach or hotel terrace, turning all her various aspects to the sun without embarrassment. Under a wide straw hat, she was trying to work out the possible tours they could do, but it was rather difficult. Not only was the heat melting her mind, but the phraseology of the English professor employed by *Alpha Excursions* was a little too euphoric for lucidity. There seemed, moreover, to be about five real "places of interest" in the island, and cleverly enough there were five separate tours, each with an intoxicating list of villages passed through, hills driven up for spectacular perspectives of sea-dashed rocks, of sloping vineyards, of olive groves or on the contrary, bare plains, "very African in character, as wild and wind-blown as the Sahara desert." Here there was a cave to visit, a wine-press there, a caramel factory, a water-pump, a church with a copy of a famous Tintoretto and some fantastical rich vestments in its Treasure (entry 1 drachma). There was no way of getting one single tour to visit the five places of interest in one day. She was trying to clarify her own mind by presenting Rupert with all the different possible permutations so that he should choose something she could then disagree with, but Rupert was in the middle of a very funny novel called *Mass Medium*, and cared little about spectacular perspectives.

They had been bickering almost from the start, already in Greece itself and on the other islands, and she was quite upset by it. She hadn't been too well, either. She didn't know whether it was the sun, the sea-bathing or the food, but her hands and wrists had come out in a rash of eczema which was spreading up her arms and felt extremely painful. The doctor in Athens had said it could only be the unaccustomed food, certainly not their beautiful sea or their health-giving sun, which would do it good, so that now she was dutifully exposing her hands to it, all pasted over in the cream he had given her. It was certainly soothing at the time, but at night when there was no sun, the itching would start again and she got little sleep.

The trouble about bickering was that they never seemed to be really alone. Lord Byron Hotel was Second Class A, very modern, very comfortable, very large and run by a German, a combination of attributes which made it an inevitable choice for *Winged Chariots Ltd.*, who disgorged their twice-weekly planeloads of what Isabel Gormsley had called travelling salesmen on holiday. Poor Isabel, she had been so enthusiastic about her party, and so mortified when it had fallen through. The couple in half of which she had been so obsessionally interested had suddenly decided to go to Norway instead, and somebody called Baker was going to Bermuda with his new mistress. Everyone else on her list had somehow had other plans and in the end Isabel had been a good girl and gone to Mallorca with her friend Tamara. Now Serena almost wished that Isabel had succeeded. Even a smart party would be better than the dreary specimens of humanity collected from France, England, Germany and elsewhere by *Winged Chariots Ltd.*

She was surprised to notice, for the first time, that Stella's generalisations about the English were true, or rather, that the particulars from which the generalisations were made really existed. Two of them were sitting in the shaded part of the terrace at that very moment, both in identical shirts of glazed red cotton with little printed windmills—or was it sailing boats? —drinking beer with a little man in grey flannel trousers that looked yellow and a shirt of yellow terry towelling that looked grey.

The terry towel was the life and soul of the party, the one who could play everything from *Bumps a Daisy* to *La Mer* very badly on the hotel lounge piano, surrounded every night by a sing-songing group of middle-aged lads and lassies who had been turning the hotel bar into a good old English pub.

This particular lot, however, was leaving the next day, at least, she hoped they were. Twice already, when one lot had been due to leave, their tables covered with pretty flower designs for the last meal, the student in charge had gone round from group to group, explaining in French, German or English that something had gone wrong, that the plane would come the next day, and for twenty-four hours the departing tour had sat miserably around, camping all over the lounges in their best travelling clothes. Serena wondered whether *Winged Chariots* wouldn't get an Olympian rebuke but she supposed not, as everyone said how glad they were of the extra day.

But if it wasn't one planeload, it was another, and one thing all the tour people had in common was their desire to talk. That's what travelling was for, wasn't it, to broaden the mind, to meet people, well, not foreigners of course, because of the lingo, though one could get a long way with signs and bursts of laughter, but people one wouldn't meet at home. And they would sniff the gentle breeze and scan the blue sky for the slightest sign of variation that would give them something to broach a conversation with, failing which they would fall back on "hot, isn't it? . . . lovely . . . I love the heat . . . always did . . .", and so forth. They had made friends with each other easily on the journey and assumed that the hotel was yet another aeroplane, and that all its guests were simply part of another tour, as pally as their own. The great thing was to be pally, and anyone who didn't feel like it was snooty, standoffish, giving themselves airs.

Serena was annoyed with herself for being so annoyed; she didn't know whether she resented her resentment most or the people who caused it. She was tired, tired out, and would have preferred a more familiar kind of vulgarity. She found herself making observations like "people have more in common with their own class anywhere in the world than with other, classes in their own country", and certainly on holiday it seemed true enough. The English who came on leave from Aden and East Africa, for instance, were dimly suburban but quiet, and kept very aloof from the jolly *Winged Chariot* lot. And one Englishman on his own, from England, who sat reading a bit restlessly on the terrace in his baggy khaki shorts and a very creased shirt which had once been the colour of suntanned flesh, always smiled and nodded to Serena and Rupert but to no one else, by way of silent recognition of his own kind, a kind that did not go on *Winged Chariot* tours. On the other hand the other national groups, though divided, and rather loudly, by language, were geologically exactly alike, allowing, that is, for local variations such as the amazing cross-table verbosity of the

French and the stiff correctness of the Germans. "You see," she explained anthropologically to Rupert, "their manners, tastes, clothes and subjects of conversation are the same as those of their own class in any other part of the world, because their reading-matter is the same—from nuclear politics to refrigerators and skirt-lengths, from the grossly garbled private lives of ex-Queens and film stars to the careers of a local starlet, champion, mayor or murderer. With such similarity of outlook there's hope for world government yet, but the internationalism seems to work in strata, each layer hating the one above and the one below. It's all very discouraging for the egalitarians."

All these things she had been saying to Rupert on and off since their arrival, besides inventing psychopathic case-histories for each of the hotel guests at all the ninety or more tables in the vast dining room, but either he didn't take in what she said at all, or he said it back to her two days later. He was being perfectly exasperating.

A German family walked out of the hotel, dressed to kill fish, that is to say, almost naked but carrying a great many spikes, goggles and flappers, as they picked their way over the sunbathing bodies on the hotel's wooden pier and bundled into a waiting motorboat. The fattest wore a leather camera case slung round his neck, with the camera itself peering out of it on his lower tummy.

"He looks like a fertility god," said Rupert. "Isn't it funny how the Germans and Americans all carry their cameras like that? At the ready, just in case. The English have them closed and slung on their backs. Interesting."

"And the French?" Serena asked icily, to see if he was going to pinch the whole of her yesterday's arch observation.

"Oh, the French. They carry them in their hands. Or not at all. They prefer to talk about it."

Then Rusty arrived, with Jean.

Wisely they had not organised a foursome holiday, and Rusty in any case was not really on holiday but "studying the layout". Still, they had arranged to meet and Serena felt astonished at how pleased she was to see them. She wanted to get out of the hotel atmosphere and suggested the taverna in about ten minutes. Then she raced upstairs to change.

Rusty was in great form, and looked extremely elegant in a well-cut tropical suit of light grey cotton.

"Everyone's delightful here, have you noticed how they all say 'tea-potty' when you say thank you?" He ordered their drinks in quite passable café-Greek. "Our house isn't ready yet. We're staying at the Corinth in great splendour. You must come over and have a meal. Guy Hart is there too, remember him? You met him at our place, I think. He's at the Embassy in Athens and popped over for a few days' leave, to see me settled in and so forth."

"How are you finding it here?" asked Jean.

"Lovely," said Serena, waving at the sea and the palm trees all round the taverna. Then she added obsessively, "if it weren't for the *English*—"

"How strange, you looked exactly like Stella when you said that," said Rusty, with a thoughtful glance, and Serena smiled slightly and stared at the bay, unsure whether the Conways knew about the break-up. Rusty had been in Leeds at the time and they had left London soon after, but Stella could well have seen them first. "But, are you comfortable?" Jean persisted, and Serena thought, of course they must know.

"Oh, yes. Private bathroom and all. We decided to go splash this time. But as the water's tepid-and-tepid it doesn't help much."

"You're lucky to have water at all," said Rusty. "I was talking to the Chief of Water Supply at the town hall this morning and he told me there's no water at all on the island, they have to import it from 'the peninsula' as he keeps calling Greece. The annual rainfall is about an inch or something like that, it's to do with the shape of the volcanoes, they're cloud-repelling in some way I couldn't understand. The clouds do come but don't break. He went on for so long about their storage system I christened him Big Chief Running Water Hopping Mad. Hello, has Ted Baker written a book?"

The Middlemen: Chapter Fifteen

"Yes, a novel, do you know him?" said Rupert, visibly brightening. "It's damn funny, all about TV publicity, you should read it, Rusty, it's right up your street and was very well reviewed."

"Ah," said Rusty, who couldn't remember Harrods Library recommending it, and would probably not have read it even if they had. He seemed to read nothing but journals called *Plastics* these days. "Oh, I say, do let's watch that couple... I bet they buy that plastic crocodile."

A middle-aged English couple at another table were being approached by a very Eastern looking gentleman all hung about with rugs and embroidered leather goods, his forearms strapped in watches, his pockets full of fountain pens. He was proffering two crocodiles, one in each hand.

"Eeeh! fatal mistake!" Rusty breathed when the woman shook her head but nevertheless looked politely at the crocodile which the man had placed on the table, and then ("oh dear, oh dear, she's done for") picked it up and examined it, still shaking her head.

The haggling went on for fifteen minutes, not because of the price, though the man kept lowering it just a little, but because the couple didn't actually want a plastic crocodile, or anything else the man had.

"Steady on," Rusty murmured. "*That's* right. No, you fool. Ye-es? Oh, no, don't say I'm losing my bet. Blast, they're using the last trump. The rotters."

The couple got up and left the taverna. To Serena's amazement, the merchant put down all his crocodiles, disentwined himself of all his leather goods and rugs which he dumped there and then on the pavement. He then chose one bag of white leather embroidered with gold and ran after the couple who had already vanished round the corner. Rusty timed him.

Three minutes later he returned, without the bag, and counting his money. Both Rupert and Rusty gave a loud British cheer and he glared at them, slowly re-entangling himself in his wares the while. When he was accoutred for action again he gave a carpet-covered shrug and walked over to a large group at the other end of the taverna.

"I was trying to get Rupert to decide whether to see the volcanoes tomorrow or the eastern grottoes," Serena said when the laughing had died down—and she herself had laughed a little less, as she was sorry for the couple. "You can't apparently do both together."

"Who says you can't?" said Rusty.

"Well, I've been studying this pamphlet here, *Alpha Excursions*."

"My dear Serena, you mustn't take any notice of them. Or at least, only to find out what you want to see. There are local buses going to all these places. I'm not letting you pay a lot of money to bundle into a horrid little microbus with some of the very people you want to get away from, on some excursion which they string out for a whole day when there's only one thing to see—"

"How do you know? Have you been on one?"

"I've been on more than one, all over the world. They're usually run by a foreigner. Just like the souvenir shops, the local handicrafts bazaars, they're run by Turks, Indians, anyone in the world except whoever the local people happen to be, because local people the world over are only interested in the sort of shop that stocks what you could buy at Selfridges. Well, it's the same with the selling of local beauty, by *Alpha Excursions* or any other. This chap's a German, I met him, he's the brother or cousin of the man who runs your hotel. But the principle's universal. If there aren't any places of interest they invent them. Two hours for lunch here, an hour to bathe there, half an hour to climb up to some point of view, a *wunderbares Augenblick* as the lady tourist said to the Swiss guide. No, no, Serena, cut out the middlemen, do it yourself."

"But I don't know any Greek."

"That's precisely what they're trading on, Serena. Learn a little, learn a little, place names aren't very difficult."

"I'd probably get on the wrong bus."

"And think what fun you'd have. You'd probably see all sorts of things not mentioned in that pamphlet at all. But anyway, not to worry. Leave it to Rusty. I've been given a car. Quite a big one too, and tomorrow we're all going together to see the volcanoes, the grottoes, the crater-theatre, the lava vineyards, anything you like, even the Byzantine Church with the Rubens or whatever it is—they're all the same, those paintings, a lot of flapping nudes and angels in the clouds with little Cupids desperately directing the traffic to avoid collisions. It's a very small island, Serena, there isn't all that much to see. But the tourists must be kept busy. So. From now on regard me as your chauffeur-guide, Excursion Alpha Plus."

This reversal of their usual roles upset Serena more than she cared to admit, even to herself, but she was so pleased, like a child, to get her excursion, that she didn't admit it to herself or anyone. She didn't even mind Guy Hart being there, oiling the conversation a little too visibly as if he thought it needed it, which it no doubt did. He sat in front with Rusty though, which annoyed her a little, for they were both swiftly adaptable abroad and talked a sort of local shop with great familiarity, while Rupert sat between herself and Jean in the wide back seat, blocking their desultory talk with his dreaming bulk.

Rupert said little, leaving Serena to Rusty and the others, because he knew that whatever he said seemed to irritate her out of all proportion to its content. But it was a sympathetic silence, for he was much aware of the hands and arms he had bandaged up for her that morning, to stop her scratching in the car.

Rusty was a very good guide. In a very short time he had not only "studied the layout" from a technical and diplomatic point of view, but had learnt all about the island, as well as quite a lot of Greek words. "It's a gesture," he would say, with a gruff modesty. "And I must say *that* for the English, they'd rather make fools of themselves and fiddle with a dictionary than address a native of any country in anything but his own language. They've got over their Empire-complex at last and don't expect every policeman and bus-driver to understand them. Unlike the French. In Buenos Aires for instance, they won't even say *vino*, but *du vin*," Rusty accented the nasal like a talking doll. "And the waiters just gape. But then the Americans are just as hopeless because they have different words. An American woman was asking the lift-boy at the Corinth if there was any mail for her, I ask you, couldn't she say letters, which might stand a chance of being understood?"

"It's you who sound like Stella, now, with your sweeping statements," Serena snapped, for they directly contradicted her own more socially stratified generalisations.

"Who's Stella?" Guy Hart asked.

"And anyway we shall soon all be saying mail and coach because nobody will understand the words letter and bus any more."

"Both good old French words," put in Rupert, "and ultimately from Latin, so what's the difference?" Which, he realised as he said it, wasn't even true.

"Trust Rupert," said Jean.

Rusty was clearly puzzled by Serena's acerbity, so he stopped the car and drew their joint attention to the fields of black lava-sand, in which were planted, here sweet potatoes, there vines, elsewhere fig trees.

"The lava absorbs the moisture from the air and stores it. You see how they scoop out these hollows, like plates, for the seed. It's really quite miraculous." His voice suddenly dropped, as if he had let it fall between his arms which he was leaning over the steering wheel. "I've a good mind to send in a report to say we can't take their ruddy lava," he murmured.

"Don't be an ass," said Guy, "there's more than enough for everyone. They've got whole mountains of it."

The mountains were frightening enough, some like giant slagheaps in a greenish grey or a fiery red as if glowing from within like furnaces, others cut in half and gaping jagged to the sky like monsters with open jaws. But the valleys were worse, for here the lava-streams had hardened into porous and pockmarked rock, spreading miles wide and down into the sea, jutting their nightmare shapes of grey and black and rotting green, as far as the eye could see, like a dead planet under the brilliant sun and the virginal blue sky.

The road itself seemed anachronistic, winding its pothole dusty way through this lava-sea, called Hades by the islanders, where not a shrub could grow or a bird could sing, then up into the orange hills along the crest, the backbone of Hephaestos, towards the peak itself, who raised his plumed hat of cloud in salutation as they approached the vast black cauldron that had given it birth.

"All this part is old eruption," said Rusty, "the original one that brought Hephaestos into being, and then I believe a second one that created the peak. It's not as high as it looks, it merely got created from a height. They call it the Godhead, but you can climb it in under, an hour. Down below, though, all that sea of lava, that was 1836. On our way back we'll stop at the Fire Mountain, it's quite little, but still very hot. You can cook a steak in a hole in the ground. I bought five eggs to cook in the earth, they taste quite unique done, that way."

They left the car to bake while they climbed the path to the top of the peak, where they stood silently round the green crater that hissed a little with sulphurous flames into the chilly breeze. Rupert bent down to choose a sea-green stone and they all imitated him, scrabbling like children in the green rocks, all except Serena, who stood and gazed at the scarred and festered corpse of the island that lay like a dead god at her feet.

They picnicked late on the Fire Mountain, at about three in the afternoon. Everyone was rather quiet, in spite of the excitement of feeling the heat come out of the oven-openings made under the rocks, and watching the dry brushwood they had brought specially to push into the hole with a spade, smoke furiously and then burst into flames. Serena particularly said very little. Her hands and arms were burning under their bandages and she was afraid that if she opened her mouth to speak she might scream instead.

Even Guy Hart gave up his smooth remarks on the return journey. They got back to Thermos at six and sat exhausted round a taverna table, sipping cool beer to a jukebox woman wailing for her demon-lover under a hiss of espresso-steam. A plastic crocodile was shoved suddenly under Serena's nose and she jumped with fright, but Rusty waved the than away with one Greek word and he moved grumbling to another table. He was not the same man as before.

A priest in a long robe with a long cross that seemed to grow straight out of his long beard was walking up and down a terrace alongside the church nearby, apparently reading his office, and they watched him with a mixture of awe, gratitude, fatigue and idleness. Slowly he reached their end of the terrace nearest to the taverna, and they saw that what he was holding so reverently in his hands was not a book but a book-sized wireless set, to the gurgling noises of which he was paying a rapt attention.

They were still laughing quietly at his turned back when suddenly Jean noticed that Serena had buried her face in her bandaged hands. She was crying, and her whole body was shaking uncontrollably. They stared at each other for a moment with raised eyebrows, and Guy Hart looked away, blushing with embarrassment.

Then they all started talking about her in the third person. "She's tired out."

"The volcanoes upset her."

"It's her eczema, you know."

"She's been working much too hard."

"The people at the hotel got on her nerves."

"She hasn't been at all well."

The crocodile and leather man stopped bargaining at the next table and stared. Suddenly he abandoned his victims and came over shame-faced.

"Very sorry lady crocodile phobia?"

Rusty shook his head, at a loss for Greek words to acknowledge this moving apology, and gave the man two drachmae. The gesture roused his practical instincts.

"Come, I'll drive her back to the hotel. Jean, you can put her to bed while I get hold of a doctor to give her an injection. Guy, will you cope with the bill?"

Rupert, so unwittingly excluded, was nevertheless as concerned for her as he had always been, from the beginning, his apparent absence being an unreasoned form of tact, and she knew it, for it was his arm she sought when, weeping still into her bandaged wrist she made her blind way to the car, followed by the curious eyes of Greek waiters and Turkish shopkeepers, French civil servants and German car manufacturers, Swedish insurance brokers, English greengrocers, tobacconists and travelling salesmen on holiday.

"Why shouldn't they have a holiday?" Serena sobbed out in the car, much to the astonishment of the other three. "Why shouldn't they? They're all going to die anyway, in their beastly winged chariots."

16

SERENA, in short, had a nervous breakdown. There was no psycho-analyst on Hephaestos but she was given the best medical attention available and a great deal of sympathy, which she didn't want. "Leave me alone," she wailed with tears still streaming down her face, and they left her alone to the darkened room and the subcutaneous flow of darkened dreams from a hypodermic needle. But when she woke she would cry again, moaning as if in pain, and muttering strange phrases about winged chariots crashing into the sun and all her patients being exquisitely tailored in molten lava. "It fits like a glove," she said, and burst into tears again.

The tears continued for two days and seemed to cleanse her of something, for her eczema suddenly vanished as if touched by a fairy's wand. She was calmer but wouldn't eat, and lay there motionless, staring at the red venetian blinds.

Rupert looked after her like a mother, though she was hardly aware of it, and Jean called twice a day, sometimes with Rusty, sometimes not.

"She's still running a slight temperature," said Rupert on the third day, as the three of them sat together on the hotel terrace.

"Good morning," murmured the Englishman in the creased and tan-coloured shirt, now worn over his wet bathing trunks as he returned from the jetty. He hesitated then stopped. "I hope your wife is better?"

"Yes, yes, much better, thank you. Just a touch of sunstroke."

"It is deceptive, isn't it?" He nodded amiably and walked away, looking pleased at having been both polite and distant at the same time.

"What *do* you think it was?" Jean asked when he had gone. "It's a bit long for sunstroke."

"Oh, general exhaustion. She's been working much too hard, and had a lot of worries, you know." He didn't want to mention them, especially the large matter of the flat, because it made him feel such an inefficient fool, and produced abstracted looks as soon as he tried to explain the details of their misfortune.

"Funny, we were due to leave tomorrow. Back to the mainland and then home through Italy. The hotel's been jolly nice, said we can stay as long as we like. Fortunately we took a lot of money, the whole of both our allowances, £500. It's odd, you know, most unlike us, we're usually so broke. We must have had a feeling something like this might happen, because we thought of staying away for several months if necessary. Serena even talked of blowing all our savings and going round the world. Instead of buying a house, you know. We may, at that."

A great burst of laughter came from a noisy group of tourists who were eating lobsters and iced beer round a table at the other end of the terrace. They were all bulging out of their bathing suits and looked rather like cooked lobsters themselves, all the more so for the red awning under which they sat, in a filtered light from the midday sun. Jean and Rusty turned back together and intercepted the look of hatred for the group on Rupert's face.

"I'm so very sorry," said Jean softly. "It must be a great worry for you. Perhaps she's upset about Stella." Rupert shrugged and said nothing, so she didn't pursue it, but added merely, "poor Stella, I'm so fond of her, but she is so very difficult to help, isn't she?"

"I think something frightened her," said Rusty. "Serena, I mean. Something to do with the volcanoes. Yes, the volcanoes," he repeated dreamily, then caught himself up. "You must tell her, sometime when you get an opportunity, or even when she's dozing, yes, tell her when she's dozing, that it's all quite safe. They're absolutely dormant, the seismographs can't lie. And besides, although the original geological eruptions may well have been fantastic, the historical one, in 1856, was a very calm affair. It went on for six years, tell her, just like the last war. Everybody got used to it. The lava came out very slowly. It would reach there one day and a little further the next. They say that the young people danced every night by the light of the fire-mountain."

The young people, however, had no time to dance on that night of September 4th when a completely new fire-mountain was thrown up just behind the little town of Thermos, which was first destroyed by the rending tremors then buried in a flood of lava two miles wide and ten feet deep that poured within twelve hours into the steaming sea, making a brand new promontory for the islanders of the distant future. The night fishermen were scalded to death, but some many miles away saw the sky lit up and knew that their homes were gone.

The world's great powers, who couldn't trust one another enough each to make one bomber less and give the money to rid the world of leprosy (in case, like God, Cliff had said at the time, they created a precedent), now vied with each other to rush in help from every side, planes, helicopters, money, supplies, rescue teams for the rescuable villages, doctors, nurses, emergency units, tents, prefabricated houses and hospitals. They did magnificent work for weeks and the international Press vibrated with emotion, printing their horror pictures and their horror stories which city workers on London tubes and ladies in New York hairdressing salons and businessmen in French cafés and government officials in Delhi, read and looked at for a minute or so before turning the pages over.

Slowly the names and numbers of the dead were traced, the natives from national census figures in Athens, and the tourists—well, the tourists were a more difficult problem, since the summer records had not yet been sent to the mainland. The Foreign Office knew they had lost one man on leave there and U.V.I. regretfully stuck from their pay roll the names of the nucleus staff allocated to Operation Thermos, as they had called it. Otherwise the international authorities were chiefly dependent on the frantic inquiries of relatives who had received postcards from Hephaestos.

The Scott-Butterys had few relatives, and were not on postcard terms with those. Their friends, with whom they had mostly lost touch through working too hard and feeling too depressed, did not miss them for many months, not knowing where they had gone. Round the world, some thought. Serena's patients rang and rang and after a while gave up, or went elsewhere, or round the bend. In literary circles, nobody noticed Rupert's absence, and those who did thought to themselves with quiet satisfaction that he was finished, unwanted, had overdone it, written himself out, had never been any good anyway. Television producers wrote once or twice then forgot about him, and the Great British television public, if they ever thought of trim at all, said at most, Yes, what happened to him? He's vanished, hasn't he? As quickly as he came up. Their big bank balance grew a fraction fatter every month, unremarked by any clerk, and they had made no Will for anyone to execute. About a year later their lawyer, Philip Hayley, worked out, clue by clue, what had probably happened, and put their affairs in order. But he could trace no relatives. It was the most unheard of death of all.

For a few weeks after the quarrel, Stella was still going over it angrily in her mind, and with her friend Molly Hardways, in whose flat she was staying. One retrospective version succeeded another, until what Serena had said, which was wicked, cruel, smug and, well, yes, wicked, became more wicked, and what she herself should have said in reply had become what she must have said, so that after a while the quarrel had slowly assumed a different shape, acquired a different essence, as it were, a taste not of hurt pride or unleashed fury, or even of crumbling resentment, but of triumphant indifference, in which hatred so often has to mask deep love.

When women make dramatic gestures and write to say that all communication must cease, they are sometimes a little pained, secretly, after the anger has died down, to have been taken literally. Without verbally thinking it, Stella assumed that Serena would, some time, send her one of her awful explanatory letters, and gave herself the pleasure of ignoring it in anticipation. Its failure to arrive seemed, however, reasonable in the circumstances and Stella found herself worrying, not about Serena's silence but Jean Conway's.

"I wonder whether she got your letter," she said to Molly a week after it had been sent. "Are you sure you posted it?"

"Of course I did. You saw me post it."

"Hmm, yes. I wish we'd kept a copy. I can't remember exactly how we put it. I do hope it didn't annoy her, I mean, it's most unlike her not to answer."

"How could it have annoyed her? I merely said I was on your side and thought Serena must be a most unpleasant person to treat you like that, and, what else, oh yes, that all your friends thought so too. And then we added that bit, don't you remember, to show we bore no real grudge, about having to forgive her because she must be terribly neurotic dealing with all those pathological cases all day. And how nice you were about it. I really can't see anything wrong in that."

"I know. People are so peculiar, though."

"But didn't you say they were going abroad?"

"Yes, but all letters are forwarded by U.V.I. They left so suddenly I didn't see them. I wrote to Rusty all about it and he's usually as sweet as pie but he never answered. Oh dear, I do hope they haven't taken *her* side. They're my only friends, I mean, my oldest friends. It would be just like her to set them against me."

"Oh, don't worry, Stella. I'm sure you'll hear soon. I expect they're just busy settling in their new place. Where have they gone?"

Stella exhaled a long lungful of smoke.

"Can't remember. Alex, I think, or was it Aden? Yes, it must have been Aden. I know he was buying a tropical suit. No, it was Athens, I remember now, and that explains the whole thing. Reeny was going to Athens, and coming back up the Adriatic, because I told her to buy an Italian swimsuit. Oh, lucky devil, she must be in Venice now. But obviously, what a fool I've been. They all met in Athens and must have had a good laugh at my expense. Ah, well, another couple of friends gone west. I'm certainly not going to be the one to write first."

And even if she had wanted to she could not have done so. Because a few days later, as August turned its leaden skies over to a bright and light

September, Stella woke up and found she couldn't move. She gave one long yell which brought Molly scurrying from her bed in her curlers and baby-doll nightdress, then she said in a dead voice but with terror in her eyes:

"Molly, I can't move. I'm paralysed, help me, get a doctor, please get a doctor." And when Molly had left the room Stella whispered hoarsely, to the ceiling, "Oh, God, no, no, no. Not me. Not me."

When the doctor came he gave her a thorough examination and took many samples of her various liquids, just to make sure, but firmly told her not to worry. It was nothing serious, nothing physical anyway. A simple attack of lethargy. It should lift in a day or two. He would give her an injection now, and another tomorrow. Absolute rest for three weeks. She was of course anaemic, and very rundown, and had she been in the tropics recently? For many years, ah, yes. Still, that didn't quite account, well, these things were very mysterious. She was to try and eat so as not to get too weak. And here was a prescription. Was there anyone here to look after her? Ah, good, well, rest, nothing but rest, he would look in again.

She didn't move for three days. She couldn't, and became more and more frightened but also quieter and quieter as she stared dry-eyed at the red velvet curtains, dead to the world like a thin waxen doll. Molly's mother tried to make her eat but she wouldn't touch anything.

In the middle of the fourth night, she woke to find her limbs not only moving but seized with such convulsions that she screamed, writhing on the bed and gasping for breath until quite suddenly they stopped and she lay back, soaked in a cold sweat, looked aghast for a moment at Molly who was standing helplessly by the bed, then she smiled weakly and fell asleep. Molly thought she was dead and rushed towards the door but then Stella moved her right arm suddenly and dropped her hand just about where the heart was. Gently Molly wiped her face with a wet handkerchief and drew the blankets up to her chin. Stella was breathing steadily.

The doctor nodded sagely when he came the next day.

"These things are very mysterious," he said again. "There was certainly nothing physically wrong. You need absolute rest for at least a month and then you'd better come and see me again, I think you should have a chat with the analyst at St. Alban's, he's an excellent man and sure to give you a lot of help."

Stella shook her her head wearily.

"She's going to Java in October, Doctor," said Molly.

"Goodness me, whatever for?"

"She's going to work there. The Dutch Population Commission, you know."

"Oh dear, oh dear. Well, well. She'd better have a whole course of injections then. And please see that she gets absolute rest."

"You've been jolly decent putting up with me," Stella said a month later in the lounge of the K.L.M. Air Terminal in Knightsbridge.

"Nonsense, it was the least I could do. But will you be all right? I still don't like the idea of your leaving so soon."

"Oh, I rested in Sussex, I assure you, the Carsons were simply sweet. And I couldn't put it off, it makes such a bad impression in a new job. Goodness, I forgot to collect my Egyptian gloves from the cleaners. Could you be an angel, I've got the ticket here somewhere. Here's ten shillings, that should cover the cleaning and the postage, shouldn't it? Ah, yes, here we are. You sure it won't be a nuisance? Karachi-Delhi, heavens, that's me, I must go, oh my God, where's my bus ticket, I think I've lost it. Ah no, here it is. Goodness, what a fright I got. Well, goodbye."

"Goodbye, Stella. I hope Java's marvellous. I must say I half envy you."

"Oh, you know, one part of the world is always very like some other part. I say, did you take my lighter by mistake? I put it down here on the table. Oh dear, I'll have to buy a new one in Karachi, what a bore, and I always smoke like a chimney on a plane. Oh, stupid me, it's in my pocket. Sorry." She gave her coy smile that always softened the hardness of her features with a sudden astonishing radiance. "Well, goodbye, Molly, and thanks again, you've been jolly nice putting up with me."

"Nonsense," Molly repeated. "You'd better hurry. Bon voyage, and write soon."

"Bye."

The Middlemen: Chapter Sixteen

She was glad to be leaving London once again. Not for ever, of course, she would return, often, she had such good friends here. And in Europe too. Europe was Europe, after all, the centre of civilisation.

On the plane, however, she got suddenly depressed. So many planes she had been on. So many times, hermetically sealed up for so many hours, fed and whiskied and cigaretted and levered back to sleep and generally looked after, to emerge, slightly deaf and dazed and woolly-legged, on some airport that looked very like so many other airports. She flicked through an illustrated magazine and stared with half her attention at photographs of rescue teams at work on some Aegean island where a volcano had erupted. The rest of her mind raced from one notion to another, sometimes in phrases, conversations even, seized in their totality before the words were formed by silence, sometimes in visual images of startling clarity. There were always earthquakes and eruptions somewhere or other these days. Chile, Agadir, and where else? That or revolutions. But what a good thing she'd known the new president when he was a mere colonel, he'd had to do something about getting her things sent on and Manolo turned out of the house. And, of course, she would never see Reeny again, even when in London. London was large enough to contain them both. Java, however, was extremely overpopulated whereas Sumatra apparently was quite empty. It was a question of persuading people to emigrate. She herself was a perpetual emigrant, so it would be quite easy. One day perhaps, in twenty years, they would end their days together, Serena a widow, she an old maid, sharing a little house. But in the meantime she would know nothing of her, and return any letters she might write unanswered. As Molly her spokesman had said for her, all communication must cease. But it was a purely temporary paralysis. Nothing serious. There was no need to keep ferreting in the garbage can. No need, at all, since a more powerful dustman was at hand to collect and cleanse regularly at a mere request. For nothing is impossible in dreams through which he walks by night.

"Bad business, is it?" said the man next to her looking at the photographs and then at her with a Levantine smile.

Her shrug was of absolute scorn and she turned the pages of her magazine. The next illustrated article was all about the moon, and mankind's race to reach it alive within the next five years.

www.ingramcontent.com/pod-product-compliance
Ingram Content Group UK Ltd.
Pitfield, Milton Keynes, MK11 3LW, UK
UKHW041302180426
11947UKWH00009B/634